MAJENDIE'S CAT

"You want me to help you in exchange for the name of my son's killer?" St. Giles asked finally, wanting to spread it all out, see what else Majendie might have in his hand.

"I would not put it quite so baldly, Mr. St. Giles. We want to see justice done, and your son avenged, of course, but there are other compelling reasons why you . . ."

"What reasons? Reforming the bloody monetary system? You think I care a damn about that? All this talk about lancing boils. Do you take me for an idealist? You know better or you wouldn't be asking my help. I don't even know who you work for."

"It is best for both of us that you not know the name of my government, Mr. St. Giles. Believe me. But you do know the government you would be working against. The United States already has attempted to have you killed once; it very nearly succeeded. . . ."

FRANK FOWLKES

MAJENDIE'S CAT

A Methuen Paperback

A Methuen Paperback

British Library Cataloguing in Publication Data

MAJENDIE'S CAT

Fowlkes, Frank V.
  Majendie's cat.
  I. Title
  813'.54[F]   PS3556.0873

  ISBN 0-413-14490-9

First published in Great Britain in 1986
by Methuen London Ltd
This edition published 1987
by Methuen London Ltd
11 New Fetter Lane, London EC4P 4EE

Copyright © 1986 by Frank Fowlkes
Published by arrangement with
Harcourt Brace Jovanovich, Inc.
Printed and bound in Great Britain
by Richard Clay Ltd, Bungay, Suffolk

PROLOGUE

On August 15, 1971, Washington's financial journalists received an urgent summons: the President would make an important announcement that evening; eight o'clock attendance was requested.

Given the cautious orchestration of the White House news operation, any spur-of-the-moment Presidential announcement would have provoked interest. But for the President to call in the press on a Sunday in August, when half of Northwest Washington could be expected to be en route from the mountains or the beach, was more than provocative; it was portentous.

It was with more than normal curiosity, therefore, that shortly before dusk that evening reporters began trickling through the Northwest Gate to the White House grounds. Drenching afternoon rains had dotted the asphalt drive with puddles, and in the fading daylight the reporters had to step with care as they made their way toward the press offices in the

West Wing—Dale and young Naughton from the *New York Times*, Rowen and Oberdorfer from *The Washington Post*, Janssen from the *Wall Street Journal*, at least one reporter from nearly every bureau in Washington. By seven-forty-five the press lounge could no longer hold the crowd, and the reporters were led back outdoors, across to the White House main entrance and on to the East Room at the building's far end. Not until they were seated in rows of grey steel folding chairs did White House press aides inform them that the President would not be present. The President at nine o'clock would address the country via television from the Oval Office. At this briefing for the press corps beforehand, a battery of the Administration's economic officials would explain the President's announcements in detail. By five minutes to eight, nearly a hundred reporters, some in golf or tennis clothes, sat silently studying the White House "fact sheets," trying to piece together what was about to unfold.

So it was that, at eight, only a few late arrivals were at the Northwest Gate to observe a strange figure limp in haste toward the White House from the direction of West Executive Avenue. The light was poor and the distance some seventy-five yards. Still, these witnesses would later agree the figure had been that of a heavyset man. As to further details, recollections would vary. But on two additional facts all would concur: the man had been holding one arm pressed to his side as though wounded, and he had appeared to be soaking wet.

The White House driveway is a slight upgrade and swings from the Northwest Gate in a wide north-to-east arc; for middle-aged men in street shoes and jackets it is not a comfortable sprint. It was nearly thirty seconds, therefore, before the clutch of late-arriving reporters reached the empty foyer inside the White House's front entrance. Breathless, they glanced around them. Off to the left, a broad corridor led toward the East

Room; it, too, was empty. Moments earlier they had seen the limping figure speak to a guard and disappear through the door they had just entered. Now the man was nowhere to be seen. Nor was there any sign of the guard. Winded, the reporters exchanged glances. How could they let so bizarre an incident pass? Yet the President was about to announce something important enough to warrant a press conference on a Sunday night in August. They would have to file that story immediately. The large Monday news hole meant front-page, above-the-fold treatment. It meant close scrutiny, too. Each reporter's account would be weighed by his editors against those of the wire services and rival papers. Locate the limping man and there might be an exclusive sidebar. But waste time in a futile attempt and they might blow the main event. At the end of the corridor they could see tables piled with papers in disarray such as only a strong wind or a crowd of pushing, grabbing reporters could produce. Others already had the jump on them. For another moment the reporters hesitated. Then, without consultation, they hurried as a group toward the East Room.

The incident had consumed less than a minute. In the rush of events that followed, any chance to discover its meaning was lost. Still, none of the handful of reporters who witnessed it would in retrospect regret his decision. None would ever enjoy more prominent play in his paper than he got for his work that night. The disclosures made by the President that evening would alter the economic landscape of the Western world, shake political alliances and precipitate among bankers and businessmen a global confusion and fear that, in time, would drive the price of gold to more than eight hundred dollars an ounce. August 15, 1971, would go down as a watershed in economic history.

As the men and the women of the press present that evening

more than fifteen years ago strained to absorb the significance of what the Administration's economic experts explained to them, they knew that the President's announcement was the biggest story they would cover all year. None could have known —and only those few late arrivals have suspected—that, fewer than forty feet away, in a small chamber off the corridor to the East Room, there sat, despondent and slumped on a couch, a man with a wet suit and a badly slashed wrist who could have given them the biggest story of their careers.

Even the injured man could not have provided them all the astonishing details. To have learned the whole story, a reporter would have had to have been in Hong Kong six months earlier.

CHAPTER 1

In her pink seminarian's uniform, the girl had seemed the picture of blushing, schoolgirl innocence. Yet already, in ten minutes, she had teased her squirming audience out of the classroom and into the seraglio. Now, as promised on the marquee outside, she was about to introduce it to "Regions Most Men Visit Only in Their Nighttime Fantasies." Gratitude was audible as the theater's fifty patrons surrendered themselves in the air-conditioned darkness to ninety pounds of sweat-slick Oriental adolescence writhing naked on a soiled counterpane. Few of the rapt voyeurs who had paid fifteen Hong Kong dollars for this diversion would have noticed the middle-aged Englishman in the rumpled tan suit rise from the back row and slip through the curtain at the rear.

Peregrin St. Giles was not bored by sex. On any other day he might have relished a little Wanchai catnip. But this day he had entered the theater already excited. Two hours earlier he had finally acknowledged what for two days he had not wanted to believe. He was being followed.

He squinted at his watch, impatiently waiting for his eyes to focus. If his pursuers had fallen for the theater dodge, he had only a minute or two before they would note his empty seat.

Six o'clock.

The hour was in his favor. The sidewalk would be all noise and people. If the two men were still waiting outside, they would have to look sharp. Following anyone through Hong Kong's rush hour was like tracking a wood chip down a storm drain.

Don't walk fast and don't look back, St. Giles reminded himself as he made for the outer door. And for God's sake stop moving your lips.

A few blocks east he paused in front of a corner jewelry store. Since leaving the theater he had not risked looking back. He did not want to appear concerned. If he could maintain a semblance of calm, there was still a chance he could shake the men following him long enough to grab a taxi and get an evening flight. Feigning interest in the window displays, he studied the reflections in the right-angled panes of glass. By shifting first to one side then to the other, he could look down all four arms of the intersection.

What was that?

He thought he had recognized a figure crossing the street half a block back. Abruptly his vision was cut off by a van. By the time the van moved on, the figure was gone.

At Mody Road he turned toward the tip of the peninsula. The flight would have to wait. Run too soon and they would close in.

Damn! This was precisely what he had come to Hong Kong to avoid.

Rounding the corner into Nathan Road he glanced back in the direction he had come.

Bugger! Halfway down the block a florid forehead was visible

6

above the crowd. One dog still on the scent. In the preceding two days, he had seen the same red face a half-dozen times. Its owner was big, two hundred and thirty pounds at least; and young, forty-five at the outside. Moments later he glanced back again, thinking he might also see the red-faced man's smaller partner. Now neither man was visible. That was how it had been for the past two days.

Damn.

It was nearly ten o'clock that evening when St. Giles left the Peninsula Hotel. Fearful of being trapped in his room, he had passed the intervening hours first in the bar, then in the mezzanine dining room. He had suspected that the red-faced man would use the time to restore contact with his partner. He had guessed, too, that neither man would attempt to eat. A professional tail had to move without notice; the bill-waving maitre d' was an occupational hazard he couldn't risk.

As expected, neither man had appeared in the dining room. He had had time to collect his wits and think about what to do. By dessert he had made his decision. He couldn't keep running. It was time to get one of the men alone and find out what was going on.

Now, crossing the lobby, he spied the smaller man hiding his swarthy, mustachioed face in a magazine at the far end of the room. A moment later he picked out the red-faced man on a couch in the middle of the lobby. The latter started to rise, then sank back as St. Giles veered purposefully in his direction.

Twenty feet from the couch St. Giles stopped. He loitered next to a library table covered with newspapers, consulting his watch as though expecting a rendezvous. Finally, satisfied that the mustache had had time to get ahead of him, he shrugged as though annoyed to have been kept waiting and headed for the glass doors to the street.

At the sidewalk, he fell in with the flow of the evening strollers moving down Salisbury Road toward the waterfront. The tower of the old Kowloon-Canton Railway Station loomed on his left, dark and undefined at first, then silhouetted against the lights of the island across the harbor. Beneath those lights, somewhere in the shadow of the station, the little man with the mustache would be waiting.

The entrance to Ocean Terminal was directly ahead now. At that hour of evening, it would be bustling, its tiered quarter mile of shops packed with passengers from the cruise ships moored alongside. Half a block short of the terminal the Englishman saw what he had been waiting for. On the far sidewalk and ahead of him a figure had appeared. The mustache had run out of shadows. Forced into the light, the small, slightly bow-legged man veered left toward the low white building at the water's edge.

"Good scout," St. Giles muttered appreciatively as he watched the man weave through the parked taxis and buses. Team tailing was difficult. The "scout" had to stay ahead of the quarry to avert a "shutout," the unfortuitous elevator door or stoplight that could bring pursuit to an abrupt halt. Being the scout required an anticipatory eye and constant guessing. It also required rapid adjustment after a wrong guess. In that event, it was the job of the "shadow," the man in the rear, to move ahead, to assume the forward role until the next wrong guess.

The mustache's guess, in this instance, had been one St. Giles had foreseen. He quickened his pace.

Both men were in the white building now, through the turnstile and climbing the concrete ramp. St. Giles measured his stride, reading the flow of bodies around him, waiting for it to tell him what he could not see. Fifteen yards from the top of the ramp, the crowd's surge announced that the mechanical gate had started to swing shut. "Bonanza," he muttered. Ahead, the mustache was caught in the human torrent. Within thirty seconds, the two of them would be among the Star Ferry's hundreds of passengers, beginning the seven-minute trip from Kowloon to Hong Kong Island. It would be ten minutes before the red-faced man could follow.

Taking a seat on the top deck, forward along the rail, St. Giles removed the jacket to his suit, one of several tropical weights he'd had made in the preceding weeks, and let the breeze work on his wetness. He resisted an urge to look around. The odds were his way now.

He did not linger at the island terminal. Immediately upon disembarking the eastbound ferry, he mounted the passenger ramp, crossed the platform and descended the ramp at the other side. Within minutes, he was on a westbound ferry, headed back to Kowloon.

On the mainland, he headed up Hankow Road into the neon-lit night world of the Tsimshatsui District, through the fried-food smells, past the nightclub barkers and into a side street. Within ten minutes, he found what he was looking for: a first-floor restaurant with no sidewalk pay phone nearby.

The restaurant's seedy clientele took no notice as he settled at a table and ordered a beer. Reflections from the bar's interior lights made it impossible to see anything through the front window except the neon signs of the buildings directly across the street. He drank in silence until he was reasonably certain the man following him had had time to settle on a spot from which to watch. Then, taking a paper napkin from the dispenser on the table, he spread it, pinched it in the center and pushed it into his jacket pocket. The mustache and the red-haired man might have discovered who he was and that he was alive, but to the rest of the world he was dead and had been for more than a month. If he had to come to life again, he wanted to do so on his terms, not because his fingerprints had been identified in some Hong Kong police lab. Downing what remained of his beer, he rose, walked to the men's room at the rear, wrapped the napkin around his hand, opened the door and stepped inside.

After leaving the ferry, the mustache had stayed as close to St. Giles as he dared. He disliked trailing on "short leash." It was dangerous, particularly with a suspicious quarry, which, after the ferry rides back and forth across the harbor, he was pretty sure he had. So it had been with relief that he had watched St. Giles enter the restaurant.

Now, however, he was worried. From the sidewalk across the street, he had seen the tall Englishman disappear into the men's room at the rear of the restaurant. Five minutes had passed, and he had not yet returned.

Reconciled to acting alone, the mustache crossed the street, entered and without ordering made his way to the rear. He listened for a few moments at the men's-room door. Hearing nothing, he pushed the door open and was greeted by the sick-sweet smell of disinfectant doing battle with filth. The room was small. A urinal was bolted to the wall on the left, beyond it a toilet stall, to the right a sink. Everything in the room wore a dirty coat of silver boiler-room paint—everything except the tile surfaces and the window, which was open wide. Moving quickly to the window the mustache thrust his head into the garbage-strewn alley outside.

The mustache hadn't time to turn his head before St. Giles's fist exploded under his left ear with the force of a grenade.

CHAPTER 2

Along the narrow flange of flatland, west of the big hotels and apartments that march up Victoria Peak from the Star Ferry terminal, a patch of old China survives the surrounding siege of glass and concrete. This section is known as West Point. It was toward it, following the mustache's instructions, that Peregrin St. Giles made his way at noon the following day.

His identity was no longer a secret. How widely known it was that he was still alive, he had as yet no idea. He might have beat more information out of the mustache the night before had he not feared further commotion would attract the police —and had not the little man's first strangle-voiced revelation so thrown him off balance.

"We know who killed your son!"

The mustache's frightened first words had clattered through St. Giles's dreams all night. He had slept fitfully, awakened at six o'clock in a tangle of sheet and risen to walk the waterfront and reflect.

There was much for Peregrin St. Giles to reflect on. In the preceding twenty-five years, he had tramped across the statute books of a dozen nations. Half of those nations' governments and security forces still employed men who had been his confederates—more than a few since risen to high station. Such men might never erase from their memories the shortcuts they had taken to the top, but, given opportunity, some would not hesitate to eliminate the witnesses. Even his own countrymen could not be trusted. Eight years earlier, he had been tipped by a contact in the British Secret Intelligence Service that the network's old pipes were being capped and plastered over, that there was talk within MI-5 of referring his particular case to Special Branch. The information had been given him in civil enough fashion, but there had been no mistaking what was meant; one didn't get more than one such warning. He had not since set foot in England.

That the red-faced man and the mustache might be Special Branch operatives had been one of many possibilities that had occurred to St. Giles since he had realized he was being followed. The one possibility that had not occurred to him was that the men knew about his son.

And for reason.

No record existed that St. Giles had, or ever had had, a son. That secret had belonged to him and to the boy's mother for twenty years. Not until the previous year had the boy himself known the true identity of his father.

It was not for his own sake that St. Giles had kept silent. There had been slate-grey and solitary days when he had yearned for someone closer than the succession of arm's-length, cash-dispensing paymasters who were the only associates his trade allowed him. But the boy's American mother had a husband and a family to protect. As for the boy . . . He had wondered often how the boy might have been affected had he, early on, been told who his real father was. The knowledge might have slipped down his innocent gullet with the day's quota of new revelations; one more peel off life's onion, no more or less startling than his discovery that soap melted in the bath, or that the kitchen door opened in either direction. Certainly a child would never have felt the emotion St. Giles had seen in his son's eyes on the doorstep of his rented bungalow in El Cerrito, California, at their first meeting, a year earlier.

The mustache's words were confounding for another reason. There had never been any suggestion—public or otherwise—that St. Giles's son had died. The *ufficiales della polizia* who had examined the burned-out hotel room in Finale Ligure six weeks earlier had concluded from the hotel's registry that the crisp and bullet-punched body on the bed was that of St. Giles himself. Even these details had never fully been released. With tourist bookings to consider, the local constabulary had handled the matter with delicacy. One week after the fire, small items in several London newspapers had reported that Peregrin St. Giles, a British tourist, had died in a hotel fire at a North Italian seaside resort.

Of his own father St. Giles had no memory; the man had passed through his mother's life in an afternoon, leaving only a name, which his mother, hoping that it might in some way confer advantage, had pathetically requisitioned for her unborn child. Of his mother, St. Giles had but sad, half-suppressed recollections. Her concerns had been too numerous and too desperate for him to rank high among them. He had been still in his early teens when she died and left him to the streets of London.

With the Depression just beginning, and Britain's economic doctors still bent on bleeding the patient, there had been few jobs for a boy whose only adult acquaintances were the pimps and touts who had smoothed his mother's road to the coroner. Work, like food, had come in scraps: loading crates, slopping vegetable stalls, running messages. For nearly three years he had eked out subsistence as one of the city's thousands of "willing-for-a-shilling" day workers, passing nights wherever he could find shelter and a bit of warmth.

At sixteen, with nearly his full growth, he turned to club fighting, taking on men twice his age for a few quid a night. He could punch, and he had stood his ground with bigger and more experienced fighters. But his nose broke easily and often, and before long it became apparent he would not be able to fight regularly enough to support himself. In 1937, having neither money nor prospects, he signed on to see the world with the drunks and deviates of the merchant navy.

With this step, his day-to-day battle for survival ended. The merchant service fed him, sheltered him and clothed him. The freedom he exchanged for these favors was a burden happily surrendered.

The late 1930s was the season to be a seaman. With dockside automation an infant technology and containerization still decades away, layovers in port were long enough for a man to feel a traveler. By the time St. Giles reached his nineteenth year, he had stood on every continent and rubbed his nose in every worthwhile Tenderloin from Piraeus to Shinjuku.

World War II's outbreak caught him in North Africa, weary of ship life and ready for change. Faced with conscription if he returned to England and disinclined to risk his life in a merchant fleet which German U-boats had made a clay-pigeon navy, St. Giles jumped ship in Tunis in 1940. There, bored, aimless and poor, he dallied for more than sixteen months. Then, in 1942, caught up in the local enthusiasm, he enlisted in the Corps Franc d'Afrique.

14

A few weeks were all it took to disabuse him of any hope that he had stumbled onto one of the war's glamorous locales. Life in the corps consisted of a monotonous round of treks back and forth over La Piste Forestière, the dirt road connecting Cap Serrat, on the northern coast of western Tunisia, with Sedjenane, a town twenty miles inland.

But if the work was tedious, the company was not. For back-street sophistication and peculating know-how, the men of the Corps Franc d'Afrique were the equals of those in the more notorious Légion étrangère. Before the war was over, St. Giles received from this polyglot faculty a host of tutorials in the art of the extralegal business transaction. After the war, with scarcity and rationing universal, it was near to ordained that the young man, with no family to go home to, should slip into intrigue and finagling.

He had started simply: black-market dealings, forbidden money exchanges, a little smuggling. Conscience was never a problem. When times were hard, men did what they had to do: everyone he knew was daily in violation of one law or another. For the most part, his were not crimes against people; they were crimes against the laws and regulations of governments straining to keep the lid on restive populations. Even after his aptitude for the work became apparent—after the little jobs became large and occasionally distasteful—he never thought of himself as a criminal. Criminals operated for themselves and against the established order. Postwar Europe offered a multitude of "orders," all of them more or less established, and always at least one among them eager to endorse and underwrite his activities. Where governments or ideologies collided, crime was not defined by laws but by allegiances.

By the lights by which most men reckon character, St. Giles's may not have been worthy of commendation. But their lights had not been his lights. Indeed, he had had no lights—

no education, no parents to set examples, no church precepts, none of the influences that permit people to check antisocial behavior or, indeed, brand it antisocial. His star had been necessity, and his teachers men who had looked upon society not as protector but as oppressor. Right? Wrong? There had been little in anyone's treatment of him to suggest the meaning of such abstractions. Fortune had dealt him a hand from the bottom of her deck and spat on him in the draw. For twenty-five years, home had been cheap flats and hotel rooms. Friends? He could scarcely have thought of five people he knew and trusted well enough to call "friends." In his business one didn't make friends. Loneliness was the uniform.

There had been other hardships. Paydays were never regular. The Belgians had paid well for the assassination of Lumumba in 1961. And the Peruvian military had ponied up handsomely the following year for the fraud evidence that reversed their election defeat. But most years had been lean. By the time he'd reached fifty, all he had to furnish the bare room of his soul was the floor-length mirror into which all men peer daily for a glimpse of the self-worth they crave. In all those years, the only hopeful reflection he had seen had been in the eyes of the boy who had died in Finale Ligure.

But hard use had given St. Giles one thing in generous measure. It had given him a knack for surviving. It had taught him never to confront a danger he could walk around, given him the gift of improvisation and, when cornered, the reflexes of a mongoose. More than one man he'd faced over the years had lived to regret his assumption that this quiet, seemingly diffident loner could be bullied. More than one man had not.

It had been the U.S. Secret Service's turn to learn this one year earlier. Thinking it could use him as though he were a no-deposit, no-return, disposable container, the Service had retained St. Giles to ferry five million dollars in "development assistance" to two countries in Central America where the White House maintained that democracy and freedom were on trial. The Service planned to get rid of him when the job was finished, but it underestimated its delivery boy. Before the episode was over, it cost the Service three of its best Latin operatives and all of the five million.

St. Giles had expected the windfall five million to end his troubles and buy him peace of mind. Having eluded the U.S. authorities and escaped through Canada, he arrived in Italy flush and ready to indulge himself. He rented a villa outside Rapallo, outfitted himself with a new wardrobe, bought a Ferrari through an agency in Genoa and a vintage Armstrong-Siddeley through *Corriere della Sera,* for the childhood longings he hoped it would assuage. But quickly—surprisingly and disappointingly quickly—he ran out of itches to scratch. He considered a boat. Boats, however, meant complicated registrations, an imprudent risk in his circumstances. Rich men bought art, so he considered art. But art was free for the looking, and, besides, he had no taste for it. Nights he communed with the ghost of his childhood, trying to summon past cravings. Things that, out of reach, had glittered, seemed dull and uninteresting brought to hand. His means had quenched his thirst without giving him satisfaction.

More bitter was what the money had enabled him to see of his personal limitations. He knew no one in the circles in which people of wealth moved. His acquaintances were riffraff; his former employers off bounds. He had none of the credentials for social small talk; no schools, no hometown, no job or profession of which he could speak.

There was also his accent. St. Giles was, even at his age, a striking physical specimen. He stood six foot three, one hundred and ninety pounds. His nose was knobby and his face a trifle too flat. But he was handsome in the way of men who carry well the evidence of rough use. He still had his hair, which was the same rat brown it had always been. And age had only enhanced the power of his quiet grey-green eyes. These rude charms had won him his share of women over the years. But in the circles to which his newly acquired wealth might have given him access, there was no working around the accent. In commercial relationships such things were overlooked. Where "nice" people gathered to socialize, he might as well have had a tattoo on his forehead.

After three unhappy months in the Rapallo villa, he had left his cars to his flabbergasted gardener, abandoned the paid-up lease, wired his son in El Cerrito, and departed with a new perspective on money: one could eat it, drink it and travel with it; but money was a silent and soulless partner. The boy had given him more pleasure in a week than money would buy him the rest of his life.

The murder had occurred in the afternoon. He and the boy had lunched in one of the restaurants along the deserted beach, then wandered back through the town, intending to climb the rocky bluff that overlooks Finale Ligure from the west. Walks had become an afternoon routine since the boy had arrived at the Genoa airport the previous week. The activity was tonic for their shyness, ballast to fill the lulls in their talk. They each had lifetimes to account for, two blank books to fill with the silt and sediment of experiences laid down over seventy-three combined years. To the boy, St. Giles had given wonder, wonder that he might have sprung from this man so unlike the accountant who had married his mother and raised him as a son. To St. Giles, the boy he'd always known he had but never until the previous year seen had given something more valuable than wonder. The boy had given him a chance—his first chance— to love. And so with wonder and with love they had each day walked and talked, slowly filling the pages, still reticent with each other, still awed with the newness of their bonding, walking, walking, finding that side by side and moving the words came easier.

This day, however, the boy, having drunk more wine than usual at lunch, grew sleepy and silent as they walked. At his father's urging he turned back to take an afternoon nap. Always cautious, St. Giles had booked their rooms in separate hotels. For ten days they had scrupulously observed the separation. But on this occasion, it being broad daylight and his hotel being nearer, St. Giles had given the boy his room key before continuing alone. He had walked perhaps an hour beyond the top of the bluff, to a point where signs indicating a quarry and danger from blasting turned him back.

By the time he reached the crest of the bluff on the return trip, the fire equipment was already in action. It took him only a few seconds to guess what had occurred. From the window of his room on the second floor, flames were shooting all the way to the roof. Nothing in the sparsely furnished concrete structure could have burned so violently. Nor could the room's furnishings have produced the dirty black smoke that the wind had already strewn along a quarter mile of the town's western edge.

He had stayed in Finale Ligure just one more day, long enough to learn of the bullet wounds and of the mistaken identification. He spent the night of the murder in a fury, blearily roaming the empty streets and vowing horrible retribution. Only with morning had the impossibility of his intention become clear. He could not make inquiries. He could not even appear in the streets, lest someone recognize him and inform the police of their error. In the past he had had the resources of a client to call upon. Now he was on his own. He did not know for whom to look. What he did know was that whoever had killed his son had made the same error of mistaken identity the police had made, and that that person would not hesitate to kill again should the error be called to his attention. He had needed time to think, some place safe and far away. Hong Kong had seemed to qualify on both counts.

The Red Pepper Restaurant was a steamy, one-room affair, so unprepossessing that, before his eyes adjusted to the dim light, St. Giles suspected he had misunderstood the mustache's instructions. He spied the little man and his red-faced partner at a corner table. The latter rose to greet him.

"I'm Majendie, and this is Bosanquet." The red-faced man held out a huge hand, motioning with the other to where the mustache, his jaw discolored and swollen, sat silent, looking none too pleased at the reunion.

At close hand, Majendie's physical bulk was even more imposing than at a distance. His massive head appeared to have been spot-welded to his shoulders without benefit of a neck. Sleeves rolled to his elbows revealed hairless forearms the size of a normal man's calves. Yet Majendie's skin was pink as a baby's, and his voice eerily cultivated, almost musical. Studying the huge blob of Neronian refinement before him, St. Giles took the proffered hand. The skin was soft, but the hand inside it, he noted, was hard, and its grip steady. That wasn't good, he thought. The rest of the body would be the same. He remembered being in the ring with such men, swinging at what appeared to be an upholstered stomach, connecting with what felt like a panel truck. They looked fat. But they fooled you. It was a bad feeling when you discovered you could not hurt them. He was glad that Bosanquet, not Majendie, had followed him the night before.

"Most unfortunate, the death of your son." Majendie spoke easily, as though resuming an interrupted conversation. "Most unfortunate. And most unnecessary. Gratuitous, even. 'Twasn't as though there was anything to be gained from killing an innocent young man, was there?"

St. Giles nodded. He was more interested in Majendie's accent than his sympathy. The locutions were British. But the accent was something else. He couldn't place it.

"Of course there wasn't," Majendie went on. "Vengefulness, frustration at its ugliest, I should say." He paused, then, shaking his head slowly, added with unconvincing wonderment, "But that is the way some people are, I suppose. What?"

Again St. Giles nodded. Majendie and Bosanquet had not followed him for two days to commiserate. They were there to talk business. The less he said, the sooner they'd come to the point. The easier it would be to say no.

"Bosanquet told you, I believe, that we know who killed your son," Majendie said.

"How?" St. Giles asked.

"We saw him." Majendie paused, as though expecting some reaction. Getting none, he continued. "Point of fact, we were in Finale Ligure hoping to see you, Mr. St. Giles; would have, too, had you returned that afternoon."

Majendie recounted how he and Bosanquet had arrived by train from Genoa the morning of the murder, located St. Giles' hotel, and waited in the small lobby at the foot of the stairs.

"We saw him come in, though of course we did not know then who he was. Fine-looking boy. I don't doubt you were proud of him."

It was an unfeeling bit of solicitude. St. Giles wondered if Majendie meant to be cruel.

"After that we saw the man who killed him. Chap came in not fifteen minutes after he did, walked straight up the stairs without so much as a how-do-you-do at the desk. We thought at first he was you. We had only your photograph to go by, and this chap looked a great deal like it; though I can see you are taller and not so heavy. Rough-looking character, he was." Majendie hesitated as though calling back the memory. "He must have used a silencer, because we heard no noise. In fact, we didn't learn until the next day that your son had been shot. From the time he came in until we got to the room ourselves and saw the smoke, we had no reason to think anything was amiss."

St. Giles felt a rush of anger. That someone who might have saved his son had been so close, so futilely close. Why hadn't they put out the fire? Tried to pull the boy out? Tried to help?

Majendie seemed to read his thoughts.

"We were too late to do anything. The bed was an inferno. Oil of some sort, I should have thought, judging by the smoke. Brought it in a hot-water bottle. It was still burning on the floor. Chap who did it couldn't have left more than a minute before we got there; that rubber bottle would have burned quickly with oil residue in it."

"How did you know it was my son?" He didn't want to ask, but he needed to know.

"From the letter."

St. Giles's face remained impassive. But his gut twisted. There was only one letter Majendie could be referring to. St. Giles had left it on the table by the door of his hotel room in Finale Ligure. It was the only "Dear Dad" letter he had ever received. Indeed, the only time the boy had ever used that term of address. The boy's clumsy and self-conscious attempt to set down his feelings had touched him. St. Giles was not given to easy emotion. Few people in his life had offered him concern or sought his, and he was unpracticed in the language of feelings. He had wept when he read his son's words. Until now, he had assumed the letter had been burned along with everything else in his room. That Majendie should have found the letter and violated his new and precious intimacy by reading it was hideous to contemplate. Had Majendie kept it? he wanted to ask. No, he told himself. Don't owe this man anything.

"Who killed him?" St. Giles's voice betrayed no sentiment.

"Yes, well, that is why we are here, isn't it, Mr. St. Giles?"

There it was.

St. Giles was glad now he hadn't asked. He knew what would come next. How would Majendie pitch it? "This is a job tailor-made for you"? "Nobody else can manage it"? "We can't trust this job to just anyone"? He'd heard all the words so often. How many times had dangerous, dirty work been pressed on him with flattering phrases?

Damn his reputation!

Once he had encouraged it; depended on it when work and money were scarce. But long before his five-million-dollar windfall from the U.S. government he had ceased to enjoy it, realizing that he was as much its prisoner as its beneficiary. Because of his reputation, clients refused to believe that any undertaking was beyond him. No amount of protest persuaded them. They saw in his manner only what his reputation prepared them to see, reading silence as confidence, numbness as courage, paralysis as sang-froid. All the lucky breaks and improbabilities that had kept him alive over the years when he should have been killed, all his accidental billiards and borrowings against fate—these only he knew. What they saw were results. Until he was well and truly dead, men like Majendie and Bosanquet wouldn't believe there was anything he couldn't do. . . . Interrupt this man now, he thought; tell him straight out; don't let this conversation get to questions of can or can't.

"I am not for hire," St. Giles said, folding his arms before him on the table and looking Majendie in the eye. He started to add that the name of the murderer would not bring back his son, but checked himself. He was jumping ahead, making assumptions.

"Mr. St. Giles, we simply want to ask your assistance in a matter of mutual interest. We know you are no longer 'for hire,' as you put it. But do us the courtesy of hearing me out. You cannot be so wise as to know whether my proposition will be good or bad for you until you've heard it."

Bosanquet had as yet said nothing. Majendie's mustachioed and clearly junior partner had not stopped scowling since being introduced. St. Giles wondered if Bosanquet's jaw hurt as much as the hand he himself was nursing.

"You are not a fool," Majendie went on, "and so that you do not think me one, I will come straight to the point. We are interested in money. . . . And who, you may ask, is not interested in money? Few people, to be sure . . . But you, as a rich man now, are one; which, as you will understand in a few minutes, is a fact that recommends you to us. Besides, our interest is not in making money, except in the literal sense; our interest is in destroying money. Specifically, Mr. St. Giles, we intend to destroy the American dollar."

It was hot in the restaurant, and the big man's shirt showed four-inch crescents of perspiration at the armpits.

St. Giles was puzzled. How had Majendie known he was rich? How had he known he was alive and in Hong Kong? Why did Majendie think he would have any interest in destroying the dollar? He had heard the dollar vilified by Continental financial types, but he had always regarded such views as reflections of national, rather than personal, animus. Besides, he could not imagine what Majendie expected him to do about it.

"Yes, well, that's not my line," was all he could think to say.

Majendie seemed not to hear.

"Do you know what the dollar is, Mr. St. Giles? The dollar

is a drunkard's promise, a lie that the world will not permit itself to disbelieve." Majendie was growing impassioned. It was plain he was much more than the simple thug he had appeared on the street. "The world has exchanged its sweat for American scrip long enough, Mr. St. Giles. The treasuries of Europe are filled with dollars that are all but useless to their holders because they may not redeem them without bringing down the international monetary system, NATO, the whole framework and fabric of the Western Alliance. The United States uses those inflated dollars, like the proceeds of bad loans, to buy up the productive resources of the world. It offers the empty promise it will convert dollars to gold, if asked. But what government has the courage to ask? Every government knows the United States cannot deliver. So the dollars pile up, and the rape goes on. This will end one day, Mr. St. Giles; you may rest assured it will end." Majendie paused, leaned forward and lowered his voice to a confiding whisper. "But some of us are not willing to wait. We intend to lance the boil, Mr. St. Giles. And you, I hope, are going to fashion the lance.

"Are you familiar with Operation Bernhard?"

CHAPTER 3

Counterfeiting!

Incredulous, St. Giles stared across the table in the Red Pepper Restaurant. He was fifty-two years old, still had more than four million dollars tucked away in accounts in the Bahamas and Vaduz. And Majendie was asking him to become involved in counterfeiting! Not just any inky-aproned, down-in-the-root-cellar counterfeiting; but a monster operation.

Operation Bernhard, Majendie had explained, was the Nazis' code name for their attempt to undermine Britain's currency during World War II. Several years into the war they had assembled nearly a hundred engravers, many of them prisoners, in the Sachsenhausen concentration camp, twenty-five miles northwest of Berlin. There they had put them to work counterfeiting British pound notes of large denomination. Initially, the Nazis had run into problems. They knew the composition of the British paper. And under chemical analysis their imitation showed no variation from the genuine article. Still, unaccountably, it did not look right. It was too white. Not until late 1943 did the Germans discover the reason: the linen in the paper on which British notes were printed was not new linen, as the Germans had assumed; it was old linen, rags, many with indelible dirt stains. Once the Germans figured out that their missing ingredient was dirt, they went to work again. In 1944, they produced more than eight million notes of several large denominations. They let these counterfeit pound notes dribble out slowly, even spent some of them in other countries to support the German war effort.

It was these purchases that ultimately proved fatal to Bernhard's purpose, for they alerted the Bank of England and gave it time to formulate countermeasures. Before more than a small amount of the Bernhard counterfeits could be put into circulation the British ceased to issue notes in denominations of more than ten pounds. Then, in May 1945, just prior to V-E day, the Bank of England recalled all larger notes, declaring them no longer legal tender. With that, any chance that Operation Bernhard might, even tardily, achieve its objective died. Except for the occasional rumor of a cache somewhere, it was a bit of forgotten history.

Majendie did not intend to make the same error. His plan was simultaneously to release twelve billion dollars in U.S. twenty-dollar bills in Europe, where confidence in the dollar's strength was already weak, to flood the market and unhorse the dollar before the United States had time to react.

There was another difference. In 1944, Germany and England had been at war; Germany's plan could invite no further recriminations. Majendie's government and the United States were not at war. Should anything go wrong, it was important the counterfeiting scheme not be traceable to its authors. From start to finish, the operation had to be an orphan.

"And that, Mr. St. Giles, is why we need your help. You are

ideal—wealthy enough to be above the obvious temptations, resourceful enough to see it through and, most important, not linked in any way to my government."

Majendie had spoken for nearly a quarter of an hour. He had made counterfeiting sound like a holy crusade. Now the red-faced man sat silent, waiting for an answer.

Bugger you, St. Giles wanted to say. While he was out risking getting hacked to pieces by the infidel, dollar-mongering United States, Majendie and his little friend Bosanquet were going to be comfortably sitting home assuring whatever government they worked for that he was too rich to steal their counterfeit money. Bugger you was what he wanted to say.

So say it, he told himself. Say it now, get up and get out of here. You're not on the hook. You don't know who these people are. Don't want to know. Walk. They aren't going to shoot you in the back in downtown Hong Kong.

Walk where?

"You want me to help you in exchange for the name of my son's killer?" St. Giles asked finally, wanting to spread it all out, see what else Majendie might have in his hand.

"I would not put it quite so baldly, Mr. St. Giles. We want to see justice done, and your son avenged, of course, but there are other compelling reasons why you . . ."

"What reasons? Reforming the bloody monetary system? You think I care a damn about that? All this talk about lancing boils. Do you take me for an idealist? You know better or you wouldn't be asking my help. I don't even know who you work for."

"It is best for both of us that you not know the name of my government, Mr. St. Giles. Believe me. But you do know the government you would be working against. The United States already has attempted to have you killed once; it very nearly succeeded. "

St. Giles started to answer, then paused. There was something in what Majendie had just said that he needed a moment to digest. Already attempted "once." Had the "once" simply tumbled out because it was a fact? Or was Majendie trying to tell him something, something he, for some reason, did not want to say directly? Majendie had only to rearrange his hand to see that his high card was not the name of the boy's killer but his knowledge that St. Giles himself was alive. It was something to think about. If the wrong people gained the same knowledge, there would be other Finale Ligures. How far would he be able to walk then? How long?

Wrong people! Majendie and Bosanquet were wrong people. . . . There weren't any right people! Wasn't that why he was still in his chair?

"I wouldn't know where to begin," St. Giles ventured. "I don't know the first thing about counterfeiting."

"But you can learn, Mr. St. Giles. You can learn right here in Hong Kong."

Majendie explained that the most successful known counterfeiter of U.S. currency was a Hong Kong Chinese named Fang Pao-Hua, that Fang already had been approached and had agreed in principle to do the engraving work.

St. Giles observed that "known" counterfeiters might not be the category of artisan from which to seek help. But his protest was half-hearted.

In any event, Majendie was not put off. "Even the best plans entail risk, Mr. St. Giles. Mr. Fang is extremely able. Besides, the artistic aspects of this endeavor will be relatively simple."

St. Giles wondered what, in addition to the "artistic aspects," Majendie had in mind. He didn't like it that Majendie had already given him a partner. If this man Fang was so good, why couldn't he do the whole job?

"I work alone," he said.

"Very wise."

"Extra hands, extra tongues."

"I understand."

"What about Fang?"

"Mr. Fang will engrave the plates. After that we do not need him."

The half smile with which Majendie accompanied this last remark told St. Giles what he already suspected. This was to be Fang's last job. When his turn came—if it came—why would it be different? Careful, he thought. Don't force this man to threaten you. You still have room to breathe. Let him see that you know where things stand and you'll lose that.

"Mr. St. Giles, we are asking you only to help Fang make arrangements for the printing. He is an artist, not a printer; he is not accustomed to dealing with such large volume. We will need your help only until the counterfeit currency is in storage. You need not concern yourself beyond that. I will see to the more difficult matter of distribution."

The two men talked back and forth for nearly an hour. Midway through their discussion they were interrupted by a telephone call, which Majendie took in the rear of the restaurant. To spare himself siting alone with the scowling Bosanquet, St. Giles seized the opportunity to visit the urinal. The telephone conversation could have taken no more than a few minutes, because as he emerged, Majendie was already seating himself. Hidden for a moment by the screen around the men's-room door, he caught a snatch of muttered explanation. It was only a few fractured sentences, but enough to establish one fact: Majendie was the point man rather than the brains behind this operation; he was taking instructions from someone named Joe Berg. St. Giles hadn't dared linger to hear more. But he filed the name away.

"So when the bomb goes off, I can expect to be at a safe distance?" he asked, taking his place at the table again.

"Bunkered, Mr. St. Giles. Bunkered away and safe as a mole. But think about it if you like. Yours, I realize, is a comfortable life. With your current anonymity, a safe one, too. This is not a decision you'll want to make hastily."

Majendie's last statement stretched almost to absurdity the pretense that St. Giles's role was voluntary. But any delay was welcome. A few days to collect his wits would be useful.

The following morning, St. Giles left the Peninsula Hotel and set out for the far side of Hong Kong Island in search of an unusual address Majendie had furnished him. On another occasion he would have taken the ferry to the island and hired a taxi for the trip across to the other side. This day he decided on a walla walla, one of the motor launches that operated as taxis around the harbor. It would allow him to watch his wake.

The harbor was calm under the morning sun. As the small boat cleared the tip of the peninsula, the water traffic thinned. Within fifteen minutes, the walla walla was out of the shipping lanes, and the harbor congestion was behind it. There was only the odd junk, now. Green Island rose off the starboard bow; then they were in the Sulphur Channel, around the western tip of the island, out of sight of the mainland. Several times St. Giles looked back. There was no sign of a following boat.

The engine noise made conversation with the driver impossible. In the noisy solitude St. Giles reflected on his predicament. Did Majendie truly believe he willingly would take this job? Even in his prime and hungry years he wouldn't have been tempted. Was he right to assume he could not say "no"? Or just paranoid? It was still possible to run for it; he could get on a plane that evening and disappear. Majendie and Bosanquet had found him after he left Finale Ligure. But he had been

31

incautious, believing the world thought him dead. He would be more cautious.

What would it gain him? Majendie and Bosanquet did not need to find him. It would be simple for them to bring him back to life in the files of people who had already proved they could find him even when he was supposed to be dead, people like the man who had killed his son in Finale Ligure, people who would make the rest of his life both short and miserable. Best for the time being to play along, he thought. Somewhere between the beginning and the end, he would find a way out.

St. Giles was surprised by the feeling of calm this half-formed decision brought to him. He had crossed U.S. authorities before and very nearly paid with his life. This time he would face the added problem of disentangling himself from Majendie whether or not he accepted and succeeded in the job. Majendie's cavalier dismissal of Fang had made it clear that, win or lose, he did not want witnesses.

Still, these were future dangers. They seemed to him no greater than the dangers he would face immediately if he ran. Strangely, they seemed no worse than the idleness and frustration that had been his daily diet for most of the past year.

The latter realization startled him. Was he, he wondered, a danger junkie? He had known gamblers to whom gambling was its own end—winning merely the means that made it possible. How else to explain the release he felt? In the past, he had accepted danger out of necessity. What did he need now that warranted accepting danger? Unless it was the danger itself. Had his life become such a burden that he could feel its value only when at risk? Except for two weeks with his son, he could not recall from the past year one day he had enjoyed or cared to repeat. He had never considered suicide. But its rationale no longer seemed alien. It wasn't crazy to believe an end to uncompensated endurance no loss.

"Habadeen." The launch driver had turned to face St. Giles and was pointing behind him, off to the left.

"Aberdeen?"

In the direction the driver was pointing he could see what appeared to be the opening of a channel. Moments later, he saw that the land ahead was not a part of the main island but a separate island.

"Hai, Habadeen." The driver nodded affirmatively.

St. Giles had approached Aberdeen before, but always by land. The water ahead was nearly solid with boats. They ranged from tiny sampans to thirty-foot junks and huge blocky houseboats fifty or sixty feet long. Few bore signs of paint, and most flew some form of dingy grey or tawny cloth as sail or sun shield. Linked by planks, they made up a floating city, the largest of several around the island.

St. Giles motioned the driver to slow down. There would be no streets or street signs to point the way. Each boat looked like a hundred others.

Aberdeen, or Chek Py Wan, as the precolonial Chinese had called it, was the Colony's largest fishing community; twenty thousand people living on three thousand boats. How anyone had managed to make the count, without addresses or permanent moorings, was a puzzle to St. Giles. One could count maggots on a pile of garbage, because one could pick them off as one counted. But how did one count the people in Aberdeen Harbour?

It took half an hour of patrolling for St. Giles to find what he was looking for. Majendie had told him that the boat he sought would be the only one in the harbor with a Scott Atwater outboard motor. The motor, Majendie had explained, hadn't run for years, but the old lady liked its gaudy green-and-yellow casing. The story had seemed implausible, but there the motor was, twenty yards ahead.

The driver slowed the boat to a near standstill. St. Giles could see an old woman seated beneath the rounded canvas canopy.

If she noticed their arrival, she offered no welcome. She watched without expression from beneath the dirty canvas, chewing on something she replaced every few seconds from a bowl in her lap.

"Hello." St. Giles attempted his most ingratiating smile as he stepped carefully onto the bow, wary of tipping the sampan. "Uh, let's see . . . *Joe sun?*"

His pidgin Cantonese elicited no reaction.

"Fang Pao-Hua?"

The direct approach seemed more effective. The woman looked up. Encouraged, he went on. "Look, I want to talk to Fang Pao-Hua," he said, speaking loudly and distinctly.

The old woman held up her palm and moved it rapidly from side to side.

"No, no, no, I know he is not here. What I want," he said, pointing to himself, "is for you," pointing to her, "to give Fang," pointing over his shoulder, "this." He concluded by producing a notebook from his pocket.

She appeared not to understand. It occurred to St. Giles that Majendie might have been misinformed.

"See here," he went on, trying to keep his patience. "I would like to see your son, Fang. I have a job for him." He was busy scribbling a note now. "But he can't have the job unless you give him this," he said, handing her the paper on which he had been writing.

"And for you," he said, reaching into his billfold and removing a $500 Hong Kong note, "there is this." The old woman was wide awake now and getting to her feet. "It will be yours when Fang appears at that address," he said, tapping the paper she now held. As she watched, he tore the note in two, handed her the smaller portion and pocketed the other piece. "Remember, I said 'when Fang appears,' which, you will see if you can read that note, as I daresay you can, must be tomorrow." As he turned to climb back into the Walla Walla, he saw her carefully fold the paper and slip it into her smock. She was right to play dumb when people came looking for Fang. If Fang was as good as Majendie claimed, there probably were a lot of people looking for him.

The following day Fang appeared on schedule in the coffee shop of the Mandarin Hotel. The counterfeiter looked exactly as Majendie had described him. He was medium height for a Chinese. But whereas most middle-aged Chinese were sinewy, with deep facial creases, Fang looked as though someone had put a bicycle pump to his navel and inflated him. His skin was smooth as porcelain. His face was the color of Spanish flan, and his hands were small, with delicately tapered fingers. He had, altogether, the look of a plump, pampered doll. And, as St. Giles quickly discovered, he was arrogant.

The two men remained in the coffee shop only briefly. When they left, it was Fang who led the way. They walked east from the hotel, through Wanchai and into a tenement neighborhood. On either side of the street, apartment buildings rose a dozen stories, their façades festooned with washing hung from poles that protruded into the space above the pavement. In a month in Hong Kong, St. Giles had learned something of life in the city's tenements. Eight, ten, twelve people would occupy each room, sharing bedclothes, sleeping in relays to stretch the space. He had learned, too, that the tenement dwellers were the lucky ones. People with less luck would pass the night hunkered down in a boat bottom in one of the city's floating slums, some never in their lives to stand upon dry land. Those with no luck at all inhabited the rickety shacks and packing crates that clung perilously to the hillside above and washed down each year with the rains.

They had walked perhaps a mile when Fang motioned St. Giles into a narrow alleyway. Ahead the alley opened into a courtyard ringed by an open sewer, ripe and slimy with excrement. St. Giles realized that they had been climbing, and in the opposite wall of the courtyard he could see the mouth of another, wider, alley leading directly down the hill. This second alley was filled with tiny shops and open-air stalls. Awnings, canopies and curtains of various shapes and colors marked each establishment and made it impossible to see more than thirty feet ahead or behind.

"Here." Fang had stopped in front of what, for the neighborhood, was a substantial shop. He was gesturing for St. Giles to enter.

"Here?" St. Giles wondered if Fang was serious.

"You are surprised?" Fang wore a condescending smile.

"Bit of a red flag, don't you think?"

The shop before them had no windows at the ground-floor level. On either side of the door, where windows might have been, stood felt-covered boards to which samples of merchandise had been pinned. Above the boards, in red and gold lettering on the wall, were the words "Victoria Engravers."

"Perhaps," Fang answerd. "but in my work, Mr. St. Giles, safety does not lie in concealment, but in camouflage. If I am a florist or a carpenter, and the police come to my shop and discover engraving tools and ink and a press, what can I tell them? But if I am an engraver, and the police come, then I tell them I am an engraver. What else does an engraver have in his shop?"

"Yes, quite," St. Giles conceded, satisfied with the man's logic, but liking him less for the didactic tone he was beginning to suspect was habitual.

"Of course, a man of my reputation needs both to conceal and to camouflage. This shop belongs to my cousin."

St. Giles nodded, mentally adding another black mark to the rapidly filling column next to Fang's name.

The shop was dark. In the half-light, he could make out a front room full of displays and a second behind it where aproned men sat hunched over desks.

Fang's boastful reference to his "reputation" had annoyed him. But from what Majendie had told him, he knew it was justified. Though Fang's was not a business in which one sought notoriety, in the small and specialized world of government counter-counterfeit operations, his work was legendary.

Counterfeiting had changed since the invention of the photo-offset process. Photo-offset made it relatively simple to turn out facsimiles of currency in great volume. The quality was poor, but this was rarely an important consideration; standard operating procedure was to dump and run—the preferred method being to sell the wholesale product at discount to a retailer, then to disappear before quality became an issue.

Fang Pao-Hua didn't operate that way. Fang was an artist. There had been some respectable counterfeits out of Los Angeles in recent years, and one job of especially high quality out of Minneapolis. But none was in a class with Fang's work. When it came to replicating the U.S. twenty-dollar bill, Fang set the standard.

From Majendie, St. Giles also had learned that Fang had never made more than a few thousand bills. No big press runs; everything retouched by hand until as nearly perfect as he could make it. And Fang never wholesaled his bills. He spent them himself for the pure joy of seeing his work pass. He took them to currency-exchange windows at hotels, to travel agents, even to banks, slid them across the counters and looked the cashiers in the eyes as if to say, "Tell me that isn't the finest-looking money you ever saw." No cashier had ever disagreed.

It had taken the chemists to catch Fang. The chemists didn't look for hash marks and highlights. Chemists were not impressed by art. Chemists counted rag content and ink trace elements. They knew how to tell one drying agent from another. The chemists were hard to fool, and Fang had failed to fool them—once in 1962, a second time in 1966.

Upstairs, the shop consisted of a single room in the rear, the front of the building having been taken over by a neighbor with lateral access. This was Fang's work area. At waist level along one wall ran a wide shelf on which were stacked leather engraving pads of various sizes. Behind the pads, racked in five tiers, were several hundred lozens, burins and gravers; flat ones, square ones, round ones, all sizes, some with Bakelite handles, others with thick dowel handles stained with sweat, still others with the characteristic half-chestnut butts, which, cupped in the palm, permitted strong controlled pressure. For light there were three Dazor lamps. Perpendicular to the bench against the back wall was a glass-topped table on which work could be illuminated from below, next to it a collection of jeweler's loupes for magnification.

"More tools than a bloody dentist," St. Giles muttered, surprised at the scale of Fang's layout.

"Do not be impressed by tools," Fang replied. "These are ordinary tools, Grobet mostly, some Glardon—Swiss. Better than the Muller tools made in America, but not good tools. My father had better tools. No matter. Art is not tools. Art is here and here." Fang pointed to his eyes and held up the fingers of his right hand.

He obviously understood what was expected of him, because, without invitation, he began to explain how the engraving would be done.

First, the bill was traced with a steel point on a thin gelatin slab. This tracing was rolled with a cylinder of wax; the traced lines being below the surface, no wax went into them. The gelatin slab was pressed face down against a soft steel plate, giving the plate a coating of wax except where the lines had been traced. The plate was then immersed in a weak acid solution to stain the lines. Finally the wax was removed and the lines scratched out with diamond-shaped gravers.

The two men moved to the light table, where Fang explained the three points of vulnerability for the counterfeiter of twenty-dollar bills: the crosshatching on the portrait of Jackson, the vignette, and the lacy border generally considered impossible to duplicate without a geometric lathe. To show where others had tried and failed to duplicate the work of the U.S. Bureau of Engraving and Printing, Fang produced an inch-thick loose-leaf notebook filled with photographs of twenty-dollar bills.

The book, Fang explained, was one of fewer than a hundred in existence and had been produced at St. Cloud in Paris by Interpol. Its black cover bore in gold lettering the title, *Faux Monnayage, Vingt Dollar, E.U.* It contained the first of Fang's efforts. The second was omitted, having been too nearly perfect for its defects to be reproducible in a photograph.

Confidently, Fang proceeded with his explanation. With sufficient time he could engrave plates so perfect that not ten people in the world would be able to tell they were not genuine. He explained that currently ninety-nine percent of dollar counterfeiting was done by photo-offset. He explained that, by repetitive shooting, a photo-offset bill might be given the appearance of an intaglio engraving. But that it could never be made to feel like one. He produced a twenty-dollar bill and made St. Giles run his fingertip across the Federal Reserve Seal and Letter to feel the raised impression only an intaglio printer could produce. He pointed out the barely visible red and blue fibers in the white portions of the bill, and explained how, though they were in the paper, they could be photographically simulated.

Finally, Fang explained that there was more than artistry to counterfeiting. One had to know the possible combinations and commutations of faceplate numbers, backplate numbers and check letters. One had to know what letter and number went with each series year and with the signatures of which Secretary of the Treasury and which Treasurer. It was helpful also to know that serial numbers, a major preoccupation of some counterfeiters, were not even recorded by the Secret Service Counterfeit Division.

St. Giles listened with interest, occasionally jotting things down in his pocket notebook. He would not need to trouble himself with such details, but it was not every day that one received private instructions from a master. He felt reassured. Whatever other problems there might be with Majendie's plan, it was solid in one respect: Fang knew his business.

"How long will it take to print the number of bills Majendie needs?" St. Giles asked when Fang had finished his explanations.

"That will depend on the size and speed of the press, and on how many hours a day it can be operated," Fang answered. "It could take months."

"Well, what sort of presses are available around here?"

Fang did not answer immediately. He looked puzzled, as though uncertain whether or not to take St. Giles seriously.

"There are no adequate presses in Hong Kong, Mr. St. Giles," he said finally. "Besides which, Mr. Majendie wants the bills produced in Europe. He didn't explain that?"

"No, I don't think he did."

St. Giles wondered if he had missed this detail or if Majendie had simply forgotten to tell him. He did recall Majendie saying the counterfeits would be distributed in Europe. What Fang said made sense.

"Of course it would be best to do the printing in Europe, wouldn't it? Wouldn't have the transport then. Do you know any printers in Europe? Someone we might use?"

Again Fang looked puzzled. When finally he answered, his tone was cold and final.

"I am not going to use anyone, Mr. St. Giles. Mr. Majendie told me that he was going to use you."

CHAPTER 4

So that was it! Fang was to make the plates. Majendie was to distribute the money after it was printed. He, St. Giles—presumably indignant over the inequities of the monetary system—was to do everything in between.

Not bloody likely!

He was being asked to take all the risk. What would Fang risk by making a few plates? Or Majendie and Bosanquet? Until they took delivery of the counterfeit money there would be nothing but his word to connect them to the project. Did Majendie take him for a fool?

St. Giles spit at the sidewalk with disgust. "Not bloody likely," he muttered as he made his way back down the hill. He knew nothing about counterfeiting, but moving ship cargo had taught him the simple geometry of three-man jobs. The trick was to avoid being the man in the middle. On either end a man could carry no more than half the load, even with a deadbeat in the middle. But a deadbeat on either end could make the man in the middle carry the whole load. Even though he might suspect he was being taken advantage of, the man in the middle couldn't prove it. Majendie's game was growing clearer.

It was raining as he headed back toward the ferry, not a light, steady European drizzle, but fat lazy drops that slapped the pavement like water bombs, sending up a rush of warm street smells. Lost in thought, he took no notice. He had promised Majendie an answer that afternoon. Forty-eight hours had seemed time enough to gather his wits. Now, as he made his way back through the crowded streets of Wanchai, he was no closer to seeing a way out. If he took the job and succeeded, he would become a skeleton Majendie's government would never tolerate in its closet. Run and his chances of survival weren't much better.

What, then?

He could go along with Majendie, hope to discover whom he and Bosanquet represented, then bargain: silence for silence. . . . No. Governments didn't buy silence from individuals; they eliminated them. It was cheaper, safer.

Then kill them? Why not? Majendie had all but told him Fang was to be killed. Majendie intended eventually to kill him, too. He had no doubt of that. So why wait? He had spoken cautiously to Majendie at their first meeting, taken care not to betray the depth of his reservations. Majendie would be wary when they met again that afternoon, but he would not expect to be shot before a discussion.

But killing Majendie and Bosanquet might only precipitate what he wanted to avert. What if Majendie had told others he was alive—perhaps the Joseph Berg character who had telephoned Majendie while they were in the Red Pepper Restaurant, or other people in whatever government they served? Kill Majendie and Bosanquet and within a week he might again be a "live" item in the files of every significant security force in the world.

There had to be a less risky way out. He just needed time.

By the time he reached the ferry it was raining in Oriental earnest. Standing next to the throbbing rail he gazed down the harbor to where brown water merged into rainy greyness. He had not been happy in Hong Kong. Still, until the preceding week Hong Kong had been far from everything he had wanted to put behind him. Crossing its harbor now for what he realized might be the last time, he knew that he was going to miss the colony's fragile isolation. He would miss, too, its noise and its smells and its color. Most of all he would miss its people, with their ability to ignore what they were not intended to see. People who lived one on top of another mastered such private arts. He would not find them in the world he was about to re-enter.

Majendie and Bosanquet were waiting at the hotel.

"So you have met Mr. Fang," Majendie began. "What did you think? Fang is imperious, but the man's a genius when he is scratching away with his implements."

St. Giles nodded, intent on Majendie's accent more than his observations, aware that this might be his last chance for a while to glean some hint of the man's nationality.

"I'm sure," he answered, "though I don't much like it that he's been caught twice already."

"Ego," said Majendie. "Putting his money into circulation isn't enough for Fang. He knows most reasonable facsimiles get past store clerks, even bank tellers, especially those dealing in currencies not their own."

"You explained all that. . . . He takes it to where he is most likely to be caught."

"Precisely."

"Yes, well I'm not too keen on that either."

"Nor am I. But that's Fang. Those people are Fang's critics; the danger, the price of their praise. But so much for Fang. What about you?"

St. Giles thought for a moment about how to answer. Majendie would be listening not just to what he said, but to the way he said it. How was he going to say "yes" with credible enthusiasm in view of the reservations he'd expressed two days before. Don't go overboard, don't make him suspicious, he told himself.

"I'll give it a go," he told Majendie.

"Splendid," Majendie said clapping his huge hands in front of him. "Splendid."

For nearly an hour, while Bosanquet sat looking on, Majendie and St. Giles discussed details. Locating an adequate and accessible press in Europe would be his first task. Majendie could offer no advice. Expenses had been provided for. Money had been deposited in a Paris bank account that St. Giles could draw against. Though Paris had been chosen as a central location, St. Giles was free to work where and as he pleased. The only constraint was that he complete the job within six months.

"You can appreciate," Majendie explained, "that the danger in what we are doing will be a function of how long we take to do it."

St. Giles nodded, tempted to say he was also aware of how the danger was being apportioned.

Communications between the two of them were to cease once the project was underway. Dealings with Fang were St. Giles's responsibility. He was reponsible, too, for dispatching the Chinese after the plates were in hand. For this, he was given a Telex number and told that the party on the other end would require only Fang's precise whereabouts. Should it be necessary to eliminate others to protect the project, the Telex number guaranteed forty-eight-hour service anywhere within three hundred miles of an international airport.

St. Giles stared at the card Majendie had handed him, trying to look unruffled. The card bore an eight-digit number, the first three of which, 448, he recognized as the country code for the Netherlands. The three call-back letters following the number, ADM, he assumed meant Amsterdam. It was as though Majendie had handed him a ray gun, or his own wallet-size, target-seeking missile. He held the card gingerly, half supposing that it might go off if dropped. Was he really supposed to use the number? How could he be sure it would work? Try a dry run? Or was the number just to help Majendie keep track of where he was? He had played in some fast and ruthless company before. But he'd never seen anything to match this. And done so matter-of-factly.

The Paris bank account would be monitored, Majendie told him. If he needed more money, he was to draw down the balance to an even five thousand francs and cease activity in the account for three days. This would be understood as a signal, and the account would be replenished.

"And when I am through?" St. Giles asked.

Majendie explained that when the counterfeit bills were printed and ready for distribution, St. Giles was to take a personal ad in the Paris *Herald Tribune.* The ad was to run one week and to announce the availability of a young American woman, willing for a fee to speak English with French businessmen on their lunch hours. Ads of this nature were common in the *Tribune,* so St. Giles was to specify the girl's name as Lynn H. The telephone number was to be of the Odéon exchange, the four-digit number to spell out the time of afternoon or evening when Majendie would meet St. Giles. The meeting would take place on the Sunday following the week the ads ran. At St. Giles's suggestion, it was agreed that the meeting be in

Paris at the Jackie Bar, on Rue Jules-Chaplain, a stone's throw from Boulevard du Montparnasse.

St. Giles congratulated himself silently on this last arrangement. He devoutly hoped the meeting would never take place. But if it did, it would at least be on familiar ground.

"Mr. Majendie"—there was one thing St. Giles wanted to make clear—"as I told you earlier, I like to work alone. I trust we understand each other on that?"

"Certainly."

"Then I may assume if someone is following me that he is working against the project."

"I think we understand one another, Mr. St. Giles," Majendie said. "I will suggest to anyone who wants to follow you that they consult my friend Bosanquet here as to what they can expect."

Bosanquet nodded grudgingly. Though the mustachioed man's eye was still an ugly reddish blue, the swelling on the side of his face had receded.

"I have every confidence in you, Mr. St. Giles. We are going to succeed. We shall break the tyranny of the dollar, accelerate the progress of history by a decade, maybe more. It is a great undertaking, this thing we do, a great undertaking." Majendie shook his head silently as though rapturous at thoughts of the good fight.

It was St. Giles who finally broke the silence. "The name."

"Ah, yes," Majendie responded, returning from his reveries. "The name. Bosanquet, would you get me the key." Bosanquet disappeared, returning in a moment with a small steel key, which he handed Majendie.

"That is the key to the name, Mr. St. Giles."

St. Giles examined the key. An inch and a half in length, flat rather than sculpted, and engraved with a five-digit number, it looked like the key to a safe-deposit box.

"That, Mr. St. Giles, is the key to a box in the Central Post Office here in Hong Kong. When you have completed your job, the name will be in that box."

Majendie paused. He wore the look of a man who, having made an inscrutable statement, expected a question.

He got, instead, a granite stare.

"Yesterday," Majendie at length resumed, "using that post-office box as a mailing address, I borrowed one hundred thousand Swiss francs, putting up dollar-denominated bonds as collateral, and prepaying the interest for one year. Do you understand what that means?"

St. Giles did not answer. He had more than a passing acquaintance with banking and a four-million-dollar interest in learning anything new Majendie might want to teach him, but he was not certain what Majendie was driving at.

"It means, Mr. St. Giles, that if all goes according to plan, the name you want will be in that post-office box by the end of the summer. When the counterfeit twenty-dollar bills are put into circulation, they will trigger a chain reaction that will move so quickly it will not matter that the money is not real. The bad money will be the ruin of the good. The U.S. dollar will fall on the exchange markets, all other currencies, as well as gold, will rise against it, my Swiss-franc loan will be undercollateralized, and the bank will send a notice asking for more collateral to protect itself. When this happens, the notice will be sent to that post-office box. That notice is what you are waiting for, Mr. St. Giles. Because my loan is written in the name of the man who killed your son. So, you see, you get what you want when I get what I want." Majendie smiled.

CHAPTER 5

Alitalia's flight 776 for Tokyo was already boarding when St. Giles arrived at Kai Tak Airport the following afternoon. Half an hour later he was airborne, watching Hong Kong and its sister islands fall away to the south.

Most of the morning and early afternoon he had spent with Fang. He had again sought advice on where to look for a press, but the Chinese had been no help. Fang never used automated presses. He knew a little about them and might have found a small one in Hong Kong. About Europe he knew nothing. That was St. Giles's problem. And he would have to move quickly. Fang could start the engraving work and proceed with the roll die. But he could not make the plates until he knew the size and manufacturer of the press. Fang would need this information as soon as possible.

Since Majendie had done nothing about arranging to pay Fang, much of their visit was consumed in working out those details. It was agreed that Fang would receive immediately fifty thousand Hong Kong dollars, an additional two hundred thousand to be paid upon delivery of the plates.

The two men had disagreed over where the plates were to be delivered. Fang insisted on delivery in Hong Kong, St. Giles on delivery in Paris, neither man wanting to take them through customs. In the end, an additional twenty thousand Hong Kong dollars resolved the issue in favor of Paris. Because St. Giles would have no fixed address, it was agreed that he would contact Fang periodically to check progress.

In Tokyo that night, St. Giles connected with a Korean Airlines flight to Hawaii, and the next morning in Honolulu boarded a Pan Am flight to San Francisco. By the time the plane touched down at San Francisco's international airport, he had been in transit for more than twenty-six hours; a day's sleep poorer, but richer by a day on the calendar, having crossed the international date line.

St. Giles's business in the San Francisco area was personal, unrelated to counterfeiting or the events of the preceding week. His son had lived across the bay, in El Cerrito, the boy's mother in nearby Sausalito. He had no desire to see the woman who had briefly been his lover. But until she was told their son was dead, the boy could not have a proper funeral. It had been preying on him since Finale Ligure.

That evening, at 10:00 P.M., he boarded American Airlines flight 94, the "red-eye," for New York City, and then on to Paris.

It was raining in Paris. Wet streets and morning traffic slowed the airport bus, and it was nearly ten o'clock by the time he reached the Invalides Terminal. Though it was not yet the tourist season, he knew that most Paris hotels would still be filled, the rooms opening that day not available until early afternoon. Gambling, he hailed a taxi and gave the driver the name of the smallest, most obscure hotel he could remember.

Half an hour later, unpacked, he was dozing comfortably in a room at the Gerson, an undistinguished, lobbyless, six-floor walk-up across Rue de la Sorbonne from the university. Except for a trip to the end of the corridor to use the toilet, with its water-repellent toilet paper, he did not leave his bed in the Gerson for twenty hours.

It was not until two days later—nearly two weeks after he first had noticed the large red-faced man and his mustachioed partner at Shek-O beach on Hong Kong Island—that St. Giles walked into a café on Boulevard St-Michel, purchased a jetton from the cashier and made the telephone call that he hoped would tell him what Fang had not been able to.

"United States Embassy, good morning." The switchboard operator was obviously a French national, for the words were heavily accented.

"Commercial section, please."

"Thank you. One moment, please."

St. Giles waited. Worried that his accent might cause a problem, he practiced biting off his r's, forcing his voice up from the back of his throat and through his nose in the American manner.

"Commercial section, Mr. Sewall's office." It was a secretary on the line.

"Yeah, right, my name is Clarkson. I'm with the John Deere Company, and I'd like to speak with Mr. Sewall for a sec, if he's got the time."

A moment later, he had the commercial attaché on the line. The man was friendly and listened attentively as St. Giles, doing his best to sound like a businessman from the Midwest, described his needs.

His company, he explained, was planning a European expansion. Because of government restrictions on capital exports, it was considering an offering of bonds in the European market.

The company had already made arrangements with Morgan & Cie and with its U.S. underwriter, Merrill Lynch. He, Clarkson, was in Paris to nail down final details. Could the embassy recommend a local printing firm that did acceptable certificate work? Dry intaglio printing being a dying art, such firms were not easy to find.

He was sure his attempt at imitation was a failure. But if the attaché noticed, he was too polite to say anything. After a few minutes of searching, the man was able to locate the names of three printers with whom American companies had dealt in the past. Two of the firms were in Paris proper, the third in a suburb called Asnières. Because of its pronunciation, he spelled the third name. St. Giles scribbled down the three addresses, thanked the man and hung up.

He ruled out the two Paris firms; transportation and storage would likely be problems, and an in-town location would only compound them. That left the Asnières firm, to which he placed a call and arranged an appointment for that afternoon.

A train from Gare Saint-Lazare got him to Asnières by early afternoon. The neighborhood was encouraging: narrow streets, warehouses, little retail life; little to keep people on the streets in the daytime, nothing to keep them out after ten or eleven at night. It was as good a location as he could have hoped for.

The same story he had used with the attaché drew the solicitous attention of the firm's manager. Proudly, the little man in an ink-stained apron showed him around the plant, pointing out its brand-new, steel-grey Koebau-Giori & De la Rue press. Flattered by the embassy's reference, he produced samples of the firm's certificate work. St. Giles was effusively appreciative: the engravings were fine, very fine indeed; he was most impressed; he would pass on his opinion to his company's higher-ups. They would, he assured the manager, be equally impressed when they learned of the excellent work being done in Asnières.

But privately, St. Giles was appalled. The press was a monster, a locomotive-scale piece of machinery, bedecked with dials, gauges, buttons, wheels, all manner of gadgetry.

At the far end of it, a man had just begun to feed paper onto a belt that ran along the top of the machine. As St. Giles watched, the belt commenced to snatch paper from a huge stack next to where the man stood. In overlapping sheets held flat by rollers, the paper traveled halfway across the top of the press, dove into a slot, disappeared for a moment, then emerged at the far end of the press and glided into a hopper bearing the printed image of . . . St. Giles tilted his head sideways but he could not make it out. A second man removed the first several sheets printed and discarded them. The press was stopped, an adjustment of some sort made, then the press was restarted. It was five minutes before the machine was working to the two men's satisfaction.

"How many sheets will it print an hour?" St. Giles had to yell the question over the noise of the press.

The manager did not even attempt to speak. Taking a pencil from his pocket he jotted a number on a piece of paper. St. Giles raised his eyebrows to indicate he was impressed. The manager smiled with fatherly pride and gave the double thumbs-up sign.

The press was running itself now. Both workmen had disappeared. But the operating hurdles, which back in Hong Kong St. Giles had hoped would be manageable, now seemed insuperable. He could not figure out even where the plates were located, let alone how they might be attached. Another problem, an obvious one, but one he had not foreseen, was that the press printed only one side of the paper at a time. After the first side had been run off, the sheets would have to be carried from one end of the machine to the other, the plates changed, the paper aligned, and the whole batch rerun. How was he to do that? And how was he to cut up the bills when he was through? How, for that matter, was he going to get the paper? Finally, there was the problem of the serial number and the Treasury seal. To apply these, he would need to use a second, smaller, press and a different color ink.

Had Majendie known what he was asking? The job obviously required professional help—a fact that multiplied the risk many times. No wonder Majendie hadn't wanted any part of it.

He spent the train ride back from Asnières staring gloomily at the dreary trackside apartment blocks. Printing was much more complicated than he had thought. Nor were his spirits lifted when, on arriving, he found the station aswarm with commuters. The crowd told him that the Métro, the only convenient way back to his hotel, would also be jammed. The way his luck was running, he would probably spend twenty minutes standing up under the river on a stalled train gagging on Parisian Métro breath.

What to do? Should he go to Majendie and describe the practical obstacles he had just observed? Majendie was an intelligent man. He would appreciate a hopeless situation when he saw one.

But how to get in touch with Majendie? St. Giles had the bank account, and the Telex number Majendie had given him. But he had no way to contact Majendie himself. This was a fix he hadn't bargained on. He couldn't move forward; he couldn't get permission to retreat. And the more time that elapsed before Majendie learned his plan wasn't feasible the angrier and more vindictive he would be.

He'd been a fool back in Hong Kong not to make Majendie give him some sort of emergency contact number. With so complex a project, Majendie should have anticipated the need to consult now and then. The oversight didn't make any sense. Unless . . . unless it wasn't an oversight. . . . Unless Majendie had deliberately cut him off. Unless Majendie emphatically did not want to hear about obstacles such as the press in Asnières. Unless . . .

St. Giles remembered a Romanian in his unit in North Africa who never had tired of telling a story about two men who wanted to move a piano up a flight of stairs. After fruitlessly struggling for some time with its weight, one of the men had gone for assistance. Upon returning, he found his friend and the piano safely installed on the second floor. Astonished, he asked how his partner had managed to do alone what they had not been able to do together.

"With my cat," replied the partner. "I tied my cat to the piano, and she pulled it up the stairs."

"Your cat pulled that piano up the stairs?" the first man exclaimed, incredulous.

"Well," confided his partner, "I did have to use a whip."

Each telling had sent the Romanian into gales of laughter. But it did not amuse St. Giles now to recall it. Of course Majendie knew the difficulties; he could not have planned such a project for long and not learned what St. Giles had discovered that afternoon. The ugly truth was staring him in the face. Majendie wanted him cut off. Because Majendie wanted him afraid. Fear was to be Majendie's whip.

He was Majendie's cat.

Some men respond heroically to terminal prognosis, begin to live more intensely, accomplish prodigies of work. Each minute is savored, each hour stuffed with a week's feelings and thoughts. Experiences grown dull with repetition become piquant again with the knowledge that each may be the last.

St. Giles got no such compensations. He had nothing he

yearned to crowd into the time remaining—no relationships to mend, no one for whom to make provision. Paris was no help. March of 1971 dealt day upon day of chill rain that turned the city's newly steam-cleaned monuments to cheerless lumps of dripping dark stone. Those weeks might have been the breaking point.

In the end, it was anger that rescued Peregrin St. Giles. He had taken the bait Majendie had dangled. It was too late to undo that. But he could at least put up a fight. More than one fisherman had been yanked from his boat by a fish he underestimated. This decision to strike back at the man who had dragooned him out of retirement fueled a welcome and warming rage. He had as yet no plan. But he had something that money and the loss of his son had killed: he had a purpose.

Two days after his visit to Asnières, St. Giles went to the café on Rue des Ecoles at the foot of the hill below his hotel, got out the Paris telephone directory and began to search it. He found several Majendies, a few Bosanquets and a whole page of Bergs. It had occurred to him that his patrons might be French, that Majendie and Bosanquet might be right there in Paris. But only for Berg did he have a first name, and, astonishingly, there was not a single Joseph Berg in all of Paris. Not one!

St. Giles left the café, walked up the hill and across the bottom of the Luxembourg Garden. Ten minutes later he was in the Franklin Delano Roosevelt Library thumbing through the Manhattan telephone book.

Berg, Joann. Berg, John. Berg, Judith. Berg, Julius M.

No Joseph, no Johann, no Josephine; nothing in New York either. Incredible!

Half an hour with a lank-haired lady at the Bibliothèque Nationale turned up additional surprising, if inconclusive, information. The name Bosanquet was, of course, of French origin, but the only Bosanquets to have left their mark on anything seemed to have been British. Majendie, the same. The name was French Huguenot, but the odds were at least even that its bearer was British.

Then what were the accents? For his morning's work he had managed only to confuse that issue.

What to do next? Back in his room, he reviewed his options. There weren't many. He couldn't make Majendie's plan work. He couldn't reach Majendie to cancel the plan. He couldn't sit still and do nothing or he would go crazy. He had to appear to be doing something in case Majendie was having him watched. He had, in the meantime, to figure some way out.

There had to be a way. Majendie had implied that the printing of the counterfeits would be relatively easy, called his own job—distributing them—"more difficult." Why was distribution so difficult? The red-faced man had talked of dumping. Surely that was a figure of speech. To have their desired effect, the counterfeits had to be put into circulation; Majendie wouldn't risk depositing them where they could be found and destroyed. The only way St. Giles knew to put them in circulation was to spend them on something. And that would take time.

"A deluge of dollars," Majendie had called it. Enough to ensure there would not be buyers to clear the market at anything remotely near the current price. That the bills might soon be discovered to be counterfeit Majendie had called unimportant. Currency markets were seismometers of fear; expectations fulfilled themselves. . . . "You get what you want when I get what I want," the man had told him.

St. Giles was pacing his hotel room excitedly now. A pinprick of light had appeared in the gloom. If expectations were enough . . . He broke off his pacing, seized a piece of paper from the table by his bed and began to make some calculations.

After a few minutes he went to his suitcase and got out the notebook in which he had jotted notes during his first talk with Fang. He read and reread what the Chinese had told him of the markings and design of a twenty-dollar bill. The vaguest outlines of a plan were forming in his head. It might not be necessary to counterfeit money. It might be possible to counterfeit counterfeiting. Once more he turned to his notes to check something. The thought that had come to him ten minutes before was holding up under scrutiny. Why would it not work? It was brilliant. He could give Majendie his dollar devaluation, keep his anonymity, and get the name of his son's murderer without printing anything at all. It would be complicated. It would take time. And he would have to make the U.S. authorities believe they were dealing with a master counterfeiter. There were sure to be other problems, too. But as Majendie himself had said, no plan is without risk. . . .

How many sheets of paper had the man at the printing plant said the machine could print in an hour? Ten thousand? St. Giles guessed at the number of bills that might fit on one sheet, then did more calculations. From his billfold, he produced a card calendar, studied it for a moment, then replaced it. For fully five minutes he sat on the edge of his bed, his face buried in his hands, deep in thought. Fang might be a problem. The rest he thought he could improvise. He would have to make believers out of some very sophisticated people; whatever could be checked had to be exactly right. Suddenly, he found himself hoping Majendie and Bosanquet were not French. Better Argentine, or Australian; better anything but French. The farther from Paris they were, the better his chances.

The last thing St. Giles did before leaving his hotel room was to spend half an hour with his French dictionary composing a cable, a cable he would send the next morning to the financial attaché at the French Embassy in Washington.

Much later that night, when it was morning on the other side of the world, he made a telephone call to Fang in Hong Kong. There was to be a little change in plans. Fang could throw away the plates he had begun engraving. The plates St. Giles wanted Fang to make would be much simpler.

On the other end of the line, Fang was baffled. St. Giles had gone crazy. The man was asking him to mutilate good money. He was asking Fang, the miracle engraver, to turn wine back into water.

CHAPTER 6

One Monday morning late in the spring of 1971, Vergil Koenig received a copy of a cable.

Koenig got it from the CIA, which had got it from Western Union, which had routinely plucked it out of the international traffic under a twenty-year-old policy of sharing with the agency all cables with possible bearing on national security.

For Koenig, receiving a cable was nothing special. As director of the Secret Service Counterfeit Division, he was accustomed to looking at communications intended for other people. Dozens of them—cables, telegrams, letters and telephone transcripts—were referred each week for his review.

Generally, he found them a waste of time.

The security community, like most large bureaucracies, was riddled with rivalry. Information was power, and agencies shared it with reluctance. If one agency passed information to another, it was because the information had been evaluated and judged useless. Occasionally someone got sloppy and let something through his fingers. But rarely at the CIA.

After six years in the director's office, Koenig knew this, so it was with only mild interest that he had happened this morning on a photostatic copy of a cable among the other materials in the blue folder sent over from Langley. The date at the top indicated that the CIA had held it only a few days. During that time, the CIA's executive secretariat would have shopped it around the agency. Had even one office taken interest, it would have gone no farther. The fact that Koenig now held it in his hand meant it had passed right through the CIA's digestive tract and into the crap bag the CIA shipped out each day as its contribution to interagency cooperation.

Koenig reread the cable, then read it a third time.

Could the CIA have sent something useful?

He read it one more time, allowing a smile to form on his lips. It had never surprised him that the referrals the CIA considered crap, he also considered crap. What made him smile now was that the people at the CIA were so convinced this would be the case that apparently none of them had bothered to keep a record of what was sent out. Had they done so, they would have known the cable he held in his hand was the third of its kind they had sent him in two weeks.

There was nothing especially significant about the number three. Another man in Koenig's position might have been moved to act after seeing the first cable, or the second. It just happened that, for Koenig, three was the number that tipped the balance against inertia. That morning, shortly before noon, after reading the cable for the fourth time, he decided the normal routine was not enough. He wanted a thorough investigation.

"What do you make of this, Jack?"

Koenig had called his assistant, Jack Childress, to his office. He pushed the cable across the desk, swiveled his chair toward the window and watched out of the corner of his eye as Childress read.

Childress had been with the service for ten years. He had graduated from the Citadel, spent three years in the army, received his discharge papers at Fort Myer and signed on the next week. Until he moved to the Counterfeit Division to work for Koenig, his duty had all been on the service's strong-arm side—working crowds, riding running boards, walking around Washington with a walkie-talkie plug in his ear.

When his previous assistant, Simon Barfield, had retired the previous autumn, having smoked up his health along with three packs a day of Salems, Koenig had let the job stay vacant for three months. Barfield had been the perfect number-two man: three decades in the service, a human card catalog of case information and a brilliant analyst.

But Barfield had been unusual. Talents like his more often occurred in constellation with other, less benign, gifts. It had been easy not to feel threatened by a cynical fifty-six-year-old man with a consumptive cough and a liverwurst complexion. But another man with Barfield's critical gifts might have administrative ambitions as well, might not look upon responsibility with Barfield's abhorrence, or be content with the same anonymity. Not that an assistant, however ambitious, was going to take Koenig's job. The civil service advancement schedule, with its rigid time-in-grade requirements, was more than adequate protection. Still, a "bright" assistant could have been a pain in the ass. Koenig had hired Childress less for what he was than for what he wasn't. He was not proud of his reasons, but he had since been happy with the decision.

"This come from the CIA?" Childress, still studying the cable, asked the question without looking up.

"Uh-huh."

"Well, you have to figure it was sent by the same guy who sent the other cables to the French financial attaché. You'd think, though, that Western Union could source these things more specifically. I've never been to Paris, but it's bound to be a big place. It would help if we knew all the cables had been sent from the same office."

"We do."

"We do?"

"The number in the upper left-hand corner identifies the sending station."

"Each station has a different number?"

"You got it, Jack."

"Son of a gun." Childress shook his head as Koenig had seen him do a hundred times in the previous months—as if to say, "You learn something new every day," which, in fact, Childress often did say, and which, in his case, was true.

Childress was not stupid; he simply was not shy about admitting what he didn't know. Koenig had learned to appreciate the trait. After Barfield's ready answers, it was refreshing to do the tutoring for a change. He tried not to be patronizing, though sometimes the temptation was more than he could resist.

Childress satisfied Koenig's Northern notions of what a Southern boy ought to be. Physically, he might have been a frontispiece for an orthopedic manual. He was all slabs and knots, with a stomach like the underside of a hard-shell crab. Koenig had seen similar stomachs on Southeast Conference running backs who cut their football shirts off below the shoulder pads, and years earlier he'd decided that musculature had something to do with climate. People in the North didn't have stomachs like that. They hadn't at Colgate in the late 1940s, at any rate. Childress's face would not have struck most people as remarkable, but to Koenig, raised in the ethnic stew of Springfield, Massachusetts, the very plainness of its heavy, even features marked Childress as different.

His hair had been short when Koenig hired him. But in a reach for urbanity, Childress had bought himself a hair style to go with the times. From the part on the left side of his head, his straight blond hair had been pulled forward, swept low across his forehead, then back over his right ear—the whole arrangement puffed up and immobilized with spray. The stylist had managed in this fashion to conceal the bald spot on the top of his head. But not without cost. A smaller, more fine-boned man might have got away with the effect; Childress wore his newly bought plumage as Jim Thorpe might a tutu.

The cables had run to type. All, sent from the same station in Paris, were short and cryptic; all were unsigned; all had been addressed to Jean-François Seydoux, the French financial attaché in Washington, and all had hinted at a massive counterfeiting operation.

"What have we heard from the fences, Jack?"

"Not a damn thing."

After the first cable, Koenig had ordered a check of everyone in the files with a record of passing counterfeit money. This was routine. Traffic in counterfeit money was like traffic in drugs, recidivism being the rule rather than the exception.

In counterfeiting, the game was to get rid of the goods quickly. No sophisticated counterfeiter attempted anything so foolhardy as to spend what he had made. He sold it to distributors, most of them all-purpose fences, who resold it in turn to wholesalers, at a markup. From the wholesalers the counterfeit bills went to the street, often to narcotics addicts, who paid twenty-five to thirty percent of face value. It was the addicts who finally put the phony bills into circulation. Too frightened to spend the bad money directly for drugs and risk retribution from their dealers, they converted it. Sometimes this meant buying an expensive item that would be returned the next day. More often it meant simply walking into a drugstore, buying a pack of cigarettes with a twenty-dollar bill and walking out with clean change.

The weakness of the distribution chain was its last link. The addicts were imprudent. Addled and least cautious at the very time they were most in need of money, they were easy to catch.

But they were only the tail end of the problem; with thousands roaming the streets, to pursue them was a prodigal use of the division's resources. The efficient approach was to get one addict, then work back up the chain to the people making the bills.

This was not hard. With a little pressure, the addict could be persuaded to identify his wholesaler, the wholesaler would identify his distributor and the distributor would finger the counterfeiter. At each stage, the price of the information was immunity from prosecution.

Since the division's job was to put the counterfeiter out of business, this price had always been considered acceptable. This method of enforcement had one shortcoming: the distribution system remained intact, ready to service the next counterfeiter who happened along.

Most of the distributors and wholesalers were well known to the division, and it was to several dozen of them that inquiries had routinely been made when the first cable was received. When big distributions got under way, word traveled fast. Almost always there was someone who had been cut out of the action and was happy to pass on information in return for future consideration.

"You haven't heard anything? Nothing at all?" Koenig was surprised. There should have been some response; even if only malicious gossip, one distributor or wholesaler trying to make trouble for the competition.

"Nothing," Childress repeated. "I've been through the files. There's nothing there."

"How about the Fed banks; anything there?"

"Nope."

Koenig already knew this to be the case. If any Federal Reserve Bank had turned up a new counterfeit bill, it would have reported it immediately to the service. The bill, its identifying marks and the point at which it had been removed from circulation would have been recorded in a volume called *Counterfeit Note Index*. If the bill turned out to be from a run not already on record in the index, a "notice of new counterfeit" would have been issued, sent to the Secret Service's sixty-five regional offices and to the head office of Interpol. Koenig had checked the index that morning, before he called Childress. He had found nothing.

"You know what I figure, Jack? I figure this is all a pile of crap."

"How do you mean?"

"Well, first off, we've been getting these cables a couple of weeks now. They talk about delivering counterfeit money, which nobody with a full deck does in a cable. Right? So where is it? We haven't yet seen any money. That doesn't make sense."

"I know. If these things are for real, then the guy who's sending them ain't the fastest worker this business has ever seen," Childress said.

"Assuming we're talking about the same business."

"What do you mean?"

"I'm not sure," Koenig answered. "Has it occurred to you there are other things besides money that get counterfeited? Maybe this guy is into credit cards. Maybe he's some kind of copyright pirate. Maybe he's just a kook."

"Then how come the French financial attaché?"

"Well, how come the French financial attaché, even if it is money? What the hell is he mixed up in counterfeiting for?" Koenig paused for a moment. "Another thing I don't figure, Jack, is why cables? Jesus, from Paris to any embassy here

. . . that's about the dumbest way to send a message. . . . I can't believe anybody who would get mixed up in any kind of big operation wouldn't know that. It's safer to send a postcard than a goddamn cable."

"Vergil, why would someone in France be wanting to tell someone here anything anyway? You don't suppose they're planning to bring the stuff into the States?"

"Dunno," Koenig replied.

The same question had bothered him since he had decided to take the cables seriously. It was not uncommon for U.S. currency to be counterfeited abroad. Just two years earlier the Australian police had seized twelve and a half million in counterfeit bills in a basement in Melbourne. And there had been a dozen cases in which U.S. currency had been produced domestically and shipped abroad for distribution.

But there had never, in Koenig's experience, been a case in which the opposite had occurred—in which money had been counterfeited abroad and brought to the United States for distribution. It defied logic to import counterfeit money. The sensible place to sell an inferior product was where the product's inferiority was least likely to be recognized. If the product was bogus U.S. currency, that place was not the United States.

A few years earlier, Koenig had read in the newspaper of a man who had used a Confederate bill to buy a train ticket in the north of England. The story had struck him as funny, and the ticket clerk as a fool—until it occurred to him that he had no idea what half of the world's currencies looked like, even what the names of the countries would look like written in their own languages.

Not every counterfeiter could get his work out of the country whose currency he had counterfeited; but no counterfeiter in his right mind would surrender that advantage once he had it.

Koenig had been pacing as he thought. He was standing now

at the far end of his office looking at the pigeons on the ledge outside the window. He had watched the pigeons for six years and for six years wondered why they sat there. There couldn't possibly be anything to eat on the ledge. And why were all pigeons the same size? Where were the baby pigeons?

Behind him, Childress's silence told him what he had known all along. With Barfield gone he could not expect advice. Nobody was going to tell him what his next step should be. For a long time he stood watching the greyish birds basking in the midday sun. He'd give it a few more days. If no counterfeits had turned up by then, he'd call the French Embassy and set up an appointment with the financial attaché, Seydoux.

Koenig left his office shortly after six that evening. He walked the two blocks north to Pennsylvania Avenue and had three quick drinks at the Roger Smith Hotel. It was nearly seven-thirty when he finally arrived in Bethesda. Ruthie was waiting.

Vergil and Ruthie had married in the summer of 1946, the year they finished high school, and in twenty-five years together they had assimilated one another's physical and personality traits to such a degree that their partnership appeared less a marriage than some sort of genetic merger. A little on the short side and decidedly overweight, neither of them had ever been much to look at, which was one of the reasons for their closeness—that and their childlessness, to which they had long ago resigned themselves, and of which by tacit agreement neither ever spoke.

"What kind of day was it?" Ruthie had seated herself next to Koenig in the dining alcove, where she could watch him eat.

"Umm, so-so. How 'bout you?"

"So-so."

Dinner was Salisbury steak, and Koenig was enjoying it. Ruthie's willingness to do for him was one of the things he loved about her, having learned its value the hard way. Six or seven years earlier, Ruthie had gone for a three-week visit to her sister's and left him to do for himself. He had eaten well enough. But not knowing how to cope with each meal's leavings, he had simply pushed them into the back of the refrigerator. By the time Ruthie returned, the kitchen had smelled like a Crimean hospital tent.

As usual, Koenig ate too much. By the time Ruthie had cleared off his dishes and they'd settled on the couch in front of the TV set, he was feeling remorse. Ten years earlier, at thirty-four, he had made himself a promise. He was going to get in shape. He had read that after thirty-five the body could not make up lost ground—it had to do with muscle elasticity or something. If you let yourself get run down after thirty-five, you stayed run down. He had weighed one hundred and ninety pounds when he made himself that promise. Now he weighed two hundred and ten.

The weight itself did not bother him. He had always been stocky. His father had been stocky. What did bother him was that in recent years he had become aware that some people associated brawn with stupidity. Indeed, it was more than "some people." There seemed to be a general cultural endorsement of frailness. It troubled him. There was nothing frail about Koenig. Playing football at Colgate, he had once torn his shoulder ligaments. The trainer had taped the arm to his side to prevent it from flapping, and that Saturday he had filled his regular offensive guard spot without complaint. He had been proud that day. It had been good to be tough then. There had been no bell-bottomed boys with pageboy haircuts and purple shirts to make him feel ashamed that he was built like a man.

"How'd the car run, Vergil?"

"Not too bad, Ruthie. It got me here." A month earlier, Koenig had got rid of a Plymouth Belvedere with plenty of life still left in it and replaced it with a 1962 Mercedes sedan bought through a newspaper ad. He had thought he might feel better in the new car—more sensitive, more worldly, less brawny, less like the lout he had begun to fear others thought him. He also had tried keeping his radio tuned to WGMS, the local classical station, instead of WDON or WPIK, which played his favorite country music.

The Mercedes turned out to be a lemon. The clutch was shot, and only the feebleness of the engine prevented it from slipping whenever he accelerated. Worse, he discovered too late that the bottom of the car was almost entirely rusted out. Within a week, the aluminum tape the previous owner had used to patch gaping holes in the floor panels had fallen off. Now, when he drove, he could watch the road whiz by between his legs. Come winter, if the car was still running, the wind chill factor around his feet was going to be arctic.

Koenig had toyed with driving the car back out to Takoma Park and beating up the kid who sold it to him. Only the loutish implications of the act had stopped him.

"Maybe it wasn't such a bad deal after all, Vergil."

"Nah, Ruthie, the car's gonna be okay."

Koenig looked at his wife and smiled. Ruthie was a good woman, he thought. She cooked good. She cleaned good. She was no shirkfuck, like the wives of some of his friends, and she was always looking on the bright side.

"You want to turn on the TV, Vergil?"

"What's on?"

"You want me to look in the paper?"

"Nah, Ruthie, don't bother. There's probably just a bunch of goddamn specials. Seems like, nowadays, they don't ever have regular programs; they're all the time knockin 'em out with goddamn specials."

Koenig's taste in television, like his taste in food, ran to basic fare. Once, Ruthie had persuaded him to watch the local educational channel. But the station had been in the midst of a fund-raising drive, and every quarter hour programing had been interrupted for lengthy appeals. After the third interruption, Koenig had exploded, announced that he wasn't going to watch any more begging and switched the channel. He had never gone back.

And Ruthie had never tried to make him. That was Ruthie. She'd known Vergil long before he got mixed up with important Washington types. She knew that, downtown, people sometimes pushed him, worried him, made him feel out of place—made him want to be, try to be, things he wasn't. Since high school, all she'd wanted was to protect him and make him happy. Just wrap herself around him; be his home, his garage, his blanket, his holster, his . . .

"You know what I'd rather do, Ruthie?"

"What's that, Verg?"

"I'd rather go to bed."

CHAPTER 7

Rat-tat-tat, rat-tat-tat.

The noise ripped across the bed and sent St. Giles spinning into a heap on the floor.

Rat-tat-tat, rat-tat-tat.

A second burst sounded through the bedclothes clutched about his head. He pulled his knees to his chest, waiting for the pain to hit, for the final volley, which would blow fear and consciousness away.

There was only silence. It was ten seconds before the sound came again, only this time it was farther away. St. Giles pulled the covers from his face and opened his eyes. Propping himself on one elbow, he looked around the tiny room in the Gerson Hotel. He was alone. Rat-tat-tat, rat-tat-tat. He got to his feet and, gingerly rubbing his elbow, walked sheepishly to the open window. Two floors below a jackhammer crew was digging up the pavement in front of the hotel.

His heart was still beating quickly when, having shaved and dressed, he reached the street. His decision to abandon Majendie's counterfeiting plan and to substitute his own version of it had been good for his spirits. But it wasn't doing much for his nerves. Or for his body. His elbow ached where it had smacked the bedroom floor. He would feel more secure if he knew who Majendie worked for and where right now the red-faced giant was. In time, it would be okay, even necessary, for Majendie to learn he had been crossed. But now was far too soon. He found himself wondering if Fang knew how to contact Majendie. He hoped not.

The Chinese counterfeiter had not taken the change in their plans with good grace. A deal was a deal, he had protested. Besides, what St. Giles was proposing was not art but deceit. In rebuttal, St. Giles had argued that, on the contrary, what he was proposing demanded the most exquisite skills, that only a man of Fang's consummate craft could do what was required. It had taken nearly an hour of intercontinental telephone flattery, but in the end Fang had relented. He was to be paid the same amount, even though there would be less work involved, and he was to be fully compensated for the cost of his materials, which would be high.

Now, with Fang due in Paris in a few days, there were other matters to attend to.

The first was a call to the Banque de Paris et Pays Bas. Parisbas, so-called after its cable address, was one of the leading currency trading houses in France, and through it St. Giles had made several transactions under assumed names the preceding year. Ordinarily, traders for personal account, such as he, were given little attention by men at Parisbas, who dealt primarily for central banks and for corporate treasurers scrambling to hedge their companies' foreign-exchange holdings. But St. Giles had more than ordinary means, and he had cultivated his man well. Now he had a favor to ask—a favor that would be worth the half-dozen dinners and countless drinks for which he was out of pocket on the Frenchman's account.

As he dialed, it occurred to him that the man he was calling might have read a news account of his death. The articles had been very small, and only in British papers. But how was he going to explain . . .

"Allo, Puesch." Too late to worry. The trader had come on the line directly. The men at Parisbas operated in a world where thirty seconds one way or another might determine gain or loss; a secretary was an impediment.

"Hello, Bertrand?"

"Oui, c'est moi."

"This is Peregrin St. Giles."

"Peregreen!" St. Giles listened to his name explode out of the Frenchman's mouth, its second syllable launched from the first like some sort of phonic Roman candle. "You are at Paris, Peregreen?" There was no suggestion in the Frenchman's voice that he thought he might be talking to a ghost.

St. Giles let out what remained of the breath he had been holding. He knew Puesch was hoping very much he was in Paris. He knew, too, that the Frenchman was already picking out a restaurant as he asked the question.

"Yes, Bertrand. I thought perhaps you might be free this evening."

"Zis evening? I zink zo, Peregreen. Martine, elle est a Fréjus avec nos gosses depuis mardi. C'est parfait."

"Good. I thought perhaps we could have dinner. Would nine o'clock at Prunier suit you?"

"Non, non, Peregreen. Pas Prunier." Puesch's tone had changed, ebullience giving way to confidentiality. Finance was important. But food! Puesch was sobered by the gravity of the decision now pending.

"You don't like Prunier, Bertrand? I thought it was a favorite."

"Ees change. Ees not so good, Peregreen. We go perhaps Chez Marius in Rue de Bourgogne."

"That's better is it, Bertrand, Chez Marius?"

"Absolument. Ees formidable, Chez Marius. You will like, Peregreen. You will love." Puesch held the last word in his mouth for at least three seconds.

"All right, Bertrand, then we'll go to Chez Marius. Now, Bertrand, I have a favor to ask of you, something I'd like you to do by this evening."

"But of course, Peregreen."

"Good, Bertrand. I want you to get me a name."

There was silence on the other end of the line when St. Giles finished his request. For a second or two, he felt a pang of apprehension. Perhaps Puesch would not be able to help him. The name he had asked for would not appear in any telephone directory, or in any other sort of directory. It was not a name people were supposed to know—not, in fact, a name at all in the sense that names exist to signify real beings. This name was the personification of a lie, a nomenclatural hat on a stick. According to lay wisdom, even the money traders, who in the course of their business dealt routinely with the name, did not know for what or for whom it stood. If that were true, Puesch would be powerless to help him.

St. Giles felt certain it was not true. He had learned enough about the financial world to know that the integrity of such secrets was a fiction. A trader would know what the name meant; he would have to. He would know by the volume of transactions, by their timing and their correspondence to similar transactions in other markets—in London, in New York, in Frankfurt. It would be almost impossible for a trader to be fooled for any length of time. Puesch would know the name, or be able to find it out.

"You can get the name, Bertrand?" St. Giles was careful not to let his voice betray doubt.

"Yes, Peregreen, I can get."

It was nearly noon when St. Giles left the hotel the following day. Puesch had been as good as his word. Through three courses, two wines, assorted cheeses and coffee, neither man had mentioned the name. They talked of the money market, of food, and of the Frenchman's family. St. Giles had been patient, aware that Puesch needed assurance that the pleasure of his company and it alone had earned him the invitation. It was Puesch's cherished illusion that St. Giles's benefactions over the previous year had been inspired by genuine affection. It had not been until late in the evening, over cognac, that the Frenchman had finally produced a slip of heavy stationery from which Parisbas's letterhead had been carefully clipped.

Now, as St. Giles made his way down Boulevard St-Michel past the Musée de Cluny, the paper, which had been worth nearly ninety dollars in custom at Chez Marius, was tucked safely in his wallet.

The name Puesch had given him was that of a German corporation, the Kieler Aktiengesellschaft. St. Giles knew that no such corporation in fact existed. The Kieler Aktiengesellschaft was a nominee of the West German Bundesbank, one of the many fictional institutions behind which the central bank sought to hide its foreign-exchange-market interventions. St. Giles wanted the name for the check he planned to give Fang. If Majendie was going to insist that Fang be killed, it would impose no further indignity on him for St. Giles to use Fang's body as a messenger.

At the Franklin Delano Roosevelt stop, St. Giles left the Métro, crossed in the middle of the block and headed on foot up the Champs-Elysées toward the First National City Bank.

A few minutes with the bank officer to whom he was referred on the mezzanine were all it took to complete the new account forms—name of firm, headquarters address, local address, signatures of all parties authorized to draw on the account. St.

Giles filled in the blanks, using the name Puesch had given him, an address on the Hindenburgufer—the only street he could recall in Kiel—and the name Werner Schlosser. The space marked "Local Address" he left blank, reasoning that whatever he put there could only lead to trouble.

He asked that the checks for the account be of the type with perforated stubs, which the payee could retain as a record, and that they be ready by the end of the week. Receiving assurances on both counts, he thanked the man and left, stopping on his way out to deposit two hundred thousand French francs, drawn on the account Majendie had set up for him.

That evening, he made his way to Boulevard Raspail to do a little reconnoitering. When it came time to meet Fang, he didn't want any surprises.

The facilities at the address on Boulevard Raspail were much as he had expected. And after half an hour of poking around he headed back toward the river and the center of the Latin Quarter.

Toward the end of the week, he returned to the First National City Bank to pick up his checks. Using one of the bank's typewriters, he made out a check to Fang Pao-Hua for the entire amount in the account. Maybe if Fang was quick about getting it cashed, he could take it with him and share it with his ancestors.

That evening, satisfied that for the moment he had done all he could do, St. Giles treated himself to a double feature on Rue Champollion, two old John Ford films he had not seen in fifteen years. His mood was one of confident resolve. He had fallen hopelessly off Majendie's schedule. But his own plan was right on track.

CHAPTER 8

Four blocks south of Montparnasse, on Boulevard Raspail, set back from the street a block from the old Cimetière du Montparnasse, there stood in 1971 an institution known as the American Students and Artists Center. In forty years of existence, the center had drifted an impressive distance from the original design of its benefactors, the only surviving vestige of high cultural purpose being a dingy library on the second floor. For several decades, the center had been little more than a refuge for anyone with forty francs for a membership card and an eye cocked for free rides, free sex, or an audience before which to parade his or her claims to bohemian sensitivities. Of an evening it was common to find several dozen ex-students and ersatz artists lounging about the main room, affecting the serious looks and low-toned conversation by which each hoped to suggest precious moments stolen from important work.

The center had been Fang's choice as a meeting place. St.

Giles hadn't argued. In exchange for Fang's agreeing to their change in plans, he would have met him anywhere.

Fang was waiting in a corner in one of the center's old leather chairs gone ratty with the years. An attaché case rested on the floor next to him. In his lap he clutched a large *Larousse French/English Dictionary*. He appeared smaller, less dapper than he had in Hong Kong. St. Giles noted the difference, but without surprise. He had known too many men who had married girls in India or the Orient only to wonder, back home, what had become of the charms that had seemed so striking on the other side of the world. Beauty might be in the eye of the beholder but beauty required an affirming culture. Cats did badly in dog shows, and Chinese looked funny in Paris. In his little blue suit and clumpy black shoes, Fang looked . . . inconsequential.

"You are punctual, Mr. St. Giles." From Fang's confident tone it was obvious he did not feel out of place.

"Always," St. Giles answered, settling into a neighboring chair. For a moment the two men regarded one another.

"You have the bills?" St. Giles at length asked.

"I have them."

"You are satisfied with them?"

"They are perfect."

"You weren't tempted to test that view with a second opinion, I trust."

"Very tempted."

"But you didn't?"

"No."

"Good."

St. Giles studied Fang's face, uncertain whether to believe him. He wondered where Fang was carrying the money.

"And you, Mr. St. Giles, you have your money?"

"Of course."

"It is a costly business to come here from Hong Kong. My expenses have been considerable."

"I will take care of them."

"Then there is no need to wait."

"I'll meet you in the library coatroom upstairs," St. Giles said, rising.

During his visit to the center the week before, he had made note of the coatroom. The library closed at six o'clock. Past that hour there would be no reason for anyone to visit the second floor until the following day.

St. Giles gave the Chinese several minutes' head start. As he climbed the stairs he could see the glow of the coatroom light. From the doorway he noted that, as expected, the hooks that ringed the tiny room were empty; there would be no one fetching a coat that evening.

Fang had looked up at the sound of footsteps. St. Giles sensed before he spoke that something was wrong.

"Mr. St. Giles, there is one detail I have not mentioned." As he spoke, Fang fingered the edges of the *Larousse,* still clutched in his hands.

"Yes?"

"There is one respect in which I have not been able to follow your instructions."

"How's that?" St. Giles's voice concealed a spasm of apprehension. Why was Fang still fiddling with that damn book? Was it just nervousness? Or had he underestimated the counterfeiter?

"You asked for twenty-five hundred bills, and I have brought you two thousand."

"How many did you make?"

"Just two thousand."

St. Giles stared at Fang, not sure whether to be angry or relieved.

"It did not occur to me when we spoke on the telephone," Fang went on, "but I realized afterward that I could not make twenty-five hundred."

"Why not? If you can make two thousand, you can make twenty-five hundred. How do I know you haven't pocketed the rest?"

"Mr. St. Giles, I could not make twenty-five hundred bills because they would not travel."

"Travel?"

Fang did not answer. He had taken the *Larousse* from under his right arm and now held it flat in the crook of his arm. As St. Giles watched, he slipped a finger of his free hand under the dust jacket and tore it the length of the book.

"Travel in here, Mr. St. Giles," Fang said, tapping the bared surface between the ragged edges of paper.

Where the dark grainy surface of the book's cover ought to have been, St. Giles could see the grey steel of what appeared to be a cashbox.

"New bills pack exactly two hundred and thirty-three to the inch, Mr. St. Giles. The *Larousse* is a big book, but it will not hold twenty-five hundred notes. As a European, Mr. St. Giles, such problems might not occur to you, but a French dictionary is one of the few things a Chinese from Hong Kong may carry through customs and not have searched."

"I see."

St. Giles silently reproached himself. He had nearly let his temper flare. This was not the time to start an argument. The missing notes were of no consequence, provided they did not appear somewhere else. For that, he would have to take Fang's word. For his own purposes, two thousand notes were more than enough.

"You see, I had no choice," Fang said.

"No, of course not; you did the proper thing."

St. Giles watched as Fang parted the sides of the dust jacket and pried open the metal box set in the hollow of the book. Inside, stacked the length of the book except where a quarter inch of page remained at each end, were twenty separate packets, each wrapped in its own blue-and-white band.

"There are one hundred bills in each of these?" St. Giles asked, making a quick count of the packets.

"Yes. You may examine the top bill in each bundle if you like, but you must not break the band. The packets are wrapped under pressure. Without the bands, it will be difficult to return the bills to the box."

"That won't be necessary. If you say they are good, that is enough."

"They are good, Mr. St. Giles, very good. As you know, they are made on very expensive paper."

St. Giles nodded, ignoring the smirk with which Fang accompanied his last remark.

"I have not asked you what you are planning to do," the Chinese added. "It is not my affair, and it is better I do not know."

St. Giles nodded again, but did not speak. He was eager to get the transaction over. It was hot and stuffy in the upstairs room. At close quarters he could smell Fang's hair oil.

"So then, Mr. St. Giles, there is the matter of my fee. An additional five thousand dollars for travel expenses will be sufficient."

The exchange was completed quickly. Fang appeared more than satisfied with the check St. Giles gave him; a little quick mental arithmetic told him he was being paid more than the amount they had agreed upon. If he noticed that the check was drawn on the account of the Kieler Aktiengesellschaft, he did not mention it. Within five minutes, St. Giles was on his way back downstairs. Under his arm he carried the *Larousse* containing the bills Fang had brought. In his jacket pocket were the metal plates Fang had used. The latter were quite small and, as befit their purpose, strange looking. Fang had opened the lining of his attaché case and hidden the plates at its ends. With the lining resewn, the plates would have been overlooked by any but the most suspicious customs official. A metal detector of the sort used by airport security would not have picked them up. With the case perpendicular to the direction of the conveyor belt, the plates would have appeared on the video screen only as thin dark lines, indistinguishable from the heavy metal wire used as reinforcing by manufacturers of leather luggage.

St. Giles's step was almost bouncy as he made his way down Boulevard Raspail. He had not expected the exchange with Fang to go so easily. He had worried that the Chinese would demand cash, want a higher fee because of the change in plans, be difficult in some other way.

But Fang had been a piece of cake. Good as his word, reasonable, agreeable. So agreeable that St. Giles had forgotten important details. Damn! He'd been so intent upon getting the bills Fang had prepared, he'd forgotten to ask him what he knew about Majendie's and Bosanquet's nationality, or whether he knew how to get in touch with them. St. Giles spun in his tracks and headed back to the American Students and Artist Center.

He was breathless by the time he arrived. It took only a few seconds to ascertain that Fang was not in the main lounge, where they had first met earlier that evening. There were only a few other rooms he might be in. He checked the billiard room on the ground floor. No Fang. He climbed the stairs to the library. Closed as it had been earlier. He poked his head into the coatroom where he and Fang had made their exchange not fifteen minutes before. Someone had turned out the light. He was about to leave when he sensed someone there in the darkness. Someone was standing silent in the far corner of the room. He put on the light. It was Fang. The check St. Giles had given him was still in his hand, but crumpled and clutched in already stiffening fingers. St. Giles felt his stomach churn. The expression on Fang's face was horrible. Someone had picked him up like a rag doll and slammed him against the wall.

Majendie! He must have just left. Had Fang talked?

Fang's head and the row of three-inch coat hooks that ringed the room had been a perfect match. Fang was upright. But he no longer stood. His legs had gone slack. His toes had turned inward, and the soles of his shoes touched the floor only at their outer edges. Fang was hanging by the top of his head.

It was nearly eleven o'clock when St. Giles, carrying the plates and Fang's papers, reached the river.

The unexpected murder of Fang had shaken him, extinguishing the charitable instincts he'd been feeling. He was in with a monster this time. He could afford to give no quarter.

That night, shortly before midnight, beneath the Pont de l'Archevêché, which connects the Quai de Montebello with the small park behind Notre-Dame Cathedral on the Ile de la Cité, a seventeen-year-old *vendeuse* from the Samaritain Department Store and her twenty-three-year-old auto-mechanic boyfriend were interrupted briefly from their love-making by the splash of Fang's plates and identification papers hitting the water fifteen yards from where they lay.

"Qu'est-ce que c'etait?"

"Rien, poisson."

"Voyeur," the girl responded and, giggling at her own wit, returned her head again to the blanket-covered paving stones.

The newspapers appeared the next morning without mention of Fang or the murder at the American Students and Artists Center.

The following evening St. Giles left Paris. After dinner he lay awake as the darkened plane droned over the Atlantic. He was playing a riskier game than he'd realized, he reflected. He was going to have to be more cautious. And he was going to have to keep moving to stay ahead of Majendie. He was a long way from getting the job done, and he still had no idea whom Majendie worked for. But he had made a start. It was his plan, not Majendie's, that was now unfolding. Even if he did not yet know where it would end.

CHAPTER 9

"Good evening, Mr. Seydoux."

"Evening, George."

Jean-François Seydoux gave the doorman a friendly nod and stepped into the semicircular driveway of the French Embassy residence on Kalorama Road. He checked his watch. Eight-thirty. He was late, but there was still time enough to walk if he hurried. After two drinks and a half-dozen hors d'oeuvres, the exercise would do him good. He would be soberer and hungrier by the time he got to Cleveland Park. Six years in Washington had taught him that the only way to survive the social obligations that went with diplomatic status was to be temperate, and late. One simply could not do all the eating and drinking one was invited to do.

Seydoux found summers in Washington uncomfortably hot. But ordinarily the heat did not really become oppressive until July and August. This June evening the temperature was pleasant, and Seydoux was comfortable and enjoying his slight buzz as he turned up Connecticut Avenue.

In recent years, his post as financial attaché had not been an easy one. Washington and Paris had seldom seen eye to eye on international money matters. But Seydoux was not a man who let official acrimony affect his private disposition. Scion of a prosperous Limoges porcelain family, he had sufficient private income not to be concerned about security. He did his job as well as he could, concentrated on what he found enjoyable, ignored what bored him and made it a point in dealing with his U.S. government contacts not to pick scabs on old sores for which he suspected time would eventually prove better medicine than reason. They were not ambitious rules, but, as a code of conduct, they had served him well over the years. Financial attaché in Washington was, after all, a quite respectable job, especially for someone who had barely scraped by his examinations at the Sciences-Pô.

But if the job was respectable, it had of late been puzzling as well. On three separate occasions in recent weeks he had received mysterious cables from Paris. Though each was ambiguously worded, all had been written in the same confiding tone, as though intended to bring him up to date on a matter with which he was already familiar. None had actually said as much, but in the aggregate they quite clearly had addressed him as if he were a conspirator in a counterfeiting operation.

At first, he had thought them a joke, perhaps some old school friend's idea of humor. For that reason, he had shown them to no one. Why give the prankster the satisfaction? Whoever was responsible would laugh about it for years. Only in the last several days had he begun to wonder.

Four blocks from the embassy, Seydoux passed the Windsor Park Hotel and started across the Connecticut Avenue bridge. From its impressive elevation, he could see, away to the left, the bright lights of the embassies along Massachusetts Avenue and, to the right, the denser if dimmer lights of Mount Pleasant. Far below, the only punctuations in the darkness were the tiny headlights of cars making their way up Rock Creek Park.

The air above the park was free by now of the exhaust fumes that poisoned it during rush hour, and as he walked Seydoux savored the warm leafy smells.

The cables had not been the only bizarre occurrences in the past couple of weeks. That very afternoon he had returned from lunch to find a telephone message from someone named Joseph Berg. The caller, his secretary said, had spoken with "one of those Michael Caine English accents," had described himself as a private business partner and had left a number, but no address. Seydoux knew no one named Berg, nor did he have a business partner. Moreover, there had been no Berg at the number on the message slip. His secretary had rung it periodically all afternoon. Not until after five o'clock had she got an answer, only to learn that the number was that of a pay phone at Dulles Airport. Why not a more permanent number? Or an address? It had been almost as though the caller had not wanted to reach him, but merely establish that he had called.

Then, too, that same afternoon, the U.S. Secret Service had called and asked for an appointment. Strange things seemed to be happening. It was enough to make a man wonder. Perhaps he should have reported the cables, after all. Maybe it had been a mistake to treat them casually. All communications directed to a government official at his office were, in a technical sense, official communications, his doubts about them notwithstanding. He might be held accountable. . . .

The hand that closed like a vise on his wrist put an abrupt end to Seydoux's musings. Before he could resist, his left arm was twisted and driven violently upward between his shoulder blades. Pain exploded behind his eyeballs. He scarcely felt St. Giles stuff four packets of the twenty-dollar bills Fang had delivered the week before into the inside pocket of his jacket, or the arm that an instant later came through his crotch from the back. His feet were clear of the sidewalk and his head already over the railing before horror struck him with full force.

He started to scream. For an instant crazed logic stopped the noise in his throat. He was already falling. Why scream? Seydoux recovered his reason in time to manage only a gurgle.

When Vergil Koenig smoked marijuana, he took precautions. Over the months, he and Ruthie had worked out a system. Whenever the telephone interrupted them in one of their moments of induced lucidity, Ruthie would answer. She would tell whoever was calling that Vergil was at the movies, and that he would call back when he got home, if it was important. In a year, it had never been important.

This night it was important.

Childress called slightly before eleven o'clock. Koenig returned the call at midnight, having first downed three cups of coffee, showered and walked around the block. The phone was picked up on the first ring.

"What is it, Jack?" Koenig asked. It worried him that his voice sounded unnatural, as though it were bouncing back at him off the receiver's mouthpiece. He didn't see how Childress could fail to notice.

"The D.C. police just left here, Vergil." From the number Ruthie had given him, Koenig knew that "here" referred to the office.

"What did they want?" Dammit, thought Koenig, his voice sounded positively weird.

"They wanted to talk to us because we were the last people to talk to Seydoux," Childress answered.

"Yes."

"You did talk to him, then?"

"No."

"You just said 'yes' "

"I said 'yes' meaning I had heard you, not 'yes' meaning I had talked to him. You talked to him, not me; you were going to set up a meeting," Koenig replied, wondering as he finished whether what he had said made any sense.

"Yeah, well, they were looking for someone who might have talked with him at some length. Our office was on his call sheet."

"Jack, what the hell are you getting at? Why do you or the police give a shit who talked to Seydoux, or when?"

"You haven't heard, Vergil?"

"Heard what?"

"Jesus, it was all over the ten o'clock news. Seydoux is dead."

"Dead?"

"They found him in Rock Creek Park under the Connecticut Avenue bridge. They think he jumped."

It took Koenig a few moments to get his head around the torrent of information that seemed to be flowing from Childress. He had the uncomfortable feeling Childress was waiting for him to arrange it all in logical, self-explanatory sequence.

"They think?" he said finally. "Whaddaya mean, they think? That damn bridge is two-hundred feet high, Jack. If he jumped, his thigh bones would be sticking out of his armpits."

"Well, Vergil, he'd been hit by a couple of cars by the time they got to him. The cops said it wasn't that easy to tell. Cars really rip through there in the evening. I guess he was busted up pretty good. Anyway, soon as they figured out who he was, they got in touch with the embassy. The embassy checked with Seydoux's secretary, and she told them he had left his office a little after six o'clock to go to a reception."

"Jesus, how'd they happen to call you?"

"They didn't. They called your office."

"And you were still there?"

"This is my duty night."

"That's right. Jesus . . . Jesus." To Koenig the conversation seemed to be proceeding in slow motion. Still under the influence of the marijuana, he felt as though they had been talking for ten minutes. "How'd you leave it with the cops, Jack?"

"I didn't leave it any way, Vergil. I just told them I had called Seydoux because we thought he might be able to help us with an investigation."

"So what are we supposed to do?"

"Nothing. At least nothing about any of that. I called you because I thought you ought to know what they found on him."

"Yeah?"

"Vergil, Seydoux was carrying eight thousand dollars when he died, eight thousand dollars in brand-new twenty-dollar bills."

"Jesus." From where Koenig stood in the kitchen he could see Ruthie watching him from the living-room couch. He looked at her, hoping to read in her eyes some sign that he was holding up his end of the conversation. It was not reassuring. Ruthie was grinning foolishly.

"That's what I thought, too."

"Did you look at the money?"

"Uh-huh. The bills were in four packs. They wouldn't let me keep the stuff but I persuaded them to leave one bill from each pack. They're in the safe now."

"Jesus, maybe those cables are for real. What does the stuff look like, Jack?"

"It looks good, Vergil."

"How good?"

"Well, I'm new at this business, you know, but to me it looks damn good. You can look at it in the morning, but if you want my opinion, I'd say it was genuine."

CHAPTER 10

If Childress was mistaken, it was not because he lacked experience. By eight o'clock the following morning, Koenig knew that much. If the bills the police had taken from Seydoux's body were not real, they were the finest counterfeits he had ever seen.

Rarely was there question. Two, maybe three times in his career, he had seen counterfeit money that had. fooled him momentarily. Ninety-nine times out of a hundred, the phony stuff was obvious at a glance.

"What do you think, Vergil?"

Childress had been there when Koenig arrived. He now sat waiting, eager to see whether his boss would confirm his impression.

"It ain't no fuckin' Xerox job, that's for sure." Koenig, concentrating hard, was speaking more to himself than to his assistant. "It ain't no fuckin' Xerox job, that's for sure. Where'd you put the magnifying glass, Jack?"

While Childress searched for the magnifying glass, Koenig ranged the bills in a row on his desk—two face up, two face down.

"Xerox jobs," in division parlance, were photo-offset counterfeits. Because they were essentially photographs, offset bills never contained errors of line or detail. Still, they were easy to spot. Their resolution was never good, their color almost always bad. More telling, offset productions lacked the texture of genuine bills. Even an inexperienced agent could identify an offset bill simply by running his fingertips across its surface. Which was not to say that offset jobs were of less concern to the division than intaglio work. Quite the opposite. One of the first lessons Koenig had learned after he came to the division was that the success of a counterfeiting operation had little to do with the quality of the counterfeit bills. Much more important were the number of bills produced and the speed with which they were put into circulation. No counterfeit bill passed many times before the banking system routed it through a Federal Reserve Bank, where even the best counterfeits were detected and removed from circulation.

There was another reason why, once in circulation, there was not much difference between good and bad counterfeits. A counterfeit bill was a hot potato. Though it was worth nothing in the estimate of the U.S. Treasury, to the dupe who accepted it in good faith it was worth precisely what it said on its face; turn it in and he got nothing but a clean conscience. This rather harsh treatment was necessary to prevent counterfeiters from turning the government into a funny-money laundry. But it penalized the citizenry for its better instincts, and not many citizens were inclined to turn in suspect bills.

All this was well known to counterfeiters, who, a decade earlier, had turned en masse to the photo-offset process and its advantages of speed and ease. It was, therefore, with relief, not alarm, that Koenig had determined that Seydoux's bills had been made by means of the old, genuine technology. Intaglio work was difficult and slow. Almost never did intaglio counterfeiters have access to the kind of expensive press required to run off bills in large volume. They tended to be basement artisans, naïve about distribution, rarely able to get more than a fraction of their bills on the street before they were caught.

Without the benefit of photographic reproduction, they tripped on details. No matter how skilled, it was impossible for the intaglio counterfeiter to duplicate the processes necessary to make a piece of U.S. paper currency. Early in his career, a tour of the Bureau of Engraving and Printing had convinced Koenig of that. One thing he did not worry about was that one day he might confront a phony bill he could not tell from the genuine article.

"For Chrissakes, Jack, sit down. You're making me nervous with that pacing." Koenig spoke with annoyance. Childress had been walking back and forth across the office ever since he located the magnifying glass.

"Is it real?"

"I don't know yet. I don't know. But you aren't making it any easier for me to figure it out by walking all over the fuckin' office."

Childress dropped into the nearest chair.

All the normal signs indicated that the bills were genuine. The check letter in the upper left-hand corner matched the letter that preceded the faceplate number in the lower right-hand corner. The numbers in the four corners of the face panel corresponded with the alphabetical rank of the letter in the center of the Federal Reserve Bank seal on the left-hand side of the face. That letter in turn matched the letter with which the serial number began.

On an offset bill, these details were right automatically,

because they were photographically copied. But an intaglio printer occasionally got something wrong.

Still, these were simple details; that they were correct did not prove the bills were real. What was more significant to Koenig was the quality of the scrollwork, the delicate mesh of lines behind the numerals in the corners, and the dots and dashes that made up the shading on Andrew Jackson's face. These were the hardest parts to render accurately. In a counterfeit bill the lines tended to be broken, the dots and dashes to run together. The bills on his desk top now were as good as any he had ever seen.

Koenig removed his wallet and rummaged through it. "Jack, you got a new twenty?"

"Yep. I did the same thing last night."

"Gimme it."

Childress handed over a twenty-dollar bill. Koenig folded it end to end and laid it on top of the last bill in the row so that the two portraits of Jackson were ear to ear. Then, taking up the glass again, he began to compare.

"They sure looked real to me," Childress volunteered.

"You said that already."

"Just thought it might help to have another opinion."

Koenig resisted an impulse to tell Childress that repeating himself did not broaden the consensus. He was examining the crosshatching behind Jackson's head. A few, not more than three or four, of the thousands of little white squares were plugged with ink. That was normal. Even the Bureau of Engraving and Printing wasn't perfect. The average counterfeit bill would have several hundred plugged squares. Koenig flipped the bills over and compared the greens on their backs. He could detect no difference. Finally he examined the paper itself, comparing tints, looking for the little red and blue flecks of rayon fiber. Using the magnifying glass, he isolated a red fiber on the suspect bill and scratched at it with his fingernail. He remembered that a Chinese counterfeiter had once very nearly fooled the division by simulating the fibers photographically on blank paper stock. When Koenig lifted his finger, the fiber was still there. It was part of the paper all right.

"The Treasury seal is typographical," Childress ventured.

"I can see that."

Koenig did not acknowledge it, but Childress's point was well taken. One of the errors frequently made by intaglio counterfeiters was to print the green Treasury seal on the right-hand side of the bill's face by the intaglio method. In fact, the seal and the serial number were the only two parts of the bill's design that were not printed this way by the Bureau of Engraving and Printing. In the case of the serial number, the reason was obvious. Serial numbers changed with each bill. It would be madness to cut a separate plate for each bill; so serial numbers were struck on by a separate typographical process after the rest of the bill was completed. Because the seal on the right-hand side of the bill matched the serial number in color and because that color changed—red for U.S. notes, green for Treasury notes, blue for the old silver certificates—the bureau had long ago adopted the practice of adding number and seal to a bill at the same time and with the same process. It saved the separate printing run that would have been necessary to print the seal in a second color by the intaglio method.

To the trained eye this was obvious, but it was something counterfeiters often overlooked. Whoever had made these bills had not overlooked it.

"They sure as hell look real, don't they, Jack? . . . They sure as hell look real." Koenig glanced at Childress, then leaned back in his chair and stared at the ceiling. When he spoke again, Childress detected a note of disappointment in his boss's voice. "I guess people do die with real money on them, don't they, Jack? Probably more people than don't."

"I suppose."

"Hmm?"

"I said, 'Right.' I mean people drop dead all the time with their wallets in their pocket, and some of them have a lot of money."

"Yeah, I guess so," Koenig said. "Except not too many of them drop off the Connecticut Avenue bridge, do they, Jack? And not too many of them have eight thousand dollars in brand-new twenties on them either. That's what bothers me. It doesn't figure."

"Well, I . . ."

"I mean, why does a guy carry that much money in the first place, huh? This ain't a guy with a payroll to meet; this is a diplomat. He leaves his office at six o'clock. By that time the banks are closed. So where the fuck does he come up with eight thousand dollars from? Tell me that, Jack."

Childress shrugged. With his judgment as to genuineness of the money seemingly vindicated, he was inclined to let the matter rest.

But Koenig was not.

"It doesn't make no sense, Jack. If I had eight thousand dollars in my pocket, I wouldn't jump off no fuckin' bridge, that's for sure. Would you?"

"Nope."

"So what do you figure then?"

"I don't figure anything, Vergil. I figure it's the D.C. police's problem why he jumped off the bridge. Look at it the other way: anybody who's crazy enough to jump off that bridge is crazy enough to take eight thousand dollars with him."

Though Koenig had asked him a question, Childress might as well have been talking to the wall.

"On the other hand, Jack, suppose you were going to throw somebody off a bridge? I mean, let's just pretend for a second that this wasn't a suicide. Would you throw somebody off with eight thousand dollars in his pocket, huh?"

"Maybe whoever threw him off didn't know he had the money."

"Possible. But if you knew, would you?"

"No."

"Me neither. In fact, I'm pretty sure nobody would."

"So what?"

"So I'm not sure. Jack, I'll tell you what—get me that Treasury series log on the bookshelf over there, would you?"

While Koenig cleared his desk top, Childress fetched the large green loose-leaf notebook containing the Treasury's Department's records matching currency series numbers against dates of issue as far back as 1950.

"What are you going to do?" Childress asked, plunking the heavy volume down on the desk.

"I just want to see something. I want to see when the series these bills belong to was issued."

"What's that going to tell you?"

"I don't know. Maybe nothing. I never had to do this before, so I don't know much about it; but I figure once bills are issued they must get into circulation pretty fast." Koenig had the book open now and was running his finger down one of the pages toward the rear. "Here we go. These babies were issued —all four of them—almost exactly one year ago, June 1970 to be precise. What does that tell you?"

"It's their birthday?" Childress ventured.

Koenig looked up, unamused.

"Only if they are real is it their birthday, Jack," he said. "If they are not real, they might have been made last week."

"I thought we had already decided they were real."

"We haven't decided a fuckin' thing. If they are real, and they are one year old, how come they look so new? Huh? How come the packets still had the paper straps on them? Huh?"

Childress didn't answer. It was obvious Koenig wanted the bills to be counterfeit.

"Look, Jack, get hold of the people at Treasury and find out how long it takes to put new currency into circulation. I want to know how long eight thousand dollars could be kept out of circulation after it had been issued. Okay?"

"Yeah, sure. What are you going to do?"

"Never mind what I'm going to do. You just find out what I asked and get back to me as soon as you do. Now go."

Before Childress could reach the door, Koenig was dialing his phone.

"Bill Verity, please."

Koenig picked up one of the bills while he waited, pinched it at either end and yanked it taut several times. The paper made little popping noises but showed no inclination to tear It was good stuff, all right.

"Verity," came the voice on the other end of the line.

"Bill, it's Vergil Koenig."

Verity was director of the Bureau of Engraving and Printing's Office of Technical Services. He had given Koenig his tour of the bureau. He had taken him through the labs, showed him how paper was analyzed, how inks could be broken down into their components and traced to their manufacturers. Koenig had been interested in the technology at the time, but since then had found little use for the information. Most dealings between his division and Verity's office were routine. If a new counterfeit bill turned up, it was sent automatically to the bureau. There, Verity's people took it apart. Within a few days, Koenig's office would get a report. The report was, basically, a recipe, describing how the bill in question had been made. The raw materials used to make the paper were identified as to kind and proportion. Often a guess was made about the region from which they had originated. The same was done for the ink; its toners, drying agents and pigments were identified and a count made of trace elements, the impurities that inevitably crept into the solution during the manufacturing process. Trace elements were particularly helpful in discovering where an ink came from. Manufacturers might use the same components, but trace elements were beyond their control and were often their telltale signature.

With the information in the Technical Services reports, the Counterfeit Division could go to work: checking with manufacturers, canvassing supply houses, poring over invoices, looking for the final retail customer who might lead them to the source of the counterfeit money. To Koenig's division, this was invaluable service. But it did not require personal contact with Verity. The two men had not seen one another since their first meeting.

"Bill, I wonder if you would mind having your people take a look at some twenty-dollar bills," Koenig said.

"Send them over."

"I thought I'd bring them over myself, if that's okay. I'm kind of in a hurry."

"I don't know what I can tell you straight off that you can't see for yourself. But if you want to, sure, come on over."

Verity was right. "Tell you what, Bill, I'll send them over and you let me know as soon as you have something, okay?"

"I think that makes more sense, Vergil."

After he hung up, Koenig called his secretary and ordered a messenger. By the time the boy arrived, he had an envelope ready. He had decided to send two bills and keep the other two. Once the Technical Services people got hold of a bill, that was the end of it. By the time they got through with whatever he sent, there would be nothing left but a ball of pulp.

Childress returned shortly after eleven.

"What's the story, Jack?"

"The story is that there is nothing unusual about year-old money that has never been in circulation."

"Why's that?" Koenig asked.

"Well, as the guy at the Treasury explained it, it works like this. Engraving and Printing prints the stuff to order. The New York Fed might for instance call and say it needs five million twenties 'cause it's running low, or maybe Treasury calls and says it needs a bunch of U.S. notes. The stuff is then printed up and shipped off. It'll leave the bureau right away but there is no limit to how long it might sit at Treasury or a Fed bank waiting to go out."

"Did you ask him what's the longest it might sit there?"

"That's what I'm telling you. There's no way to know. It depends on how the banks handle their inventory. If they reorder every time their stock gets low, they may pile the new bills right on top of the bills left over from the previous order. Except the bills on the bottom of the pile may not be from the previous order; they may be from the order before that, or the one before that. In other words, there's no telling how old the stuff at the bottom of the pile is."

"Shit."

"Well, I'm just telling you what the guy said."

"Yeah, but I still think that money on Seydoux should have been out a long time ago."

"Maybe so, but what are you going to do about it even if you're right?"

"I'm going to think about it."

At noon, Verity called back with more bad news.

The people in the lab had finished with one of the bills. It was genuine, no doubt about it. Koenig listened as Verity ran down the results of the tests. He sensed from Verity's tone that his counterpart at Engraving and Printing regarded the entire rush-rush effort as a little silly. By the time Verity was finished, it was time for lunch.

Koenig returned to the office shortly after two o'clock. He had broken one of his rules by allowing himself two drinks, but he felt better for it.

Childress was right. It was unseemly of him to hope that Seydoux's bills were counterfeit. Still, anyone in his position would do the same. Finding counterfeiters was his job. Outfielders hoped for fly balls; defensive backs hoped the quarterback would throw the bomb. For all he knew, cops hoped for crimes and firemen for fires. It was human nature. People wanted to do their thing. And if you had no hobby, no children and nothing to do at home but smoke dope and watch the tube, well, doing your thing was important.

Back at his desk, Koenig busied himself with his in-box. There was nothing but crap. An invitation from a savings and loan trade association to speak on counterfeit detection at a convention in Florida next fall. He scribbled "No" across the top of the invitation and dumped it into the out-box on the other side of his desk; if there was one thing that terrified Koenig, it was public speaking. The next item was a staff memo alleging syndicate involvement in counterfeit distribution. So what else was new? Everybody knew that organized crime controlled a substantial percentage of the funny-money wholesalers in the country. Nevertheless, the memo was a perennial. Every year, some eager beaver on the staff could be counted on to rediscover the fact and call it to the attention of the director. Koenig scribbled "File" across the memo and chucked it, too, into the out-box.

By four o'clock, having cleared maybe thirty items, he was interrupted by his secretary's buzz.

"It's Mr. Verity, Mr. Koenig. Can you take it?"

"Yeah, sure, put him on."

In a few seconds the director of Technical Services came on the line. "Vergil?"

"Yes?"

"I've got some bad news for you."

"Yes?"

"It's about those bills you sent over here this morning."

"What about them?"

"Well, we took a picture of them before we did the analysis —you know, just in case it turned out we found something. I sent it down to Records just before I talked to you last."

"Uh-huh."

"Well, the people down in Records noticed something I hadn't noticed, something that wouldn't have shown up in the analysis either. I'm kind of embarrassed about it, but what they found isn't something we normally look for. . . . Vergil?"

"Yeah, I'm listening."

"Well, it's kind of complicated unless you are familiar with the mechanics of our printing process. I could try to give it to you over the phone, but I think you'd understand better if you came over here and took a look for yourself."

"Okay, I'm coming, but for Chrissakes stop playing games with me. What's the bottom line?"

"The bottom line, Vergil, is that I'm now pretty sure the bills are counterfeit."

CHAPTER 11

St. Giles was having second thoughts.

He had planted enough evidence for the U.S. authorities by now to believe there was a counterfeiting ring in operation, probably a ring based in France—though on this second point they might soon change their minds.

He also felt reasonably sure that the U.S. authorities would have decided that the bills found on Seydoux's body were counterfeit and would have determined from their quality that they were up against a more skillful counterfeiter than any they had previously encountered.

He could not be certain, however, what the U.S. authorities would do. He was afraid that they might do nothing.

With his plan and very likely his life in the balance, that was a chance he did not intend to take.

One morning in early July, St. Giles appeared at the offices of the Federal Reserve System on Constitution Avenue in Washington, D.C., headquarters for the Federal Reserve

Board and for the family of Federal Reserve banks, which control the nation's money supply and see to the replacement of old bills with new. After checking at the desk in the lobby, he spent more than an hour in a room on the second floor going through all the publicly available material he could obtain on the system's personnel. He had hoped he might find a single person who suited his needs. He did not. But he did find two, each of whom met half his criteria. By noon he was back in his hotel room. Posing as a London travel agent, he was able in several hours on the telephone to obtain additional valuable information about those two from credit-rating services. Face-to-face contact would tell him everything else he needed to know.

While St. Giles lay on his bed making telephone calls that afternoon, Vergil Koenig was hurrying across town to find out what mysterious discovery had made Verity change his mind about the Seydoux bills.

Verity had left word with the guard at Engraving and Printing, and Koenig was ushered straight to his office. The director of Technical Services, older and thinner than Koenig remembered, rose to meet him as he entered.

"That was fast," Verity said, pulling on his jacket. "I'd say sit down and catch your breath, but since you seem to be in such a rush, maybe we better head on down to the press room."

As the two men made their way through the labyrinthine network of corridors that stitched the old building together, Verity began to explain what he had discovered.

"Are you familiar with quadrant numbers, Vergil?"

"Yeah, sure," Koenig answered.

Strictly speaking, his answer was the truth. Like any other agent in his division, he knew that the minuscule number that followed the check letter in the upper left-hand corner of a bill's face indicated which quadrant of the paper stock a bill had come from. He knew that bills were printed thirty-two to a sheet in four vertical rows of eight bills each, and that each quadrant, therefore, had two vertical rows of four, or a total of eight bills. But in all his years in the division he had never had occasion to use the knowledge.

"Good, because quadrant numbers are the key to what I'm about to show you," Verity said.

They reached the floor of the press room. Verity guided Koenig to its far end, where huge stacks of uncut bills rested on wooden pallets against the wall. Verity checked the tops of several stacks, then stopped next to one that apparently suited his purpose.

"Okay," he began. "The bureau has standardized press runs. They vary from denomination to denomination, but for any single denomination a press run always contains exactly the same number of sheets. If we didn't do it that way, then every time there was some doubt about how many sheets were in a stack we'd be obliged to count the whole thing. You with me?"

"Yeah."

"Okay. Now it happens that for twenty-dollar bills, we always run ten thousand sheets. That's what we've got here," Verity said, slapping the top of the stack he was leaning against, "ten thousand sheets—six million four hundred thousand dollars. Now the next thing you have to understand is how these things get their serial numbers, and this gets a little complicated, because, as you know, the numbers go on after the sheets are cut up into individual bills."

"Right."

"We don't have to go into all the mechanics of the process, but the effect is that when these bills get their numbers, the serial progression will run right down through the stack, quadrant by quadrant. Do you follow me?"

"I'm not sure."

"Let me show you," Verity said, beckoning him toward the stack of printed sheets. "You see this bill right here?" he said, pointing to the bill in the upper left-hand corner of the top sheet. "That is the first bill in quadrant number one. The next bill in numerical sequence is not on this sheet; it's on the sheet next down in the stack, right underneath the one I've got my finger on, and the bill after that in the sequence is on the third sheet down, and so forth, and so forth, all the way through all ten thousand sheets. You see?"

"That's a helluva complicated way to do it, isn't it?"

"No. It has to do with the way they come out of the cutting machine. But let's save that until later. Anyway, after we number from the top of the stack down to the floor under the upper left-hand bill, we go back to the top of the stack, this time to the second bill in the left-hand column. The numbers then run through the stack again. Then you start with the third bill in the same column and go through the stack, then the fourth. After the fourth bill, we go back up to the top of the sheet and go through the first four bills in the second column. When we've done that, we've got the whole first quadrant sequentially numbered. Then and only then do we start numbering the second quadrant. And then, of course, the third and the fourth—each of them just the way we did the first."

"So, in other words, the serial number of any bill on a single sheet of paper is exactly ten thousand either more or less than the bill right above it or below it?"

"Exactly, but only within a given quadrant. That's important to remember."

"Yeah, right. I got it."

"Good, because here's what I've been leading up to. This is the photograph we took of the two bills you sent us." Verity handed Koenig a large glossy photograph of extraordinary clarity showing the bills face up one above the other. "Do you notice anything strange about them?"

Koenig's brain slammed in the clutch. From what Verity had just finished saying, it was clear something was wrong with the numbers. But what? New information was still spinning in his head; yet no amount of effort seemed to make it mesh. The harder he tried to concentrate, the less able he was to think. It was like trying to piss for the doctor. He was about to confess his confusion when Verity took him off the hook.

"Look at the serial numbers."

Koenig was already looking at the serial numbers: E78581403C for the top bill, E78470216C for the bill on the bottom. "Now, those bills were printed from the same plate— at least their face plate numbers match. And according to their quadrant numbers, they were part of the same quadrant. But if you subtract one serial number from the other, Vergil, you will see that they are separated by more than one hundred and eleven thousand bills. And that is not possible. As I just explained, in any single run there are exactly eighty thousand bills in each quadrant. The serial numbers of bills in a given quadrant, therefore, have to be within eighty thousand of each other. These aren't. They just plain aren't."

"Is it possible they are from consecutive runs?" Koenig asked.

"Nope. But the numbers wouldn't work out even if they were. The last bill in a given quadrant of one run has to be separated from the first bill in the same quadrant of the next run by the sum of the bills in the three intermediate quadrants —by two hundred and forty thousand bills. There is no way in the world you can get serial numbers one hundred and eleven thousand apart out of the same quadrant."

"So they're counterfeit?"

"At least one of them has to be. You don't have any more of these bills, do you?"

Koenig, who had pocketed the other two bills before leaving his office, produced one of them and watched as Verity made a quick calculation.

"Now see, we have the same situation here. The number on this bill is ninety-five thousand higher than the closer of the other bills. That means at least two of these bills have to be counterfeit. If they all come from the same source, chances are they all are counterfeit."

"Then what about the tests your people ran?"

"I have to admit I'm confounded by those. I've been in this business a long time, as you know, and we've never until today had a bill that tested even close to the real thing. It's true, of course, that you can't always be sure about the ink tests. We get our ink from commercial sources, companies like Interchemical, Addressograph-Multigraph, APF. Different batches, even of the same color from the same company, don't always match. The raw materials the companies buy show different trace elements from month to month, and there's no way to control that. So it's possible that with luck somebody could get their hands on ink that fell within the range of what our people would judge to be genuine. But that doesn't explain the paper. There just isn't any way anybody could match the paper."

Verity's last statement annoyed Koenig, because it came in the middle of an explanation he very much wanted to believe. It was part of the folklore that the paper on which U.S. currency was printed was, like Coca-Cola, the product of a secret formula that no one had ever been able to discover. Koenig was no scientist, but he had common sense enough to know bullshit when he heard it. The Crane Paper Company manufactured the government's currency paper in Dalton, Massachusetts. Koenig, so far as he could recall, had never seen or heard of any "famous Crane scientists." He was reasonably sure there were no Werner von Brauns hidden away in Dalton. Men who could walk on the moon and send color pictures back to Koenig's living room could make any kind of paper they goddamn well wanted. If no private citizen had ever done so, it wasn't because it was impossible, but because it was expensive. There wasn't much point in making counterfeit money that cost more than the real thing.

"Bill, in your view, what is the best work you have ever seen?"

"Counterfeit work?"

"Right."

Verity put his hand to his mouth and massaged his lips for a minute. "I'd have to say the Hong Kong job five years ago. In fact, there's really no question that it was the Hong Kong job. I'm pretty sure we could have spotted that stuff even if it had been on good paper; but if it had been on good paper, I'm not sure we ever would have got a look at it. You remember those bills? They were fantastic."

Koenig remembered. The bills Verity was referring to were the ones to which simulated red and blue fibers had been applied photographically. Though the tactic had not succeeded, the quality of the engraving and printing had been excellent. Barfield had talked about it for weeks. At the time, Koenig had found it annoying that his assistant took such pleasure in the work of a crook. Now, he understood. The longer one was in the business, the more one respected a good job.

Koenig thanked Verity for his help. Together the two men left the press room and made their way back toward the entrance. At the top of the glass-enclosed corridor leading to the street, Koenig said good-by. "Thanks again, Bill. I'll keep you posted."

"Do that, Vergil. I'll be interested to hear what you find. I guess you realize that in order to get serial numbers as far apart as the three on those bills, somebody had to print a hell of a lot of money."

It was after six when Koenig got back to the office. Childress was waiting. In his haste to leave, Koenig had neglected to tell anyone where he was going, and Childress had been looking for him for over an hour.

"The police have been trying to get hold of you, Vergil; the guy down there has called you three times."

Koenig peeled off his jacket and tossed it over a chair to dry. If there was one thing he had never got used to about Washington, it was the summers. He sweated like a pig every time he went outside. And Ruthie—no matter how many times he told her he didn't like them—always bought him polyester shirts. "It was all they had, Verg," she would say when he complained. She could never seem to get it through her head that there were other stores besides Sears that sold shirts. Cursing his discomfort, Koenig plopped down in the chair behind his desk and took a deep breath.

"What do the police want?"

"I don't know," Childress answered. "My guess is they want to know what we've found out about the money."

"Yeah, well, there's nothing about the money that the police need to know."

"Well, what have you found out? I'd like to know myself."

"Hmm?" Koenig's mind had wandered, and it took him a moment to focus on the question. "Oh, the money. It's counterfeit. I'll tell you 'bout it later. Right now we got about ten things to do."

"Like what?"

"First thing we've got to do is get off cables to Paris, Hong Kong and Honduras asking for lists of all commercial printing operations large enough to handle a big run of counterfeit money." Honduras was a long shot. But as the only other country whose currency paper Crane produced, it was worth a try. It was not impossible that someone had pried loose a shipment. "No, hold on, Jack. That isn't going to get us anywhere. We're going to have to ask them to check with each of the operations themselves . . . ask them to see what they can find out."

"You mean ask them to ask everyone if they've been printing counterfeit money?"

"Yeah, something like that. You got a better idea?"

Childress looked at Koenig, waiting for him to smile, but Koenig was serious. "Well, who's 'them'?" he asked finally.

"Who's who?"

"I mean, who do we send the cables to?"

"I don't know; we got to look that up. I guess in Hong Kong we send it to our consulate and let them figure it out. In Honduras . . . Christ, who knows? I guess we have an embassy there; we must. In Paris, just send it to the Sûreté. They're a surly bunch of fuckers, but we've worked with them before."

That reminded him. Koenig picked up a pencil and scribbled himself a note. He would have to call the Secret Service's Paris liaison. The service had no legal authority to make criminal investigations abroad, but for years it had maintained a rough character named Hawkins in Paris to ensure that someone took action where U.S. interests were involved. He would give old Hawk a call in the morning and ask him to birddog the Sûreté.

"And then?" Childress asked.

"Then we do the same thing for the regional offices here."

"All of them?"

"All sixty-five. It won't be so bad. Send the same telegram to all of them. Have your secretary do it. And while you're asking the regional offices to do that, you might as well ask each to shake down a couple of fences, too. Tell them we'll offer a future free ride to anybody who cooperates. If any of these new bills are out yet, we ought to turn up something."

Childress was scribbling madly, trying to keep up with Koenig's instructions. It was becoming obvious that most of the things "we" had to do were going to be dumped in his lap.

"You got that?"

"Yep."

"Okay. Now while you're doing that, I'm going to get off a cable to Interpol. You remember the Chinaman counterfeiter?"

"No."

"You don't?"

"I've just been here a few months."

"That's right, that's right. . . . Well, anyway, there was once this Chinaman counterfeiter who was some kind of good. We put him away back in the middle sixties, but if I remember right, he's been out since about sixty-nine. And unless I'm dumber than I think, he's our man. You know these guys don't give up. It gets in their blood. They're like a bunch of fuckin' George Chuvalos; they just keep coming back for more. You know George Chuvalo?" he asked, referring to a Canadian heavyweight, legendary for his ability and willingness to absorb punches.

"I know who he is."

By the time the two men left the office together it was after eight and nearly dark. At the corner of 19th and G streets, they split, Childress walking north to his bus stop on K Street, Koenig a block and a half east to the parking garage where he kept his car.

Koenig walked briskly. That spring, before he had bought the Mercedes, and while he was still listening to WPIK, he'd taken a liking to a song called "I Never Promised You a Rose

Garden." He hummed it now as he walked. The street was nearly empty, and the night air had started to cool. He was on a good case, and he felt good.

At the garage window, he pushed his ticket under the glass, paid the woman and plopped himself down on a bench by the wall to wait. In six years as director, he had never had a really tough case, one with a little mystery to it. They'd all been a bunch of Xerox jobs, a lot of trash collecting. Now he was going up against Mr. Fang Pao-Hua. It was showdown time: Mr. Fang Pao-Hua versus Mr. Vergil Koenig. Silently he mouthed the words like a prize-fight announcer. They would have sounded better if his parents had thought to give him a middle name, at least a middle initial; but they sounded good, good enough to celebrate. Maybe he and Ruthie would go out to dinner, get some ribs.

"You got the Mercedes?" It was the red-jacketed man who fetched the cars from the bowels of the parking garage.

"Yeah."

"It don't start."

CHAPTER 12

Armistead Carrington hung up the phone in his office on the fourth floor of the Richmond Federal Reserve Bank, ripped open the day's second pack of Luckies and winced with the first puff.

It had been a bad week. To begin with, his wife and children had got back from the river the previous Saturday and were already vociferously bored with summer. For four nights running he had listened to complaints. No one had anything to do. The older children couldn't play tennis at the club because the courts were always full of women. Marylee refused to play tennis at the club because, she claimed, the heat made her dizzy. The children complained that the pool, a successful diversion for the first couple of weeks of summer, was now too hot and smelled like "wee wee." Marylee, who had tolerated the pool a month earlier, now had a respectable tan and no further interest.

Carrington had feared as much back in April, when they had taken the house on the river. He had mustered all the arguments against it: the river was dirty, full of stinging nettles; neither he nor Marylee enjoyed the frustrating ritual of picking crabs, which seemed to get smaller and more heavily armored each year; the mosquitoes were unbearable—hadn't the Jamestown settlers bolted inland at the first opportunity?

Camp had been his prescription. He had pushed hard for camp. Baseball, tennis, archery, riflery, woodcraft. It would do the older two boys good; two long months of healthy activity, two beautiful silent months.

Marylee hadn't wanted to hear of it. Nobody went to camp anymore. Everybody went to the river. And so they had gone to the river—Marylee and the three boys for the month of June, he for the weekends.

Carrington drew deeply on the already half-gone cigarette and looked wearily at the stack of folders before him on the desk. His mood had been further blackened the day before when the bank's executive director had informed him that the guard force would have to be cut by six men. Carrington, as the bank's vice president in charge of security, was to pick the bodies. Because many of the guards had been hired at the request of one or another of the bank's officers, he would have to go through the folders of every man on his staff, remind himself of who was whose maid's husband, and decide who, if let go, would be likely to cause the least trouble.

And if that weren't nuisance enough, he had just agreed to spend the afternoon showing some Canadian journalist named Joseph Berg around the bank.

He pushed the folders aside and gazed out the window down 9th Street, between the old Raleigh Hotel and the new Bank of Virginia building, at the James River glistening like chocolate in the afternoon sun. How had he got himself into such a lousy job? Vice president for security at the Richmond Federal Reserve Bank sounded exalted enough. But the job was no plum, even for someone only thirty-three years old. His salary,

116

twenty-three thousand five hundred, was fifty percent lower than that of any other vice president in the bank—a fact of which Marylee was kind enough to remind him frequently.

And Marylee's jibes were not the worst of it. Most men at thirty-three were at the beginning of their careers, three or four rungs up a ladder they would go on climbing for thirty years. Carrington had no such prospects. He couldn't move laterally into one of the other vice-president slots. He knew nothing about central banking. He could scarcely remember the little economics he had learned at The University. Nor was he in a position to learn. The work he did had nothing to do with banking or bank policy. He never went to meetings, never discussed whether the bank should be discounting member-bank paper to increase the money supply or calling in funds to contract it. He never did any of the things other bank vice presidents did. In fact, he was not really a banker at all; he was a white-collar cop, part of the office's overhead, the bank's in-house Pinkerton man.

As he had been for months, Carrington was depressed. Somewhere, something had gone wrong. What had he done? Or failed to do? In high school he had been thought a catch —athlete, stud, Missionary Society president. The name Armistead Peyton Carrington had dampened panties all over Richmond's West End.

The name had been intended to impress. His mother had picked its components judiciously and from the most verdant reaches of the family tree. Together, they were a laminate of everything about their family she had been raised to believe prideworthy—and to believe that Richmond, or the eight or ten percent of the city she acknowledged as Richmond, held in the same regard.

In the weeks preceding Carrington's birth, there had been lively family debate over whether "Peyton" might not be improved upon with "Bryan" or "Scott" or "Skelton." The first two had been ruled out early as overpopulated and, for that reason, lacking distinction. "Skelton," however, had gone down to the wire and might in the end have been the choice had not Cousin Skelt, as he was fondly, if infrequently, referred to, attracted the untimely attentions of the Internal Revenue Service and raised serious questions about the social utility of his ancesterhood.

So "Armistead Peyton Carrington" it had been. And for twenty-five years it had seemed that Armistead would do his mother's work honor. Marylee's parents had been delighted when he proposed.

All that had been before the debts.

Just that morning, American Express and two credit-card banks had called. He'd put them off. But the mortgage was going to be due again in another week, and he couldn't put that off. He was also on the brink of being posted at the country club. Jesus, the debts, he thought.

"What would you like to see, Mr. Berg?"

Carrington had been waiting inside the front door when St. Giles, alias Berg, arrived at the bank's 9th Street entrance. He was still worried about his money problems, and it annoyed him to have to leave his office for another tour. Journalists, Cub Scout packs, eighth-grade field trips—he was fed up with the lot. Why can't they handle this crap in Public Affairs, he thought, having already asked and knowing that it would do no good to ask again.

"Why don't we start where the money comes in and then just follow it around," St. Giles answered. He was carrying a spiral notebook, and, while his rumpled tan tropical suit would have looked more appropriate on a parboiled British colonial planter, he might easily have been the Canadian reporter he said he was.

Carrington nodded to the guard that St. Giles was with him, and the two men climbed the steps to the main lobby.

Ten paces from the end of a corridor off the lobby, Carrington stopped St. Giles with a grip on the elbow. "Stand here."

St. Giles watched as a heavy glass door at the end of the corridor opened to admit Carrington. Through the soundproof glass he watched Carrington speak briefly with a guard; then the door reopened and the guard motioned St. Giles to enter.

"What was that all about?" he asked when the two were together again.

"Normal procedure," Carrington replied. "Our guards have instructions never to let a bank employee enter the Money Department unless alone. They won't open the door for anyone, even the president of the bank, as long as anyone is standing next to him. That's so no one can pull a gun on an employee and make the employee bring him in here."

The room they had entered was a rectangle approximately one hundred feet in length. Men and women were busy moving stacks of money around.

"What happens in here?" St. Giles asked.

"This is the incoming room. These people are doing bundle verification. They count to make sure the number of incoming bundles of bills agrees with the shipping manifest."

"Tedious, I imagine," St. Giles remarked, smiling at Carrington.

"It's not too bad," Carrington answered. "The people here only have to count the bundles, not the little packs. If you want to see a tedious job, wait till you see where this stuff goes next."

Next stop was downstairs at the vault. Both men were required to sign their names at a custodian's desk before entering. The vault looked like other bank vaults St. Giles had seen, except in one respect: its walls, instead of being lined with safe-deposit boxes, had large cabinets going up from the floor.

As they watched, two employees opened one and rolled out what looked like a large steel office file.

"Money bus," Carrington said, nodding toward it. "It's nothing but a big tin box. That's how we get the money from one room to another."

St. Giles remembered seeing similar metal boxes scattered throughout the room upstairs. "Does a money bus hold a specific amount of currency?"

"Nope. They just fill them up. How much goes in depends on the condition the bills are in.

"Now then, this is the Currency Sorting and Counting Division." The two men were back on the first floor, standing in the corridor next to a long row of windows. On the other side of the windows forty to fifty women sat at metal desks. Though they wore looks of intense boredom, their hands were flying.

"After the money leaves bundle verification, it's brought here in the money buses. The bundles are broken down into packs, and these people take over. Their job is to count the bills in each pack. Actually, they don't have to do it by hand. See those machines next to each desk?"

"Yes."

"Those are Tickometers. The machines count the bills. But those ladies out there still have to go through each pack before it's counted to take out the bills that are bad—either worn out, torn or counterfeit."

"What do they do with them?"

"What do we do with the bad money? First, for every bad bill set aside, a new one must be put back in the pack, so it will still have a hundred bills. See the woman in front of you?"

"Yes."

"See that stack of bills with red stars on them on her desk?"

"Yes."

"Those are replacement bills."

"She's not looking at what she's doing."

"She doesn't have to. After you've been at this a while, you can tell more with your fingers that with your eyes. Good money feels good, bad money feels bad."

"Where are the bad bills kept until they are destroyed?" St. Giles asked.

"They are kept right here until we get a bus full. Then we take them down to the cancellation room."

"Down?"

"Yep. Believe it or not, we have to go back downstairs."

"Surely they don't take those buses down the stairs."

"No, no, there's an elevator. We're going to take it now."

Inside the elevator, St. Giles had another question. "Who takes the money buses down in the elevator?"

"You mean with the bad money?"

"Yes."

"Half a dozen different people."

"Who?"

"The division supervisor, his assistant, the guard who covers the corridor, me, a couple of other people. I make the assignments."

"And whoever you assign just wheels the buses into this elevator and rides down with it?"

"Right."

"What's to prevent his opening the bus and taking out a few packs?"

"Nothing, except he wouldn't get away with it."

"Why is that?"

"Because before the bus leaves Currency Sorting and Counting, the people down in Currency Cancellation are called and told how much is on the way. When it gets there, they count it."

"Who counts it?"

"Three different people."

"At the same time?"

"At the same time."

The currency cancellation room was smaller than either of the previous two rooms. Against one wall, packs of bills were stacked to the height of a man. In the center of the room, three young men sat at a strange-looking machine. One man, his back to the door, had a large pile of packs on a table next to him. As St. Giles watched, he fed them one by one into a slot in the machine. Each time he did so, the machine spat two narrower packs out of a larger slot on its side. These narrower packs, which at a closer look St. Giles realized were the two halves of the original packs, were divided into two separate piles by a metal partition, then scooped up by the two other men and removed to separate parts of the room. This whole operation took place under the constant scrutiny of two elderly men perched on high stools.

"Is that machine punching holes, too? It looks as though the bills coming out the side have holes in them."

"They do. Each half gets two clover-shaped holes punched in it. There is not much left to chance here. The reason those men are putting the two halves of the bills in separate places is that we don't burn the tops and the bottoms at the same time; we burn the tops of the bills one day and the bottoms the next. That way nobody in the burning operation can put a whole bill back together. You want to see the ovens? That's where it all ends up."

St. Giles declined Carrington's offer of a look at the ovens. He had already seen what he had come to see.

As Carrington led the way back to the front door of the bank, St. Giles thanked him effusively. The tour had been most interesting. He was most grateful. He was sure, too, that his editors were going to like all of the bowels-of-the-bank detail Carrington had furnished him. But he had one more favor to ask: he planned to rough out his story that evening and was sure that in the process new questions would arise; they always did.

Could Carrington have lunch the next day?

CHAPTER 13

On the same day that Carrington showed St. Giles, posing as a Canadian journalist, around the Richmond Federal Reserve Bank, Vergil Koenig received a reply to the cable he had sent Interpol. Childress, who had left it unopened on his desk, entered while Koenig was still reading.

"Pretty fast over there, aren't they?" he remarked.

"Yeah, they're fast, but they ain't worth shit. This just says the Chinaman got out of jail in 1969. I'd be fast, too, if that's all the information I had to dig up."

"There weren't any other cables," Childress volunteered.

"No, I know. It's going to be weeks before we get answers from some of those people."

There was nothing to do but wait. Field-office reports on conversations with fences around the country trickled in slowly, with disappointing results. Either the fences didn't know anything or they weren't cooperating. The third morning after the cables had gone out, a call from Milwaukee raised hopes. By afternoon, they had been dashed. The bills submitted to the Milwaukee agent turned out to be part of an operation busted more than a year earlier. That kind of thing had to be expected. Dangle the promise of future forgiveness under fences' noses and you were bound to turn up a few dishonest ones.

Meanwhile, the requests for information about presses were producing nothing Koenig could use.

Honduras was the first to respond. There was only one press in the country that might have done the job, but it belonged to the government. Scratch Honduras.

The reports from the regional offices were also discouraging —but for the opposite reason. Within forty-eight hours of its request, the division had received the names and addresses of nearly one hundred printing firms that were possibilities. This deluge had forced Koenig to reconsider. Even if he discovered which press had done the work, he would have to find the people involved, and some way to make them talk. It could take weeks. For a single firm, or a handful of firms, it would be worth trying. For a hundred? Out of the question.

It was nearly a week before the first piece of useful information turned up. It came, not from the field agents, or in response to the cables, but from Burton Hawkins, in Paris. And it came over Koenig's home phone.

After he had received the disappointing cable from Interpol, Koenig had called Hawkins direct and asked him to do what he could to get more effort out of the bureaucrats at St. Cloud. Hawkins was a tough and wily old veteran. A lot of people had considered him mean in the days when he'd been with the division in Washington. But Koenig liked him. He had had a hunch Hawkins might shake things up.

"You mean you want me to kick a little ass, Vergil?" Hawkins had chuckled after listening to the request.

Hawkins had kicked ass well. After talking with Koenig he

had gone to the U.S. Embassy. Using the phone in a friend's office, in case he was told to wait for a return call, he had dialed Interpol's president's office, identified himself as a member of the embassy staff and requested an appointment four days hence for a delegation from the U.S. House of Representatives' Banking and Currency Committee. The committee, he had explained, was drafting the fiscal 1972 Treasury authorization bill, which contained the U.S. share of Interpol's funding. Some members of the committee wanted to see what they were paying for. There had been complaints about outdated information, Hawkins had explained, and he'd mentioned specifically a recent case, that of a Mr. Fang Pao-Hua.

It had worked like a charm. Within twenty-four hours, the Paris police records, which St. Cloud had not checked against its files for a year, had been swept. That morning at eleven Paris time, Hawkins's friend at the embassy had received a call. The body of Fang Pao-Hua had been found, his prints matched against those in the file. The Paris police were holding his effects.

Koenig received this information by relay at about 6:00 A.M., as he was getting ready to leave for work. It was deflating. He had spent a week working himself up to do battle with an enemy who all the while had been reposing in a suburban Paris landfill. Fang was ashes.

While Vergil Koenig was adjusting to this disappointment, Armistead Carrington was waiting for Peregrin St. Giles alias Berg to arrive for their second meeting.

At Carrington's suggestion, they had agreed to meet on the terrace of the Country Club of Virginia. The club was the one place in Richmond where Carrington still could sign for lunch and immediately be reimbursed by the bank. With his chronic cash shortage, every little bit helped.

125

Carrington had been brooding on his financial and other domestic problems for nearly ten minutes when he saw the taxi come through the gate and start down the club driveway. He watched, suspecting that the driver might not notice the four-inch asphalt bump placed across the drive to slow traffic. With perverse satisfaction he saw the taxi's front wheels all but disappear up into its fenders and heard the heavy thud as the car's tool kit and spare tire smacked against the roof of its trunk. He watched St. Giles extricate his large frame from the rear, pay the driver and make his way toward the terrace. He wore the same suit he had worn the day before. But this time he was carrying a large case, such as a salesman might use for carrying samples.

"Hello, Mr. Carrington. Sorry I'm late. Richmond is larger than I thought."

In fact, St. Giles was late because he had been racing around the city all morning. Since he had left Carrington the previous day, he had been, it seemed, to nearly every bank in Richmond. He had cleaned out the account Majendie had set up for him and added to it the money he had recovered from Fang, plus a substantial amount of his private resources. If his guess about Carrington's character was wrong, or if there had been a dramatic change in Carrington's financial circumstances as the credit services had described them, the effort would be for naught.

But St. Giles was confident he had the right man. He hadn't spent thirty years in his business without developing a nose for weaklings. He was too well acquainted with desperation not to recognize it in others.

"Hello Mr. Berg," Carrington replied.

The two men remained at the table on the terrace for more than an hour. To anyone watching from the clubhouse, it would not have been apparent after the first ten minutes that the men were conversing. Each sat facing the golf course. Only occasionally did either turn to look at the other. There were no gestures, nothing to suggest that a business proposition had been made and was being considered.

For a long time after St. Giles left, Carrington remained at the table on the terrace. When finally he rose, he did not return to the bank. Instead, he went from the terrace directly to the clubhouse, got a bottle of bourbon from his locker and poured himself four stiff drinks. Then he went home.

It was after six o'clock when he was wakened by the sound of the back door opening. He had fallen asleep in the bedroom fully clothed.

"Armistead?" It was Marylee. "Armistead, how long have you been home? Your mother called this afternoon and said she'd tried to get you at the office. I told her you might have left early to play golf."

"She say what she wanted?" Carrington had managed to raise himself to his elbows.

"I didn't ask. She probably just wanted to know how her little sweetums was. I wish she'd take half as much interest in the kids. Where are you?"

"In the bedroom."

"What are you doing in the bedroom? I've been at the grocery store for two hours. I swear, I'll never take these children anywhere again. This one wants Popsicles, that one wants pretzels; they tore the candy counter apart, and Army, bless his mindless little self, cried steadily for forty-five minutes. Arrrrg."

"Daddy, Daddy." It was little Armistead, at three, their youngest.

"In here, Army." Carrington listened to the little meat sounds of bare feet on the bare floor.

"What are you doing, Daddy?"

"Just resting, Army. What have you been doing?"

"We got possicles."

"No kidding. That's great. What colors?"

"What's this, Daddy?" Little Armistead's attention had fixed on his father's shirt pocket.

"Army, watch it; your knees are sharp. They're hurting Daddy's tummy. That's a pen."

"Can I have it?"

"Army, I just gave you a pen two days ago. I need this one."

"What are you looking at, Daddy?" Undismayed by the pen's unavailability, little Armistead had rolled onto his back and lay now with the back of his head propped in his father's armpit.

"Just the ceiling."

"What's that?"

"What's what?"

"That thing."

"Oh, that, that's just a cobweb."

"What's a cobweb?"

"It's like a spiderweb. You know what a spiderweb is, Army?"

"Why did the cob build it up there?"

"Armistead, if you think you can summon the strength, I would appreciate a little help with these bags." It was Marylee from the kitchen.

"Be right there." Carrington, slightly hung over, roused himself. In the kitchen, there were already half-a-dozen bags piled along the counter. Marylee was wrestling a huge bag of dog food through the door. "Where are the other guys?" he asked.

"In the station wagon. You don't think they'd offer to help, do you? You look like you had a nice snooze."

"That's right, Marylee. You know how we children are; we just lie around all day waiting to be fed. Why, without your unflagging energy and good spirits, we'd . . ."

"Don't be an ass, Armistead."

"What's put you in such a good mood?"

"Look, just get the bags, would you? It's almost six-thirty, and I told the Cooksons we'd be there at seven."

Armistead caught the end of her sentence over the slam of the screen door. "Christ," he muttered to himself. He'd forgotten all about the Cooksons. Dinner at the Cooksons' was the last thing he needed. Caught between ruin and the criminal life, and he was going to have to spend the evening listening to Tommy Cookson go on about his goddamn law practice, about how he worked so hard and how there was no way in the world he was going to be able to find the time to run for the state assembly in the fall, even though the pressures on him to do so were irresistible.

It was old ground. Carrington knew it by heart. Marylee would tell Tommy, as she always did, how clever he was and that he should be flattered so many people were after him. Then Tommy would puff on his pipe and tell Marylee that clever people were a dime a dozen and that, really, the man who should run for the assembly was old Armistead, which would remind Tommy to ask old Armistead how things were going at the old bank. That unwelcome query would evoke the usual shrug and give Tommy the opening he needed to get back to his favorite subject, the rigors of the law. That was the way it had been for the last three or four years.

As it turned out, the evening at the Cooksons' was a blessing. With Tommy occupying Marylee, and Tommy's wife, Louise, spending most of her time in the kitchen, Carrington was left largely to himself. On several occasions, others made efforts to include him in the conversation but received no encouragement. Carrington seemed to want to be left alone.

It was one-thirty when he and Marylee finally got up to leave. Neither spoke during the drive home. Marylee, having spent nearly six hours on the receiving end of Tommy's attentions and flattery, hummed contentedly. If she noticed her husband's silence, she did not remark on it.

As Carrington pulled the car into the driveway, he could see from the window of their bedroom the blue glow of the TV. The baby-sitter doubtless was asleep on their bed.

"Marylee, you pay the girl and send her out. I'm going to wait here," he said, slumping down in the driver's seat.

"My, aren't we gallant."

"Just send the girl out, would you, Marylee?"

"What's bugging you, Armistead? You've been acting like an ass all evening. First you don't talk to anybody; then, when people try to get you to talk, you're nasty."

"Are you going in or not?"

"I want to know what it is."

"All right, it's your goddamn flirting." It was only half a lie, since, in truth, Marylee always flirted, and it always annoyed him. The fact that this particular night he had more pressing concerns did not change that.

"My flirting?"

"That's right."

"My God, Armistead, all I was doing was talking to Tommy. We've both known Tommy for twenty-five years. Is that flirting? That really makes me mad. I mean, coming from you, Armistead Carrington . . . You should talk! What about Judy Galpin? What about that, huh?"

"That was four years ago."

"That is not the point, Armistead. You seduced Judy Galpin and you didn't even feel bad about it until I found out."

"I did feel bad about it."

"Baloney."

"It's true."

"But you seduced her anyway."

"Actually, she seduced me, if you really want to discuss it."

"I don't believe that."

"Marylee, the woman's pussy tasted like she'd been feeding it Necco wafers. Why, if she wasn't . . ."

"Oh, you're disgusting."

"I'm also tired. Now would you get the baby-sitter."

Carrington watched his wife's slender silhouette as she walked toward the house. It was the same figure, same walk that had been part of his life for ten years. It seemed that little else about his life had survived so well. Ten years earlier he had believed he had the world by the nuts. Since then, however, his old friends and contemporaries had seemed to keep on growing, while he'd stayed the same. He had expected success, like adulthood, simply to arrive. He had waited too long. Now it was too late. He wasn't a doctor, he wasn't a lawyer or a minister; he didn't know the first thing about how to start a business; he couldn't even think of a business he might want to start. Who the hell was he?

He heard the screen door open and looked up in time to see it close behind his wife's moonlit arms and calves, all that was visible against the darkness of the house. Maybe that's what he was, and all he had been for ten years: Marylee's husband. And for it, up to his eyeballs in hock.

By the time the baby-sitter emerged, Carrington had made up his mind. He would do what St. Giles had asked. Not for Marylee's sake, and not for the children's. He would do it because it accorded with the principle he had let govern his life and which it was too late to abandon: given a choice between two pains, choose the more distant. He would call the John Marshall Hotel in the morning.

CHAPTER 14

Five blocks south of the Panthéon, there is a small hardware store tucked between two retailers of the prosthetic devices in demand locally on account of the neighborhood's numerous government-operated hospitals. It was to this hardware store that St. Giles went late in the morning of Friday, July 23. He had remained in Richmond just twenty-four hours following his meeting with Carrington at the country club, during which time he had met once more with the young banker and paid a brief visit to the Trailways bus station.

From the hardware store, St. Giles purchased a ten-millimeter Renault power drill and, after checking to make certain the drill's chucks would accommodate it, a seventy-five-millimeter grinding wheel mounted on a steel bit. To these purchases, he added an extension cord, a hacksaw, a flashlight, a set of one dozen screwdrivers with snap-on Phillips tip adapters and forty feet of flexible plastic tubing. Then, at a nearby pharmacy, he bought a candle and a bag of half-inch-broad rubber bands.

His shopping complete, St. Giles strolled west from the Place Pierre-Lampué toward the Luxembourg Garden, which he entered from Rue Auguste-Comte. The occasional clank of metal on metal announced a game of *boules* in progress somewhere in the trees on his left. There were few other signs of life. Midway down the garden's promenade, a white-clad sherbet vendor was erecting an umbrella over his pushcart. St. Giles nodded as he passed. Either the man did not notice or he wasn't ready for business, since he made no reply. Around the octagonal pool in the center of the garden, at intervals wide enough to suggest that they sought the solitude, a half-dozen old men sat dozing, skinny ankles visible below their heavy year-round trouser legs. Picking a chair that would not threaten anyone's privacy, St. Giles lifted his own pants legs and sat down. Propping his packages on his knee, he slid low in his chair and tipped his face toward the morning sun. He had about thirty-six hours to kill.

Paris, gay Paris, it never sleeps . . . so the tourist literature proclaims. But if the bars and *boîtes* of Montparnasse, Les Halles and Pigalle seem never to close, there is at the ends of the Métro lines a very different Paris from that of the tourist literature. There, in suburbs like Montreuil, Alfortville, Villejuif, Malakoff, and Clamart, the working class keeps to a different schedule. Men and women rise in darkness, don their working blues and set course by sunup for their jobs in the city. These Parisians have no energy to spend on the night. Their days end with a glass of wine at the kitchen table. By ten in the evening, they are in bed.

It did not surprise St. Giles, therefore, that at two o'clock in the morning of Sunday, July 25, the streets of Asnières were empty when he pulled his rented Simca into an alley between two rows of warehouses several blocks from the printing plant he had visited the previous March. No one who had seen him leaving the Gerson Hotel earlier in the evening would have recognized the figure who five minutes later emerged from the alley. Gone was the light-colored tropical suit; in its place, a dark blue warm-up suit and a pair of royal blue Bata running shoes. Over the jogging outfit, he wore a lightweight bicyclist's backpack, purchased the preceding afternoon at the small camping-and-sporting-goods store on Rue des Ecoles, three blocks from the Gerson. It had taken an hour of working with a razor blade to remove the parallel white stripes from the sleeves and legs of the suit, nearly as much time to cut the manufacturer's gold insignia from the backpack. Now, in the dim light of the abandoned street, he was all but invisible.

He turned into the narrow cross street and slowed to a walk. In the darkness he could make out the outlines of a chain link fence on his left. It stretched, shadowy grey, the length of the block, broken at twenty-foot intervals by vertical dark stripes, which he recognized as the fence's support posts. He had counted them on his earlier visit; the printing plant's loading area began with the sixteenth post.

He climbed the fence and crept cautiously to the rear of the building. He could make out the outline of the plant's loading bay, partially obscured by a parked delivery van. During his earlier visit, he had watched other vans being loaded. The manager had explained that the plant did more than certificate work. Its principal client was the French government, which contracted for official stationery, invitations, and also for the *certificats, diplômes* and other citations by which French citizens' rites of passage were commemorated.

Behind the parked van, the bay was sealed by a corrugated steel curtain, secured by two large padlocks. To cut the high-alloy steel of the lock bolts would take hours. With the hacksaw, St. Giles set about cutting the flanges through which the bolts were threaded.

The press sat in a well, six feet below the level of the rest of the plant. He felt his way along the metal rail, found the metal ladder and descended to the lower level. Relying on memory, he made his way to a point midway along the press, removed his backpack and dumped the purchases of the day before on the floor.

Working by flashlight, he located an electric outlet at the base of the wall, plugged in the extension cord and attached its female end to the cord of the electric drill. A pull on the drill's trigger confirmed that the outlet was live. He took the seventy-five-millimeter grinding wheel, inserted the steel rod on which it was mounted into the drill and made it fast with the chuck key. Then he broke open the bag, removed one of the broad rubber bands and stretched it around the circumference of the grinding wheel. He was ready to go to work.

It was nearly dawn when St. Giles finished with the press. After nearly two hours of the drill's noise, his mind was half asleep. But when the plant opened the following morning, the device that counted paper as it moved through the press would show that over the weekend an astonishing ten million sheets had been run. He had just one more thing to do. Fetching the plastic tubing, he ran one end into the gas tank of the delivery van by the loading bay. A few sucks and he had a siphon pouring a quarter-inch stream of gasoline into the press well. He ripped a sleeve from his jogging suit, wrapped the cloth around the base of the candle to hold it upright and set it on the floor. Then he lit the candle and gathered up his tools.

It was first light and raining when he crossed the Seine at Pont de Levallois. He swung south down the quai to pick up

Avenue de Neuilly. From there it was a straight shot to Avenue de la Grande-Armée, and the Champs-Elysées, an asphalt slash from the city's northwest corner to its center, one that would take him to within four to five minutes of his hotel. For the first time that night, he allowed himself to feel the weariness. His consciousness had retreated to a private vantage deep in his head. In his narrowing vision the city reached barely to the curbs of the wet street ahead; he was driving as though down a glistening tunnel.

St. Giles crossed the meandering river a second time at Pont de la Concorde and bore left into Boulevard St-Germain. Eight blocks farther on he pulled the Simca to the curb at the intersection of Rue du Dragon. Sawhorses were stacked along the sidewalk where a section of the street had been cordoned off. During the day, the area inside the cordon would be filled with workmen resetting the ancient Belgian-block paving stones torn up to permit installation of a twentieth-century sewage system. The project had been going on all over the city for a decade.

On rubbery legs, he left the car. Next to a stack of sawhorses, he dumped out the backpack's contents. In several hours workmen would arrive. They would do then what workmen in any city would do. By the following evening, the drill, the screwdrivers, all the tools that might have been traced, would be in the hands of new owners, who would be disinclined to confess where they got them.

He was mentally and physically spent as he slowly climbed the circular stairs of the Gerson. Bent on bed and sleep, he was halfway to the second floor before his brain caught up with his eyes. On the stairs, next to his shoe, still wet as though left there no more than five minutes before, was a footprint, a huge footprint, one made by a shoe at least two sizes larger than his own. He glanced behind him at the stairs he had just climbed.

There were similar prints on each. Heart pounding, he tiptoed on.

The trail of footprints ended at the filthy brown carpet that covered the second-floor corridor. At the end of the corridor a slit of artificial light shone beneath his door. Had he left his light burning? There were times when he routinely left lights burning twenty-four hours a day to mask his comings and goings. He could not recall having done so that evening.

Uncertain how to proceed, he hesitated, eyes on the slit of light, watching for a telltale shadow. His room was small; it would be impossible for anyone to move around in it without getting between the light and the door. If someone was there, he was not moving.

Cautiously he advanced. With each step the awful reality screamed at him more insistently. Majendie had followed him. Majendie had found him out. No wonder no newspaper had reported Fang's death. Majendie would not—could not—leave messes lying around. Now Majendie was waiting to get rid of the final bit of evidence. Would he be alone? Did Majendie already have someone downstairs?

"Click."

The metallic noise came from behind the door at his left. He whirled. No time for stealth now. With one quick motion he seized the door, yanked it wide and, lunging forward, swung head-level with all his might.

"Madre mia, oof . . ." The exclamation was cut short by the force of St. Giles's crashing body. His punch had found only air. Unbalanced, he had toppled upon a soft black form that now gasped beneath his weight.

He pushed himself upright, fear giving way to mortification and to the assault being visited on his senses.

"Excusez-moi," he muttered at the lumpen figure he had nearly crushed. The hotel's Spanish charwoman, her black dress hiked above her knees, one hand still on the toilet chain, was far too terrified to answer.

"Excusez-moi," he repeated as he backed hastily out of the second-floor toilet he had used every day for more than a month. Before he closed the door, his eyes fell on her feet. On them, stuffed with what appeared to be rags, were very large, shapeless black men's shoes.

His last thought before he fell asleep that morning was to wonder if he would be able to hear the fire trucks when the alarm came in from the printing plant.

One week later, St. Giles used, for the first time, the Telex number Majendie had given him in the event he needed someone eliminated. He included the name and address of the second man he had discovered the preceding month in his research at the Federal Reserve offices.

Carrington didn't know it yet, but compared to this other man, he was getting off easy.

CHAPTER 15

On Monday, August 2, Leonard Swartzman arose at six-thirty in his apartment on West 16th Street in New York City. He tiptoed to the kitchen and turned on the coffeepot that his wife, Etta, had prepared the night before. Then he shaved, gathered up the clothes Etta had laid out for him and carried them into the living room. By the time he had dressed, the coffee had finished perking. He poured himself a cup, added a teaspoon of sugar and, while waiting for it to cool, fixed a single serving of hot cereal, which he left in a double boiler on the stove. At seven, having gulped down the coffee, he let himself out of the apartment. He walked east two blocks to Union Square, angled across it to the green wooden newsstand, bought the *New York Times* and descended the stairs to the Lexington Avenue Subway. The height of the rush hour was still an hour away when he reached the platform, but already several dozen people stood waiting. He walked to the uptown end, opened his paper, creased it down the middle and began to read.

139

For thirty-five years Swartzman had followed the same ritual. He liked getting to his office at the New York Federal Reserve Bank early. It enabled him to avoid the worst of the crowds, which around Union Square he found threatening. It gave him a jump on his co-workers. Not least, it burnished his reputation for dedication and vigilance. Both were traits that, as vice president for security for twenty years, Swartzman had come to embody.

Swartzman also liked being able to call his wife each morning to wake her and tell her that her cereal was ready. And he knew she liked to hear from him as much as he liked to call.

This morning he would especially enjoy the call. The previous evening he and Etta had discussed their future. In a year and a half, Swartzman was going to be sixty-five years of age. That meant mandatory retirement. Though he could never have brought himself to retire voluntarily, having the decision made for him somehow made the prospect of idleness acceptable, even attractive. It had been on the subject of idleness and its pleasures that he and Etta had ended their bedtime conversation the night before. And it was to this subject that Swartzman looked forward to returning, if only briefly, in his morning phone call.

In the meantime, there was his paper. Swartzman had the routine of subway newspaper reading down to a science. By leaving home at seven he avoided most of the people who had to be at work at seven or eight. That meant an emptier subway, which meant less jostling, which meant more reading. By boarding the subway at the rear of the train, he saved the time he would otherwise waste walking the length of the platform at the popular Wall Street stop. More precious moments for reading. Finally, by not joining the charge to exit and waiting instead for the other Wall Street passengers to debark, he saved himself moments he would otherwise spend standing on the stairs to the street. In thirty-five years Swartzman had figured out almost everything there was to know about riding the subway from Union Square to Wall Street.

What he hadn't counted on was that this day at the Pine Street station a slender man in his middle forties with slicked-back blond hair and a three-inch lift on the heel of his left shoe would limp up close behind him and press something hard against the middle of his back three-quarters of the way up his spine. Nor had he figured on the muffled thump, or that the last thing he would see in this world was a Spearmint chewing gum advertisement turning crazily on its side and rising out of sight.

Etta Swartzman got her call that morning. But it wasn't from her husband.

The Raleigh Hotel, one block from the Richmond Federal Reserve Bank, was, by the summer of 1971, past pretensions to elegance, a shopworn relic of days decades gone when down-town Richmond had been the center of the city's commercial life. That the hotel clung to life at all was only because Thomas Jefferson's capitol building and the state legislature sat directly across the street. Lobbyists and legislators had to drink some-where. In the barless Richmond of 1971, the Raleigh's rooms were as convenient a place as any.

The coffee shop, neon-lit and dingy, with aging Formica tables of dinette-set green, had been nearly empty the after-noon of August 3, when Armistead Carrington entered. He carried the salesman's case that St. Giles, posing as Berg, had brought to their meeting at the country club the month before. He had with him also several out-of-town newspapers, pur-chased in the lobby upstairs. He wore a look of extreme con-cern as he slumped in a booth reading and rereading accounts of Swartzman's murder in the New York subway. The coffee shop was still nearly empty at ten-thirty in the evening, when, after five hours of coffee and cigarettes, Carrington got up to leave.

He negotiated the uptown drive in a daze. He scarcely took note of the green-grey statues marking the cross streets on Monument Avenue. As a child, the statues had been his friends. He had waved to them from the window of the car, struggled with their names. He had been five before he had learned to say "Stonewall Jackson" instead of "Stone Jack Walton," nearly seven before he had understood that these men on their bronze horses were not, like all his other adult friends, his relatives.

Of whom could he make a friend now? Things had come to a head with Marylee that morning. It had happened at breakfast, and, like a dozen quarrels over the previous month, it had begun with Marylee's complaining. This time it was Edward's piano teacher who had got under her skin.

"There is nothing wrong with Mrs. Mason, Marylee," he foolishly had ventured, thinking he could head off an argument and get on with breakfast.

"She doesn't like me. I can tell," Marylee had said, "and she's taking it out on Edward."

"She likes you fine. Actually, she probably doesn't care one way or the other. If Edward gets a little disciplining now and then, it's probably 'cause he needs it. None of us is perfect; are we, Edward?" he said, winking at his six-year-old, who was sipping his orange juice and showing no interest in the conversation.

"She's a witch, Armistead. Tommy Cookson had her twenty-five years ago, and he says she was a witch then."

"I had her, too, Marylee. She's perfectly nice. She's just strict, old-fashioned. If you'd been teaching piano to six-year-olds for twenty-five years you'd be strict, too."

"Well, Tommy said I'm right to be upset."

"Tommy would."

He had meant nothing special by the response, but Marylee had jumped on it.

"What do you mean by that?"

"I mean, Marylee, I'm not surprised Tommy supports you. For what you've been giving him, you have a right to his support."

He had spoken without thinking. His words had surprised him as much as they did Marylee. But once spoken, they had seemed like short, crisp lines connecting the dots in an all-too-obvious picture. Carrington had felt the impact in the pit of his stomach. He had known immediately that there would be no second chance at innocence. When, ten minutes later, he left the house, Marylee had not yet answered. He wasn't going to find a friend in Marylee, that was certain; not that evening, not ever. Now that he knew, and she knew he knew, she would need to hate him for something.

Carrington turned north off Monument Avenue onto the Boulevard. In a few minutes, he was passing Parker Field and the lots where as a child he had played Little League Baseball. The first Dairy Queen in Richmond had been across the street from the field. Or had it been a Carvel? A Tastee Freeze? It didn't matter. It was gone now, run over by the Interstate ten or fifteen years before.

He slowed at the intersection of Boulevard and Westwood, where the Esso station had been, and the traffic circle, and Grants, where he'd got his first squirt gun. Angling left onto Hermitage Road he looked for them, or for some naked spot that would share their memory.

The Esso station was an Exxon station now, the circle and Grants gone. But the old A. P. Hill monument was still there, straight ahead; and past it lay Ginter Park.

"Ginna Park, Ginner Park." The name sounded strange

after all the years. Once Ginter Park had been his world, its name as familiar as his own. Things hadn't worked out for old Mr. Ginter. He had wanted Richmond to move north on the road he'd built for it. But Richmond had not wanted to move north; it had wanted to move west, and there had been nothing Mr. Ginter could do to stop it. Forty or fifty big houses were all he had built before giving up. His dream had long ago choked on bungalows.

Nottaway Street flashed by, and Carrington slowed. A moment later, he turned right into the familiar circular driveway.

As the car's headlights swept the yard, he could see an open space where the old lightning-blazed oak had stood. Then the lights played across the house, and Carrington could see the huge covered porch that ran around more than half the house and the yellow of the brick and a hundred familiar details.

The old house had been out of his family for years. His grandmother had sold it when he and his mother and his sister and his aunts had moved out after the war. Fifty years in the family, and then one day, all of a sudden, gone! Sold to Mr. Pembroke, just like that! Then, he had been a child and had not understood how anyone could sell a house he had spent his whole life in.

For a long time, Carrington remained in the car at the foot of the front steps. There were no lights on in the house. Five years earlier, the drafty old structure, with its cavernous, uninsulated attic, had expelled its last tenants, priced them into a prefab in the West End.

The thicket at the edge of the side yard was gone. He could look across the openness to where Miss Dot had lived. Miss Dot was gone, too. Someone had told him she had moved. He wondered if she ever came back to look, and if she did, whether she, too, missed the thicket.

The thicket had been his hiding place. "The briar patch," he had called it, taking the name from the Uncle Remus stories people read him. There had been lots of people to read to him in those days: his mother, two aunts, his grandmother, a whole houseful of women. Maybe there had been too many women. Perhaps if his father had been around, he would have learned to do whatever it was that men admired. Perhaps he'd have been a doctor or a lawyer; perhaps he'd have done something. But his father hadn't been around. His father had gone off to the war when he was an infant, and the closest contact Carrington ever had after that was a stack of baby-talk V-mail tied up in ribbon and the pair of huge black shoes that had disappeared from the floor of his mother's closet about the time he was six or seven. Carrington had grown up trying to please women. By the time he was seventeen, he had learned that he didn't have to be a doctor or a lawyer to do that.

He got out of his car. The front yard had not changed. Same magnolia tree, same hedge, same holly trees side by side next to the driveway. The cedar tree close to the hedge caught his eye. He approached it and slid his fingers up and down its trunk. Disappointed, he started to turn away; then, remembering that trees grow from the top not the bottom, lowered his hand and felt again. The old hammock hook was still there—rusty, worn half through with the years, but still there.

At the top of the side steps, he paused to peer in the window of the downstairs bathroom. There was only blackness, but the nearness brought a rush of memories. He remembered he had been standing in the bathroom when his mother and his aunt told him the war was over. He remembered, too, the day he had poured mineral oil on the bathroom's linoleum floor to turn into a barefoot boy's skating rink. And the crash and the cursing later that day when Laura, the maid, had gone in to do her cleaning.

He walked along the darkened porch toward the front of the house, past the spot where the semicircular rocker called the "joy cup" had sat through the childhoods of two generations.

He passed the front door, found with his hand the impression its knob had made in the brick wall; passed the windows of the "red room," the spot where the glider had sat in front of the parlor window and the spot at the far end of the porch where his baby sister's basket had been set to let her catch the sun. Memories stripped away the years, bringing back the old feelings and smells of happy days when it was always summer morning and his only worry had been that the sun would make the steps too hot for his bare feet.

His earliest recollections were of the world as it appeared from that porch; its roof and railings bounded life's possibilities. He squatted, half hoping to recapture the old perspective. Rising, he walked to the heavy white railing that ran around the outside of the porch and slid his hand along the dusty chalking paint. He removed his shoes and socks. It had been a long time since he had felt the porch—cold in the morning, warm in the middle of the day. With his bare feet he felt again its familiar surface, the chips and craters of a dozen paintings. Twenty-six years, twenty-seven? How many coats of paint separated him from that five-year-old?

He stood for some minutes at the top of the front steps. Below him, the newel post of one broad banister was missing the ornamental ball that had topped it. Probably it had rotted off. Once someone had taken a picture of him sitting astride the banister, hugging that ball. His mother still had the picture in her apartment.

Descending the steps, he threw his leg over the banister, slid forward until his groin mashed against the post and waited for the old feeling of innocence, for some sign that the child of his past might forgive him for what he had done with their life and let him start over from that porch as he had started once before.

Sitting on there, one foot resting on a step, the other dangling nearly to the ground, Carrington faced at last what he had known since that afternoon in the coffee shop. There were limits to a prodigal's entitlement. Unless he turned himself in and sought protection, Berg would have him killed just as surely as he had Swartzman. This time he had gone too far.

It was eleven o'clock that evening when the coffee shop at the Raleigh Hotel closed. Mavis Byrnes, the waitress, had been on duty since one o'clock that afternoon, and she was tired. Halfway through wiping tables, she had decided that the health inspector could go to hell; the floor would have to wait another day. She might never have seen Carrington's briefcase had her foot not struck it as she was reaching to wipe under the sugar bowl and the napkin dispenser.

Godamighty, one more chore. She would have to take the case upstairs to the hotel lost-and-found. Why did people have to forget stuff on her night? She put it on top of the table and went on with her wiping. She remembered the man in the booth earlier that evening. He had been an odd one. All that coffee!

She finished wiping up at eleven-fifteen, wrung out the sponge, washed her hands, stuffed her apron into the laundry bag, then removed her pocketbook from the locker under the counter. She was nearly out the door when she remembered the case. Fetching it from the table, she started for the door that opened onto stairs to the lobby. Then she stopped. The case was light. It was scuffed and battered. She shook it a few times. It felt empty. The heck with it, she thought. As long as she was cutting one corner, she might as well cut a couple. She walked to the counter, hoisted the case and tossed it over. It would be safe enough.

CHAPTER 16

"**W**here the hell is the money, Jack? Answer me that. Why isn't there any money out there?" Vergil Koenig slapped his desk and glared at his assistant across the room.

Since Hawkins's call from Paris, there had been one frustration after another.

To begin with, the consulate in Hong Kong had cabled for more specific instructions regarding the presses. They had wanted brand names, model numbers, other details about which Koenig hadn't the slightest idea. That was the trouble with trying to work with the State Department. You asked them to find something; they asked you where to look.

Then at eleven that morning, Verity had called. Verity was wavering. Quadrant numbers notwithstanding, he was no longer certain the Seydoux bills were counterfeit. He had put the matter to other members of the Technical Services staff, and opinion was divided. Some members held with Verity's original view—that it was mechanically impossible for the bills to be real. But others on the staff were not convinced. It was more likely, this group argued, that an error had been made in printing the quadrant numbers, or that an accidental run of more than ten thousand bills had occurred, than it was that Fang, or anyone else, had obtained genuine paper and reproduced without a single flaw what no one had ever before been able to reproduce.

Verity's new uncertainty annoyed Koenig. He wasn't going to call off his efforts on the basis of some bureaucrat's estimate of probabilities.

More annoying, the fences were still pleading ignorance. That wasn't logical. Counterfeiters didn't sit on their work. It was too risky. If someone had made as much money as the quadrant numbers on the Seydoux bills suggested, it had to be out there somewhere.

"You got any bright ideas, Jack?"

Childress, who had been browsing the bookcase at the far end of the office, thought for a few seconds before answering.

"I suppose we could use the commercial banks. You know, get the word out to tellers to watch quadrant numbers."

For a moment, Koenig considered this suggestion. Regulation of the nation's banking system was divided among the Federal Reserve System, the Treasury Department and the Federal Home Loan Bank Board. It would take just three phone calls to put a million eyes to work for him when the banks opened for business the next day. But it was impractical. The tellers could compare quadrant numbers as Verity had done. But the likelihood of two counterfeit bills showing up in succession at the same teller's window was remote. For the tellers to help, they would have to record not only the serial and quadrant numbers of each bill coming over the counter, but also the faceplate number, check letter and series. For bills from the same press run, the tellers would then have to go through the same subtraction exercise Verity had showed him. It would take forever. By noon of the first day, bank customers would be lined up into the street.

"That ain't going to work, Jack; it's too goddamn complicated."

Several days later, Hawkins called from Paris with another report on Fang.

"Vergil, I don't know if you're still interested in the Chinaman, but I just got back from looking through his stuff, and I thought I'd better let you know what I found."

"Good man, Hawk!" Thank God there was one person around he could rely on to get things done.

"Well, there wasn't a hell of a lot. Guy didn't have his wallet when they found him. So there weren't any airline stubs or anything like that. No telling how long he might have been in Paris. The cops here never bothered to find that out, so I'm having airline reservations searched right now. I don't know how long they keep those records around. I doubt we'll get anything."

"Don't tell me what you don't know; tell me what you do know."

"Well, that's what I'm getting to. The only thing on the body, except for the guy's clothes, was a check."

"Yeah?"

"It was a check for a couple of hundred thousand francs drawn on the Paris account of something called the Kieler Aktiengesellschaft. You want me to spell that?"

"You better," Koenig said, scribbling down the letters as Hawkins read them off. "What's that?"

"What's what?"

"The Acting-gesell-whatever-it-is?"

"I don't know yet. From the name, I'd say it was a corporation in Kiel, but I don't know any more than that right now. If you want, I'll try to check it out; but you'd probably have better luck having somebody there do it. My sources here are kind of limited."

"Who is the check drawn on?"

"That company I just been telling you about."

"No, no, I mean what bank?"

"First National City, Paris branch."

"An American bank?"

"Sorry, Vergil, you're going to have to speak up a little. This is a bad connection. I can barely hear a thing you say."

"It wasn't important, Hawk, but look, could you do me a couple of favors?"

"Yell 'em loud."

"First, find out when that check was written. Then I want you to get on somebody's ass over at the Sûreté. They are supposed to be getting us a list of printing firms in Paris, and we haven't heard shit. If you could do one of your numbers over there, I would appreciate it."

"Okay, Verg, I'll see what I can find out."

"You're a great American, Hawk. You can tell them it was their man we found holding the money. Seems to me the least they can do is offer us a little cooperation."

"I'll tell 'em."

Koenig ate lunch at his desk, a sandwich—pastrami and muenster cheese with Russian dressing on pumpernickel—potato chips and a Coke. Then he put in a call to the Bureau of International Commerce at the Commerce Department to find out what he could about Kieler Aktiengesellschaft. Ordinarily, he avoided calling Commerce. Nobody in that department ever seemed to know what anyone else was doing, or even supposed to be doing. Commerce was the bureaucracy's trash pile, a jumble of all the rope ends and garbage other departments had over the years discarded, the hair on the drain of the sink of government.

After ten minutes on the phone Koenig had learned nothing. No one at Commerce had heard of the firm. There were no records of any American company having done business with a firm by that name. It was possible, he was told, that the Kieler Aktiengesellschaft was a financial rather than a manufacturing concern. Had he tried the Treasury Department? By the time Koenig received this useless suggestion, he had been transferred through three different divisions and no longer had any idea to whom he was talking. He thanked the man for his thought and hung up.

Calls around Treasury and State were no more helpful. After nearly forty-five minutes on the phone, he had nothing more useful than the promise of a Mr. Kurz at Treasury that he would keep checking and call back if he found anything.

For the next hour and a half, Koenig stared at his ceiling and tried to assemble the scatterings of fact into some plausible theory.

If Fang had made the plates for the Seydoux bills—and that much now seemed obvious—then Fang had finished them at least a month earlier. Why then was there no money? Even a medium-sized commercial press could run off millions in twenty-dollar bills in a couple of hours.

It was possible, of course, that Fang had made not just the plates but the bills as well. Perhaps he had run off just ten or fifteen thousand dollars on a hand press, as he had in the past. Perhaps he had only been visiting Paris as a tourist and had got rolled by someone who'd seen him flashing the money around. The Seydoux bills might, in that case, be all that was left of Fang's work.

Then why the check? Why would Fang have been flashing a roll of U.S. currency in Paris? And who had sent the cables to Seydoux? People didn't send cables for an eight-thousand-dollar caper. It was much more likely that Fang had been hired to make the plates, then was killed when he was no longer needed.

None of which shed light on who might have hired him, or why they would want to bring counterfeit dollars into the United States. Unless . . . a thought occurred to Koenig . . . unless the Seydoux bills had been brought in just to check their quality. What if someone had wanted to find out whether the bills were going to pass. The Seydoux bills could have been a test marketing. Stupid, but it was the sort of thing that would have appealed to Fang. If Fang was working for hire, he might have convinced his employer to try it.

Koenig picked up a pencil and scribbled himself a reminder to have somebody check the U.S. military bases in Europe. A military base was a good place to pass bad money; it could be put in circulation there without going to a bank or official exchange. With bills as good as Seydoux's, using a military base was an unnecessary precaution. Still, habit was sometimes stronger than reason.

Shortly after four o'clock, Koenig rang for Childress.

"You got anything yet, Jack?"

"Not yet."

"Well, keep plugging."

"Okay."

Koenig's next question caught his assistant by surprise. "What's the name of your barber, Jack?"

"Beg your pardon?"

"Your barber, Jack; barber, barber. You know, like haircuts. What's his name?"

"Seguy. Joe Seguy."

"He do regular haircuts, too?"

"Huh?"

"He do regular haircuts, too?"

Taken aback, Childress had instinctively raised his hand to his head. Caught with it there, he affected an itch behind his right ear, then stiffness on the right side of his neck. Finally, simulated concern for the straightness of his tie got the errant hand back to more comfortable regions and he gave his answer: "Yeah, sure, I guess so."

"I mean he doesn't do just those fairy jobs with the hair dryer and all?"

"No, no. He'll do whatever you want."

"Uh-huh, I'll bet he will."

Childress didn't respond to Koenig's last remark.

"Does this guy have a fingernail girl?" Koenig went on.

"Yes."

"You ever done that?"

"Once."

"What's it like?"

Childress shrugged, not certain quite how to react to this strange turn in his boss's conversation. "It's okay."

"Yeah?"

"Feels kind of good, I guess."

"Well, where's this place at? I think I'm up for it."

It was nearly five-thirty by the time Koenig left Seguy's, on L Street. He was grateful the haircut notion had not hit him earlier in the day. Once in the chair, amid the flowery shirts and fluffy-headed hairdressers, he had lost the macho assurance with which he had ribbed his assistant. Not wishing to appear loutish to the peacocks, he had kept his mouth shut and let them work their way. Now he regretted his timidity. Half a block from the barbershop he paused in front of a store window to take stock again of the damage. He ran his fingers through his hair several times. Each time it sprang back into place. He let out a little groan. Until he could get to a shower, he was going to be a perma-press "froot."

Back at the office, he was surprised to find that Childress had already left. There were no messages, or any further word from Hawkins. Embarrassed about his appearance and eager to remove himself from view, he cleaned up his desk as quickly as possible and left.

When he reached home it was nearly quarter to seven. Ruthie greeted him at the door with the information that Childress was on the phone.

"Jack, I just got back from the beauty parlor. I'm be-you-tee-ful. Where the hell are you?"

For the next three minutes, Koenig stood in the middle of the kitchen and listened. His expression had become serious. Ruthie entered and smiled, making little pointing motions at his head. Koenig frowned, motioning for her to cut it out.

"Okay, Jack, hold him right where you are," Koenig said finally. "Don't do anything. I'll be there just as fast as I can. . . . What? . . . No, no, don't call anybody. Just sit down and stay calm and wait for me. . . . And, Jack, no fuckin' newspaper people, okay? Don't let any newspaper people in there."

"What is it, Vergil?"

"Huh? Oh, I gotta go to Richmond, Ruthie. I gotta go right now."

"Richmond, Virginia?"

"Yeah, Richmond. I may be there a while, Ruthie. Be a good girl and get me a bite to eat. I gotta wash my hair."

CHAPTER 17

Pushing his Mercedes as hard as its clutch would permit, Koenig reached Richmond shortly before ten o'clock. Childress's call earlier in the evening had come from the regional office, and it was to its downtown address that Koenig went directly. He sat now in the regional director's office, with the regional director, whose name was Briscoe, Childress and a third man, whom Koenig did not know.

"Name?"

"Carrington. Armistead Carrington."

"Spell it."

"Spell which?"

"Spell the whole goddamn thing."

Koenig drummed his fingers impatiently on the tape recorder as the man spelled his name. Childress had told him on the phone a little about Carrington's background. But ten years of dealing with junkies, pimps, touts and pushers had conditioned Koenig's expectations. He had not been prepared for a rather patrician-looking young man with a suntan and a conservative business suit. Carrington had finished spelling his name.

"Okay, now let's have your story."

"You want me to start at the beginning?"

Childress interrupted before Koenig could explode. "Vergil, this guy's story is awful damn complicated. I think you'd be better off letting him start at the end. It will make more sense to you that way."

Koenig nodded. "He can start wherever the hell he wants. Just get on with it."

Carrington's story took half an hour to relate. He began by describing the proposition St. Giles, still posing as Berg, but having dropped all pretensions to journalism, had put to him at the Country Club of Virginia the month before. Then, skipping ahead, he told of reading the previous day about the murder of his counterpart at the New York Federal Reserve Bank, Swartzman, and of his realization that he, too, was in danger. From that point, Carrington backtracked, filling in details.

For a long time after Carrington was finished, all four men were silent.

"Is this what you explained to me over the phone, Jack?" Koenig asked finally.

"It's what I tried to explain. You can see what I was up against."

"Jesus." Koenig was leaning forward in his chair resting his forehead in the palms of his hands. "Jesus. That's the most complicated fuckin' story I ever heard."

"We can have a transcript for you by noon tomorrow, Mr. Koenig," the regional director ventured. "I can get the girls in by six o'clock."

Koenig wasn't listening. He had sat up again and was looking at Carrington.

"Let's go through some of this again, Mr. Carrington. You say there isn't any counterfeit money because it all got burned up?"

"Yes, sir."

"You burned it at the Federal Reserve Bank instead of the old money that was supposed to be burned?"

"Well, I didn't burn it myself. The bank burned it."

"You just swapped it for the real money the bank was supposed to burn?"

"Yes, sir."

"Every day for a month?"

"Approximately a month."

"What did it look like?"

"What did what look like?"

"The counterfeit money. What did it look like? I mean, you people burn old money, right? Ripped-up stuff."

"Well, yes. That's right. But Berg had managed to make his counterfeit money look exactly like the bills we usually burn. At least I couldn't tell the difference. It was amazing. It was like everything else. The man was amazing. Things you didn't think could be done, he figured out how to do."

"How'd he do this?"

"What? Make the money look old? I'm not sure. He told me once, but I'd never heard of the machine . . . a wheelator, wheelerator, some name like that. Made it sound like it was no problem at all."

"So anyway, after you substituted the counterfeits, you took the real money that was supposed to be burned and gave it to this fellow Berg?"

"Yes."

"And all this because you owe money and your kids might have to go to public schools?"

Carrington didn't answer.

"Don't they have guards in that place?" Koenig went on.

"Yes, lots of guards. You might say I was sort of a guard myself. I wouldn't have thought it possible, either, until Berg showed me what to do."

"Go through it again."

Carrington took a deep breath. "Well, Berg left the counterfeit money in a locker at the bus station. We each had these cases, these identical leather cases he had bought. We carried the money in them. In the morning, I would stop by the bus station on the way to work and pick up the case of counterfeit money he had left. In the evening, having made the swap, I would go by the station and leave the case of genuine old money for him to pick up."

"Where was he getting it?"

"The counterfeit money?"

"Yeah."

"I never asked. But it must have been nearby, because he had to get there and back every day."

"Where did he get rid of the real money?"

"I don't know."

"I mean, did he mail it off, put it in the bank, buy postage stamps? How the hell do you get rid of that much money every day?"

"I don't know."

"Did he do it during the day or at night? Before or after he picked up the next batch of counterfeit money?"

"I don't know. During the day, I imagine, but I don't know. As I said, I never asked. I tried to stay as uninvolved as I could," Carrington answered.

"Oh, yeah, well, you did a helluva job," Koenig replied sarcastically. He thought for a moment.

"How much money did you swap each day?"

"Forty thousand bills."

"In one briefcase?"

"Well, the bills had been banded and bound up with metal straps, just like we do it at the bank. They didn't take up as much space as you might think. And these cases weren't ordinary briefcases, either. They were those traveling salesmen cases."

"You got him these bands and straps?"

"No, but they would be easy to get. The bands are just brown paper and the straps are regular packing straps."

"Okay, go on."

"So then I'd make the swap, as I said."

"I want to hear you say it again."

Carrington exhaled audibly and resumed. "There's a section of the bank called the Currency Sorting and Counting Division. The people who work there go through all the money that comes in and take out the bills that are torn or old. The bad bills are wrapped up, as I told you, and put aside to be burned."

"But the burning is done on another floor."

"That's correct. The money is burned in the basement, which means that somebody has to take it downstairs in the elevator."

"And you do that?"

"Well, I have been doing it for the last month. That was our arrangement. Berg figured out that the elevator was the only place I could be alone with the money. . . . I told you about the money buses, the big metal boxes we move stuff around in?"

"Yeah."

"Well, it was no trick to stop the elevator between floors for twenty seconds, open the bus, and exchange the counterfeit money for the good money."

"In twenty seconds?"

"It's all wrapped up, as I said—a hundred bills to a pack,

forty packs in each steel strap. That's only ten straps to make forty thousand bills. And I always knew exactly what I had in the case. All I had to do was count the ones I took out of the bus."

"Were there always ten there?"

"In the bus? No. Sometimes there were more, sometimes fewer. But I never took out more than I put in, and I never put in more than I took out. Generally, it was right around ten. . . . Berg had that figured out, too."

"Then what?"

"That was it."

"The counterfeit stuff went right into the oven?"

"No, not right away. The bank just burns on Wednesdays and Thursdays. As I said, the bills would be counted. Then the people in the basement would drill holes in them, chop them up and all that."

"And you?"

"I'd just ride the elevator back up with the case full of real money and go on back to my office."

"Then you'd put it in the locker on your way home?"

"That's right."

"Every day for a month?"

"Every weekday."

"And nobody ever said anything?"

"About what?"

"About you hauling this case around. Doesn't that seem a little funny?"

"Well, sir, the whole arrangement was funny. I'm just telling you what happened. But the answer is no, nobody ever did ask. Of course, you have to understand that just about the only people I see during the day are the guards, and they work for me. I don't think it's too surprising that they wouldn't question their boss."

Koenig paused in his questioning, rubbed his eyes with his fingertips, started to say something, then turned to the regional director and asked if there was any coffee in the office. There was none, but Briscoe, who was hearing Carrington's story for the fourth time that day, volunteered to see what he could find.

Koenig turned his attention back to Carrington. To this point, his questions had dealt with areas he could understand. The subject to which he now turned had confused him.

"Now you said the French were behind all this?"

"That's right."

"Who? The French government?"

"Yes. Or part of the French government, at any rate."

"How do you know?"

"Berg said so."

"What exactly did he say?"

"He said, 'The French are behind this' or 'I'm doing this on behalf of the French,' or something like that."

"The French government, though?"

"I believe he said it was the government. Certainly that was the impression I got. I can't remember exactly what his words were."

"How much money do you figure you've swapped in a month?" Koenig asked.

"I never added it up, but it was forty thousand bills a day —whatever that comes to."

"You're the fuckin' banker. What does it come to?"

"Well, forty thousand times five is two hundred thousand a week, times four is eight hundred thousand. And that's just bills. If you multiply it by twenty, it's sixteen million dollars."

"But that's just the stuff you swapped?"

"Yes."

"And you say the dead guy, Swartzman, was doing the same thing at the New York Federal Reserve Bank?"

"Yes, for quite a long time, Berg told me," Carrington answered.

"But he was here every day, this guy Berg?"

"Yes."

"So who was working with Swartzman at the other bank?"

"I don't know. Maybe that was Berg, too. Maybe he had a partner. Maybe they had a different system in New York. I really don't know."

Koenig was silent for a while before he asked his next question. Something puzzled him. Carrington seemed to know quite a lot about the general sweep of what Berg had been doing, yet he was curiously short on details. Why had Berg bothered to tell Carrington anything?

"So when the guy at the New York Fed, Swartzman, got shot yesterday, you figured it was only a matter of time?" Koenig went on.

"I didn't know anyone was going to get hurt."

"You just thought you'd rip off a few million dollars and nobody would be the worse for it. Is that it?"

"Well, it seemed to me almost a victimless crime. It wasn't as though the money we were skimming came out of anyone's pocket. It was money that was going to be burned anyway."

Koenig fumbled for a response. Every agent in the Counterfeit Division was, in the course of his training, subjected to at least one lecture on the economic consequences of counterfeiting. Koenig had had it explained to him why the average citizen was hurt when the nation's money supply was increased without the official approval of the banking system. He had sat through the lecture on three occasions, hoping to absorb its mysteries. Still, he was at a loss now for a reply to Carrington's seemingly sensible analysis.

"Did you have any idea that Swartzman was going to get it?"

"No. Berg did tell me that the swap arrangement was not

going to go on much longer. He said they had a new counter-feiter who was so good that his bills could be circulated directly. He said he only needed me for a little while to help Swartzman swap the old counterfeits they still had in inventory."

"Just a month or two of work, then you and Swartzman could retire, was that it?"

"Sort of, I suppose."

"Except you didn't know what Berg had planned for your retirement party until you read about Swartzman in the paper. Right?"

"Yes."

Koenig shook his head, incredulous at Carrington's naïveté.

"And you say Swartzman had been at it quite a while?" he asked.

"About twelve years."

"Twelve years!"

"That's what Berg said."

"Twelve years! That must have made it seem pretty safe—that somebody had done it for twelve years."

"It did, yes."

"How much money would that be, twelve years?"

"I don't know, the New York Fed burns a lot, four or five times as much as the Richmond bank."

"Christ, that's billions of dollars." Koenig did a few moments of mental calculation. "That could be ten, twelve billion, or more."

"It would be an awful lot."

Koenig, who had been pacing, pulled up a chair, straddled it and threw his arms over the back. "What did you mean when you said the French are going to dump the money in the middle of August?"

"That was Berg's word, 'dump,'" Carrington answered. "He said it meant they were going to sell it."

"Sell it to whom?" Koenig asked.

"Just sell it was all he said. He said it would be enough to break the dollar. I asked him what that would mean, and he said it meant that nobody would want dollars anymore, that they would want gold instead."

"Well, where did this fellow Berg say the counterfeit money was coming from? And, for that matter, how did he get the real money back to the French? I assume this 'dump' is not going to happen here."

"He said the French would sell the money in the European money market."

"The Eurodollar market?"

"I guess so."

Koenig had "guessed so," too. "The Eurodollar market" was a phrase he had never before found occasion to use—for the simple reason that he had only the vaguest notion what it meant. Like "balance of payments deficit," "full employment budgeting" and "block grants," "the Eurodollar market" was one of those newspaper terms that, to him, signified nothing other than continuation of a story whose beginning he'd missed and whose progress was too far advanced for him seriously to consider catching up. He did not press Carrington for further details.

"So where was the money coming from?"

"I don't know. He must have been storing it somewhere around here, but we didn't talk about that."

"Did he say how he was getting it out of the country?"

"No, sir. He didn't say; I didn't ask. Maybe he just deposited it in a bank here and let the French withdraw it. I just don't know."

"A whole suitcase full of money, every day?"

"Pardon?"

"You think he walked into a bank and deposited a whole

suitcase full of money every day, all twenty-dollar bills, and nobody ever says anything?"

"I don't know. Perhaps he did it some other way. I've told you, I haven't any idea how he did it."

It was after midnight, and Koenig had been going at it for over two hours. For Carrington, having talked to Briscoe in the morning and Childress in the early evening, it was his third performance, and the strain was beginning to show. He sat slumped forward, cheekbones propped on the heels of his palms. His answers were becoming unresponsive. Contrite, courteous and cooperative to begin with, he now showed clear signs of fatigue and irritation. Even Koenig could see that the interview was approaching profitlessness.

"Does this look familiar to you?" Koenig had taken one of the Seydoux bills from his pocket and now held it out to Carrington, who looked at it without expression.

"No."

"No?"

"Okay, yes. It looks like a twenty-dollar bill."

Koenig shrugged and returned the bill to his pocket. He wasn't sure what he'd expected. Even Verity had not been able to tell it from a real bill by looking at it. Carrington had explained earlier that the counterfeit money Berg had given him had been made to appear old. Obviously, the crisp new Seydoux bill would mean nothing to him.

For a long time, Koenig did not speak. When he did, it was to Briscoe and in a tone that made it clear the interview was over. He and Childress would return to Washington that night. Briscoe was to put a man on Carrington and to have him watched twenty-four hours a day. Carrington was to go to work the following Monday as though nothing had happened. For the moment Carrington was the only bait Koenig had.

"What are you thinking, Vergil?"

Koenig had asked his assistant to walk him to where he had parked the Mercedes, but he had not spoken since they left Briscoe's office.

"I'm wondering how we're going to keep the CIA out of this."

Childress nodded sympathetically. Though he did not understand it, he had, if only by osmosis, come to share his boss's hatred of the CIA.

"Well, they don't really have jurisdiction, do they, Vergil? I mean, counterfeiting is our bag, not theirs. Right?"

"Right."

"So we're probably okay, don't you think?"

"Except for one detail."

"What's that?"

"There isn't any counterfeit money anymore, Jack. They burned it, remember?"

Childress started to remind his boss that Carrington had mentioned a "new" counterfeiter, but thought better of it.

The two men had reached the car before Koenig spoke again. "I think I'll start with Treasury in the morning. Since we're technically part of Treasury, if we can show them we've got things under control, maybe we can keep the CIA out for a while."

"Can I help?"

"Yeah. I got an important job for you, Jack."

"What's that?"

"Find out what a wheelerator is."

Koenig nursed the Mercedes through the vacant Richmond streets toward the point where he could pick up Route 95 north. Though he was weary and confused, things were looking up in one respect. His on-again, off-again battle with Fang was, at least for the moment, on again. Fang himself would not be there to offer a sportsman's congratulations, but the scale of the battle would more than compensate. If Carrington's story was true, Koenig was onto his biggest job ever. And though he did not know what his next step would be, he was, for the time being, in charge.

He switched on the radio. It was one-fifteen; a lot of stations would be off the air. There was a good chance he'd be able to pick up WWVA in Wheeling. He was in the mood for a little country music.

CHAPTER 18

It was August 5 before St. Giles learned of Swartzman's death. Confirmation that his cable from Paris to Majendie's Telex assassin had worked came in the form of the *New York Times* airmail edition, which he found at the Franklin Roosevelt Library in Paris.

He read the obituary with mixed feelings. "Trusted employee . . . devoted to the bank . . . meticulous attention to details." The quotations from Swartzman's colleagues jibed perfectly with what St. Giles had deduced from the Federal Reserve System's personnel records. Swartzman had been an inspired choice—the corruption of the incorruptible. What was more unnerving? The old man's death would terrify Carrington.

While St. Giles was in Paris reading of Swartzman's death, Vergil Koenig was in his office in Washington filling in the blanks.

At nine o'clock that morning, only six hours after he returned from Richmond, Koenig received a cable from Paris. Bingo! The French police had located a press in a suburb of Paris called Asnières. The plant that housed the press had burned two weeks earlier, but investigations had turned up a vast amount of unaccounted for usage on the press's digital counter, an unexplained run of nearly twenty million sheets.

"Good old Hawk," Koenig thought as he reread the cable. He tried to imagine what his friend had done to stir up that much action from the languorous French bureaucracy.

He read the cable again, then made a few quick calculations on his blotter. Twenty million sheets . . . thirty-two bills to each sheet . . . over twelve billion in twenty-dollar bills.

Were these in addition to the ten or twelve billion Carrington and Swartzman had swapped? They had to be. But if the French government was behind the counterfeiting, why would the Sûreté cooperate with Hawkins? Had they not been informed?

At ten o'clock Briscoe called from Richmond to say that he had the briefcase that Carrington had left in the hotel coffee shop. The label inside indicated the case had been bought at a Richmond leather-goods store.

After talking to Briscoe, Koenig called the Interpol office in the Treasury building and requested any information they had on anyone named Joseph Berg. The request would be relayed immediately to St. Cloud, where, if the message center was doing its job, it would be forwarded to the General Records repository. Within two hours a clerk, perched on a sliding stool, would begin thumbing through the repository's circular files. Koenig had heard it said that there were more than a million names on file at St. Cloud. One in a million were just about the odds he put on Interpol finding anything useful. No inquiry he had ever made to Interpol had yielded anything. Still, it could do no harm.

Then, at about ten-thirty, Koenig made the call he had been putting off. He called Paul Walker, under secretary of the Treasury for monetary affairs. It being the weekend, he placed the call through the White House switchboard, which routinely went on telephone searches for high officials all over the executive branch.

While he was waiting for a return call, Childress phoned from his home with more corroborating facts. A call to the Congressional Reference Service at the Library of Congress had turned up some interesting information. There was no company or any machine made in the United States under the name wheelerator. But there was, in Hampton, New Hampshire, a firm called Wheelabrator-Frye, Inc., which listed among its products a machine that polished iron castings by tumbling them in a cylinder full of metal filings. A phone call to the firm's Washington legislative office a few blocks away on M Street had failed to turn up a list of firms that owned such machines. But Childress had learned that one firm in the area had purchased one several years earlier—an iron foundry, located in Petersburg, Virginia, twenty-five miles south of Richmond.

The company's representative had also been able to give Childress an interesting description of the polishing machine: it resembled nothing so much as an enormous front-loading clothes dryer.

Koenig thanked Childress and hung up. The clothes dryer had been a basic part of the counterfeiter's equipment for thirty years. Though there were other ways to age new bills, an hour or two in a heatless dryer with a few cups of dirt, hair dye, cigarette ash, coffee grounds and small bits of light steel scrap was generally acknowledged to be the easiest way to simulate the wear and tear that months of handling produced. Childress's information was not conclusive; the Petersburg firm would have to be investigated. Still, it looked like a good bet.

At eleven-thirty, Under Secretary Walker called from nearby Rehoboth Beach. He seemed at first annoyed by the interruption, but listened intently after Koenig explained why he was calling. After a few questions and some further explanation, he agreed to return to Washington that evening. A meeting was set for eight o'clock at the department, and Koenig was instructed to contact two other men: Henry Erlich, a Yale economist and monetary expert on loan as a consultant to the Treasury Department, and Seth Ferguson, chairman of the White House Council on International Economic Policy. Koenig was to brief each beforehand.

By the time Koenig hung up, he was in a good mood. Ordinarily he disliked dealing with people like Walker, the higher-ups at Treasury and the White House. He sensed that they regarded Secret Service agents as blue-collar bureaucrats. They were not rude. But there was condescension in their voices, the casual bonhomie of the Georgetown homeowner talking to the mailman. What bothered him most was the nagging thought that their condescension might be warranted.

But Walker had been pleasant, almost respectful, and Koenig felt assured. After calling Erlich and Ferguson, he spent the remainder of the afternoon preparing himself for that evening's meeting by listening to the Carrington tapes.

He need not have bothered.

The meeting in Walker's office on the third floor of the Treasury building was not ten minutes old before it became clear to Koenig that the other men in the room were interested almost exclusively in the feasibility and consequences of the French plan to sell dollars. The counterfeiting operation through which the dollars had been accumulated seemed to interest them hardly at all.

Walker opened with a summary of the facts. He then asked

views on four points: a motive, the volume of dumping that might be expected, the probable impact on the dollar, and, finally, the countermeasures available.

Erlich was first to respond.

In his view, the motive was obvious. The French were gold bugs—always had been, always would be. They had never liked the way the Bretton Woods monetary system had evolved, because it conferred special status on the dollar, giving the United States the power to make other countries absorb its deficits. This was offensive to the nationalistic French on principle, doubly offensive for the practical reason that, by absorbing U.S. deficits, they were, in effect, lending the United States the money that American multinational firms were using to buy French companies. This view had been broadcast in 1967 in a book by the director of the leftist news weekly *L'Express.* But the complaint had quickly been embraced by the Gaullists as well; and by 1971 it was generally subscribed to by everyone in France who worried about such matters.

The French preferred that official reserves be restricted to gold. This was no secret. They had argued for it for years in the councils of the International Monetary Fund. It was Erlich's guess that, in their frustration, the French were now attempting to achieve their objective by destroying the acceptability of the principal alternative to gold—the dollar.

"What do you think, Seth?" Walker asked, looking at Ferguson.

"Henry's right, Paul. Frankly, I'm amazed the French would consider anything as brazen as this, but certainly it is not inconsistent with their view of national interest. . . . I'm sure they'd like to do just exactly what this man Carrington says they're going to do . . . if they had the balls."

"Well, it's pretty obvious they've got the balls or we

wouldn't be here," Walker said. "The question is can they pull it off?"

Ferguson shrugged. It was Erlich again who answered.

"You know, this dumping scheme may appear bizarre, Paul. But it is not new. Twenty years ago there was a great deal of talk—in rather narrow circles, admittedly—about something called the 'money bomb.' Superficially the money bomb differed from what we face now, but the principle and intended consequences were quite similar. The notion was that huge amounts of counterfeit currency could be dumped out of airplanes over the major cities of the target country. The idea being that if the bills were good enough even to confuse people for a while, they would destroy the value of real money and bring economic activity to a standstill. I mention it only to suggest that, crazy as all this may seem, there is some history behind it. In my opinion, the answer to your question is, 'Yes, I think they can do it.'

"I called the Fed this afternoon and got some rather frightening numbers—which, incidentally, tend to confirm what you told me earlier," Erlich added, nodding at Koenig. "According to the Fed, there was a total of more than 1.2 billion dollars in twenty-dollar bills burned during calendar year 1970 at the New York bank. The midyear-to-midyear totals for the period ending this past June are probably larger. If their man has been swapping in that sort of volume for twelve years, as alleged, it's possible that the French have accumulated something on the order of ten billion, even twelve billion."

"Good God!" Walker exclaimed.

"That's right. It surprised me, too, Paul. But it turns out that forty percent of all the currency destroyed each year is in the form of twenty-dollar bills." Koenig was watching Erlich with respect. The professor had done his homework.

"Now, to put this in perspective," Erlich went on, "France's official reserves as of year-end 1970 were only $4.9 billion—that includes everything: dollars, sterling, gold, drawing rights, the lot."

"How did it break down, Henry?" Walker asked.

"Which?"

"The French reserves. I was just curious how much of the $4.9 billion they were holding in dollars."

"I don't have the figures here, Paul; but if you are wondering whether our gold reserves would cover their dollars plus another ten or twelve billion dollars, the answer is, 'No.' Our current gold reserves are around ten billion. But even if we had twenty billion dollars in gold reserves, it might not be enough. Remember, their plan is not to present us with the dollars for redemption; they're going to dump them on the market."

"Henry's right," Ferguson broke in. "We'll have the whole goddamn overhang crashing down on us. With the right timing, ten billion dollars dumped in Frankfurt, Paris and London would scare the bejesus out of every bank in the world. It'll be the dynamite that triggers the avalanche. When the private holders start unloading, who's going to stand with us then? The Japs? The Germans? I wouldn't count on it. They've been good to us until now, but they're not so stupid as to jump in front of an avalanche."

"How large is the overhang, Seth?" Walker asked.

"Something like thirty-seven billion dollars, Paul, and going up every week. That's just central bank holdings. Counting foreign private holdings, it's around seventy billion dollars."

"Mr. Koenig," Erlich asked, "did this man Carrington suggest a date when the dollars were to be sold?"

"No, sir. He just said 'the middle of August.'"

The question had been gratuitous; Walker had already gone over the matter of the date in his opening summary. Koenig guessed that Erlich had intended the question as a kindness, a means of including him in the discussion. But it only exposed his uselessness. For months he had been charging around trying to prove the existence of a counterfeiting operation no one else seemed to believe in. When Childress had doubted, he had pushed. When Verity had wavered, he had persisted. With Carrington's confession, he had felt vindication. Now he could see that the real effect of Carrington's confession was to reduce him to an irrelevancy. These other men were dealing with what was relevant. They were not interested in counterfeiting; they were interested in consequences. They did not care about the ingenuity of the plan or the quality of the Seydoux bills; there were no more questions he could help them answer. His usefulness was over.

Depressed, Koenig tuned out the discussion still in progress. He felt shame, embarrassment at having been patronized and anger with himself for not understanding what the others in the room were talking about. He glanced at the slender, agile-minded men around the table. Those on either side of him wore dark grey suits, the man across from him a blue suit. Why had he let Ruthie buy him a green suit? And such a shiny one; he hadn't noticed before how shiny it was. Suddenly he was conscious that he was the only man in the room whose shirt sleeves did not show at the cuff. Damn Ruthie and her short sleeves. He crossed his arms, buried his fists in his armpits and lowered his eyes. They came to rest on his knee, his stubby, shapeless knee, a meat loaf. An inch and a half of pale skin was visible above his sock. He uncrossed his legs, and thrust them under the table. Had it been his imagination, or had his shoes also had a greenish tint?

The meeting was winding up. Concluding discussion had focused on possible reactions. An options paper would be prepared that night. Erlich and Ferguson would meet the next morning at seven-thirty to go over the recommendations before final typing. The President would have to be briefed as soon as possible. No mention was made of a role for Koenig. Take it away, you bastards, he thought. It was late; he'd scarcely been home in thirty-six hours; he was tired and depressed. He didn't care if he never again set foot in the Treasury Department.

He was halfway down the corridor to the elevator when he heard a voice behind him.

"Mr. Koenig."

He turned to find Erlich ten steps behind him.

"Mr. Koenig, I thought perhaps we could have a chat, if you are not too tired. I was very interested in what you said this afternoon about the quality of these counterfeit bills. Have you ever heard of Operation Bernhard?"

"No, sir."

"Well, if you have a few minutes, why don't we go to my office? You might be interested."

There was nothing to do but agree, and a few minutes later the two men were seated in a litter-filled office with books stacked high on the sills of both windows.

"Can I offer you a drink, Mr. Koenig? I have only Scotch. Can you drink that?"

"Thanks."

"There are some people on this floor who would frown on this little practice of mine," Erlich said as he removed a bottle from the file cabinet and began to pour into two glasses taken from a bookshelf, "but one doesn't break the habits of a lifetime for one little sabbatical year. Do you think?"

"Right."

"Now then," Erlich said, seating himself opposite Koenig and nestling his iceless, undiluted Scotch between his hands. "Operation Bernhard was a very, very interesting proposition." And he proceeded to tell Koenig the same story of Nazi counterfeiting Majendie had related to St. Giles more than five months earlier.

"I never heard that before," Koenig said when Erlich was finished.

"No, not many people remember it, or, for that matter, ever knew about it," Erlich said, "but it was an interesting episode —particularly in light of what this fellow Berg seems to have managed to do."

"What do you mean?"

"Nothing, except that it does seem odd that this man, even with the support of the French government, has been able to pull off what the Nazis, with a major commitment of resources, could not. The Nazis were efficient people, you know."

For a moment he appeared to be musing to himself about something. When he spoke again, it was on another subject. "There, but that's not what I wanted to talk to you about. I sensed in the meeting that you might be having some trouble keeping up with all of our financial jargon. And small wonder. We economists live in a rather murky world. We try to keep our confusion a secret from other people by hiding behind our lingo. But that kind of talk gets to be a habit, and we sometimes use it even when there is no need. This evening, you got a bigger dose than any law-abiding citizen deserves, and I thought you might like to have an explanation in simple English of what is going on."

Koenig nodded. Erlich was being considerate. It would be rude to decline his offer. But Koenig had had layman's-language explanations of the international monetary system before. He knew better than to expect enlightenment. Erlich would start off with something like "Now imagine you're country A, and I am country B." After that: the eternal forest. In five minutes Erlich was going to have him nodding like a native at morning mission prayers.

"Forget about what reserves are and why we have them, Mr. Koenig. Fix one thing in your mind: a central bank wants to hold, in addition to its own currency, only money that will not decline in value. Have you got that?"

"Yes."

"Good. Now there is one more thing to remember. For a long time, most central banks outside the Communist bloc have been willing to hold just two things besides their own currency: one is gold, the other is the dollar. That is a bit of an exaggeration, but essentially true."

Koenig nodded.

"Central banks hold gold because there is a limited amount of it, and because there has never been a time when one could not find a buyer for gold. But why do central banks hold the dollar? They hold it because the U.S. government has promised them that anytime they don't want their dollars they can bring them to us and we will give them gold instead. So, you see, holding the dollar and holding gold have been the same thing."

"I understand."

"But our promise to give people gold for dollars is only as good as our ability to do it. We can't give them gold if we don't have it. Right?"

"Right."

"And that is where we are today. We just don't have it."

"I see."

"There are seventy billion dollars out there in the hands of foreigners, and there is only about ten billion worth of gold in Fort Knox. Now we don't have to worry about all of that seventy billion, because some is held by commercial banks or by people like you and me, and the United States never promised private holders it would give them gold for dollars. But about forty-seven billion is a problem, because it is held by central banks, which can demand gold."

"What did you mean when you were talking about the 'overhang'?"

"That's just a term of the art. The overhang is the difference between the amount of the gold we might be asked to surrender—the forty-seven billion—and the amount of gold we have—the ten billion. That's how we came up with the thirty-seven billion figure you heard."

"How did we get so far in the hole?" Koenig asked.

"You mean why didn't countries start asking for the gold as soon as it began to look as though we might not have enough to go around?"

"Yeah."

"Logical question. Some countries did. But the main reason there wasn't a serious run on the bank was that most countries realized that depleting our gold supply would destroy the dollar's value as a reserve currency at a time when, without a stable dollar, there would have been too few reserves for countries to carry on their normal exporting and importing. Then, too, most countries that held dollars were beholden to the United States for military support. But the need for large world-wide reserves—or what we economists call 'liquidity'—was the main reason. It's a complicated area, and you don't need to understand it to understand what's going on right now."

"What will happen if the French plan works?" Koenig asked.

"Well, that will be the end of the dollar as a reserve currency. After we use all our gold, we won't be able to support the dollar's price. Our allies are not going to throw themselves on the pyre by trying to help. With the price falling and the gold gone, the dollar will be just another currency."

"Will that be bad?"

"Depends on whom you ask. If you want my personal view, it might be good, but mine is hardly the prevailing view around here. You see, all sorts of prestige considerations get mixed up with this. Foreign policy considerations, too. A chaotic end to the dollar's special role will increase the price of gold, and that will benefit the wrong people: the French, the people who created this problem; the Soviets; and the South Africans, the people who produce most of the world's gold. From the President's point of view, those are not politically attractive results.

"In any case, Mr. Koenig," said Erlich, with a kindly, professorial smile, "you certainly need not feel bad if you don't understand all of this perfectly; none of us does." The Treasury consultant paused for a moment, as though waiting to see if Koenig wanted to say something. But Koenig was silent.

"Have you ever heard of Begelman's dream, Mr. Koenig? No, of course you haven't; how could you have? Begelman was a professor when I was in college—brilliant man, a lecturer in ethics and philosophy and generally reckoned to be the best mind around. It was terribly difficult to get into his lectures, but I was fortunate enough to obtain permission one term. I will never forget one particular day. It was toward the end of the term, and we were meant to be discussing some minor German logical positivist. Instead, Begelman appears in the lecture hall, puts aside his notes and proceeds to recount a dream he had the night before.

"In his dream Begelman had imagined himself, like Jack, climbing a beanstalk. Except that, in this dream, the beanstalk represented knowledge, and his ascent of it, learning. There were other people on the beanstalk, but because Begelman was the highest of them, they had to look up to him. As he recounted it, he found it satisfying to have everyone beneath him suppose that he knew more than they. But it was troubling, too, because Begelman could see what those below him could not —namely, that the section of the beanstalk that he clung to looked precisely like every other section he had passed on his way up. Still, he climbed on. Until, finally, reaching the top of the beanstalk, he pushed open a trap door above him and climbed through. He expected paradise. Instead, he found himself standing at the bottom of another beanstalk."

Erlich fell silent. He peered out his window through the darkness at the lights of the White House across East Executive Avenue. "Begelman laughed about that dream when he told it to us. But that evening he shot himself."

It was nearly eleven-thirty when Koenig finally rose to leave Erlich's office. Much of the despair he had felt earlier in the evening had lifted. Begelman's dream may have helped. On balance, he was inclined to credit the Scotch.

CHAPTER 19

A weekend meeting with the President could not be arranged. Due back from California, Friday evening, he had decided to stay on the West Coast for the weekend to visit a friend in Palm Springs. Not until Monday morning, August 9, were Walker and Ferguson able to get an appointment.

Because the President preferred small meetings, it was agreed that Erlich would not attend. Erlich was only a consultant; the President might regard his presence as redundant.

The options paper, complete with a summary of the Carrington tapes, just forty-eight hours out of the typewriter, had crossed the country twice; once as the sole passenger of an air force Jetstar, then back with the President overnight on Air Force One. There was every reason to suppose, as Walker and Ferguson entered the Oval Office, that the President was as familiar as they with the imminent French threat.

Walker took no chances. He reviewed in detail Carrington's dealings with Joseph Berg, explained the probable French motive and noted as corroborating evidence the death of Fang, the press in Asnières, and the Wheelabrator in Petersburg.

The President asked about timing. Was there reason to believe that one day in the middle of August was more likely than another? Why would the French settle in advance on a date? The dollar had been slipping in world markets for months. In May, both the Germans and the Dutch had elected to let their currencies' values fluctuate rather than continue buying dollars to maintain the old rates of exchange. Rumors were flying that the Swiss were contemplating the same step. With exchange markets uncertain and volatile, why would the French fix a certain date? Much smarter, the President reasoned, for the French to watch for a market day when the normal fears and suspicions of the money traders had already caused a minor flight from the dollar, and to act then. That way, the impact of the dump would be leveraged. What did Ferguson and Walker think?

Both men agreed with the President, but Walker only in part.

"Your point is well taken, Mr. President, but we have a reaction-time problem," he advised. "If we wait for it to become clear what is happening in the market, it will be too late to do anything about it. By the time we see the whites of their eyes, we are going to have a bayonet in our chest." Walker flushed slightly as he spoke. The President had a weakness for grandiloquent images. It was generally agreed among his staff that the way to sell him a point of view was to wrap it in language he could not resist repeating. Walker was a believer in the theory. But he had no gift for its practice.

"What do you think, Seth?"

"Paul's right, Mr. President."

For a few moments the President sat silent, eyes fixed on his desk.

"Goddamn those bastards," he said finally. "You know, it's a helluva note. First, the French drop out of NATO because they know they can sponge off us. Now they're going after our money because it offends their goddamn chauvinistic sensibilities to have American businessmen over there. That's Gaullist crap. You expected this kind of thing when that big bat-eared bastard was around. But Pompidou? . . . I don't know. I figured he was a reasonable sort of guy. . . ."

"Yes, sir," Walker said.

"What?"

"I said I agreed with you," Walker said.

"Yeah, well okay. So what do we do? You think we have to guess at a date? Is that what you're saying?"

"Yes, sir. I would say the sixteenth."

Berg had told Carrington the middle of August. The sixteenth of August, Walker explained, was a Monday. When a country had an important announcement to make that might adversely affect its currency, the announcement invariably was made on a Friday afternoon, after the markets were closed. Because there could be no trading until the following Monday, the country gained an entire weekend during which to offer reassurances and let the panic dissipate. It was reasonable, therefore, that a country bent on creating trouble would move on a Monday. That way, the country whose currency was under attack would have to defend it for five full market days. A few big orders from friendly central banks might moderate the effects of a huge private sale for a while. But five full days? Very difficult.

"You want to argue with that, Seth?" the President asked.

"No, sir, I agree with Paul again. My guess is they'll spend the preceding week sponging up dollar demand with short sales. They'll have the dollar flat on its floor and friendless by the Monday opening."

"So, we are down to what we do about it, then."

"Yes, sir," Ferguson answered.

"Well, get on with it. You fellas are the brains around here. I'm just a dumb politician, remember?"

Since the President had already read the options paper, Walker was brief.

Option one was for the United States to begin immediately selling its remaining gold. With four market days remaining in the week, it might be possible to accumulate foreign-currency holdings large enough to enter the market as a buyer of dollars on August 16, to absorb much, if not all, of the French dump. But it was inconceivable these gold sales could go undetected for four days. The resultant diminution in U.S. gold reserves would have to be published shortly. Even if the French were blocked, word of the gold sales would probably precipitate a spontaneous and genuine flight from the dollar. Option one had to be considered unappealing.

Option two was to approach countries holding large reserves and ask for support during the opening hours of trading on the sixteenth. This would be little different from numerous currency swaps arranged in the past to support other weak currencies. But the only country that could buy dollars in volume large enough to blunt the French offensive was West Germany. And two and a half months earlier West Germany had stopped buying dollars because it already held more than it wanted.

Option three was to confront the French. They were sure to deny all, since they almost certainly intended to mask the origin of their dollar sales. Moreover, a confrontation could cause word of imminent sales to leak. If the leak were picked up by the market, it would trigger panic selling by private holders, at least as serious a threat as what the French were planning. Option three had possibilities. But whoever confronted the French would have to be extremely diplomatic.

The fourth option was for the United States simply to announce that it would no longer sell gold, that it was following the lead of the Germans and the Dutch and allowing the value of the dollar to find its own level in the market. This would concede half of what the French wanted, by effectively taking the world off the dollar standard. But it would fall short of French objectives with respect to gold. There was even the possibility that, in the long run, option four would diminish the importance of gold by precipitating agreement through the International Monetary Fund to get rid of the whole archaic system. The IMF had already moved in this direction by issuing its own reserve currency called "special drawing rights." There were plenty of countries that, lacking both dollars and gold, would be happy to see the IMF go the whole way and make special drawing rights the principal reserve unit.

Walker had a banker's abhorrence for option four. Its first consequence would be world-wide uncertainty. Without fixed currency values, bankers and businessmen would be reluctant to accept promises to pay in currencies other than their own. Buyers and borrowers would be chary about assuming obligations to pay in foreign currencies. Every international transaction would have to be hedged. A decline in trade would result, followed by world-wide depression. Of this, Walker was certain.

The fifth and last option was to do nothing. In his years in government, Walker had never seen an options paper that did not include the "do-nothing" option. It was irresistible, because it allowed the writer of the paper to appear to have one more idea than he had.

"That's it, sir," he said.

"No more options, Paul?"

"No, sir."

"Well then," the President mused, doodling with his pencil on the pad before him. "If I understand you right, we have two alternatives that you think are terrible. We have two more that aren't too bad, except they won't work. And then we have the last one, which sounds familiar, and which I don't mind saying always sounds pretty good to me."

Walker suspected that the President was off on one of his occasional attempts at facetiousness.

"You know," the President went on, "I always wonder why people put the do-nothing option last, when you know damn well that it was the first one they thought of."

"Yes, sir."

"The trouble is, if we always do nothing, then we've got to wonder why anybody needs us here, huh?"

"Well, actually, sir, it is possible that . . ."

"I'm just kidding you, Paul; I'm just kidding you. I know, maybe the whole thing is never going to happen and we'd be stupid to make it happen by overreacting."

"Yes, sir."

"But it does look bad, doesn't it, Paul? I mean, we really don't have five options; we have two: we can take it in the mouth or we can take it up the ass. Isn't that what it amounts to?"

"That may be overstating it somewhat, sir."

"Uh-huh. Well, I've been accused of overstating things before. Look, here's what I want you fellas to do. I don't go for this groveling business—asking for help here, asking for help there. If we go down, we are not going British style.

"Paul, I want you to talk to the French. Don't accuse them, but put it to them straight, so there is no confusion in their minds. Say we've heard something is up, we're understandably concerned, so we're checking it out. You see, if they know we know, then they'll know we'll know who did it if it happens. That, by itself, might not stop them, but it will give them pause. You see?"

"Yes, sir."

"And, Seth, I want you to brief the people at the Council and the Fed. Look into how we go about floating on our own if Paul's trip doesn't pan out. We are going to fight like hell to avoid it, but I'd rather do it to ourselves than have somebody else do it to us like we were some goddamn banana republic."

The meeting in the President's office broke up shortly after eleven o'clock. By one-thirty, Walker was airborne.

Walker was met at Orly by George Poulos. Poulos was officially the deputy chief of mission at the U.S. Embassy in Paris. But a month earlier, the ambassador, a political appointee, had resigned, and Poulos had since been doing both jobs.

The two men went straight to the embassy, paused at Poulos's office long enough for Walker to wash up, then proceeded to the third floor. At the top of the stairs, Poulos opened a heavy wooden door and motioned for Walker to enter. A curtain blocked his way. Walker pushed it aside, and a blast of air greeted him, rumpling his hair and reminding him that his face and neck were still wet. They stepped up, opened a second door and entered the embassy's secure room, a Plexiglas box surrounded on six sides by hissing air. Four men sat at a brightly lit conference table. Poulos made the introductions and motioned Walker toward a chair at the far end of the table.

The briefing turned out to be nearly useless. The President had forbidden Walker to tell the embassy staff why he was there or why he would see the French finance minister the following day. He was limited to questions designed to elicit confirmation of a French motive. By the time the meeting broke up, after two o'clock, he had learned little. There were no prospects of declining support for Pompidou, nothing that suggested the French government might be looking for some favorable development as an opportune time to call elections. Yes, the French favored an increase in the price of gold and an end to the dollar's dominant role. But that was nothing new. The French affection for gold went back hundreds of years, to a time when France, unlike the Protestant countries of Europe, had no banking system to stabilize the value of paper currency. Frenchmen had many times seen war and revolution destroy the value of the government's paper. Americans might laugh at the French peasant, with his bits of gold buried in the barnyard or the mattress. But Americans had never held an assignat. The French government that caused the price of gold to rise was a popular government. Good times benefited incumbents.

At two o'clock the following day, Walker met with the French finance minister in the minister's office at the Palais du Louvre. Over Poulos's protests that it would break protocol and undercut the embassy's standing, Walker went alone.

Walker and the minister were not strangers. As private bankers, both had served on advisory committees to the IMF and to the GATT, the multilateral institution that laid down trading rules for the Western world. In all, they had seen each other probably ten times.

Superficially, the meeting was friendly and relaxed. As the President had directed, Walker was careful to say nothing that might be construed as direct accusation. He explained in detail Berg's counterfeiting operation. The means by which the dollars had been accumulated was of only academic interest to Walker, but it was important that the minister understand that the scheme had been uncovered in all its details. It was one thing for France to destabilize the market by selling its normal reserves—the international community might not like it, but France was within its rights—but selling ill-got dollars was something else; the furor that would raise might be too much for even the French.

If the minister was unnerved, he did not show it. He seemed more intrigued with the details of the swap at the Federal Reserve Banks than with the larger economic implications. When Walker mentioned the suggestion that the French had masterminded the operation, the minister laughed.

Walker was nonplused. He had made his point as forcefully as the President's constraints permitted. Yet the minister was treating the whole matter as though it were a fanciful TV plot. The longer they talked, the more difficult it grew for Walker to rescue the seriousness of the conversation. Long before the minister's *chef de cabinet* ended the conversation by announcing that his boss's presence was required elsewhere, Walker had given up trying.

"He never even twitched, huh?"

It was the morning of August 11, and Walker was back in the Oval Office.

"No, sir."

"Never let on he knew anything?"

"That's right."

"And you're sure it was clear to him that nobody was fooling anyone? He knows we know, and all that?" the President asked.

"Oh, yes. I went over it in great detail."

"Well, jelly bread always falls jelly side down, I guess. I don't know what else we can do except move ahead with our planning and hope that the CIA or the FBI can run down Berg before the weekend. You're following that, I trust?"

"Yes, sir."

"Well, keep me posted. We'll just keep our fingers crossed."

As Walker crossed East Executive Avenue to the Treasury he marveled at the President's coolness. His debriefing that morning had contained nothing but bad news. His trip to Paris had left them no better off than they had been two days earlier —nor any wiser. Yet there had been no hand-wringing, not even the cursing that, from meetings over the past several years, he had come to expect. Just "jelly bread always falls jelly side down." Strange man, Walker thought, as he passed the large bronze replica of the Liberty Bell in front of Treasury's west door and started up the stairs.

A report from the CIA was waiting on his desk. Someone named J. Berg had left Kennedy International Airport back on July 12, on a TWA flight for Paris. But a search of registration cards for major hotels in that city had so far turned up nothing. The agency had checked with other contacts in France and Hong Kong. Requests had gone out asking for information on anyone named Berg, Joseph, Josip or Josephus. But the CIA was finding that, though the name sounded common, there were very few people who bore it. With the exception of a Swedish tour-bus operator whose wartime Gestapo collaboration rated him a mention in Interpol's files, no one who might conceivably have masterminded anything so complex had turned up.

Walker remained at his desk the rest of the day, reviewing patterns in currency trading over the previous two weeks, matching them against published reserve holdings of central banks, looking for where damaging sales might come from, for banks to which the United States might look for help.

At six o'clock, still poring over the figures, he was considering whether to send his secretary home. Some officials worked their secretaries unconscionable hours, but Walker had always made it a point not to keep his secretary overtime unless absolutely necessary. He liked to think of himself as a thoughtful employer. But he did not entirely disbelieve an office legend that the tyrant who preceded him had, during his four-year tenure, consumed two full two-ounce bottles of Schaeffer Scrip Deluxe Blue ink and half a flowerpot of loam, mixed with the coffee his secretary was required to bring him four times a day. Walker was still deliberating when the call came.

"Put him on," he said wearily.

A moment later his secretary put the other party through.

"Hello, Mr. Koenig," he said. "What's on your mind?"

For nearly a minute, he listened. Pushing the papers he had been studying aside, he placed his free hand over his left ear to hear better. His face registered intense concern.

"No, Mr. Koenig, you did not tell me about the check. . . . Yes, it's relevant; it sure as hell is relevant. . . . Where did you find this out? From whom? Kurz? Who is Kurz? . . . Okay, thanks."

Walker slammed down the phone in exasperation. A few minutes later, when his secretary came in to ask if she could leave for the day, she found him staring blankly at the desk top.

"Everything all right, Mr. Walker?"

"What?"

"You all right?"

"Yes, I'm fine, fine. I just spent two days flying all over trying to find out what the French are up to. Now the Secret Service tells me that some flunky downstairs, in my own department, says it's not the French at all; it's the Germans!"

CHAPTER 20

Vergil Koenig awakened with an easy mind the morning following his talk with Erlich. He was still confused about the consequences of the French plot, but the calm of the Treasury consultant had been reassuring. Apparently there was to be no great catastrophe. If the Japs and the Europeans decided they preferred gold to dollars, that was their business. No skin off his back, or Ruthie's. Erlich had said the President would want to avoid loss of face. Whose face?

Anyhow, there was nothing he could do. This wasn't a counterfeiting problem any longer. His chance to affect events had ended before he'd known it existed.

Though he still had several inquiries outstanding, he turned to other office matters. Paperwork, allowed to pile up during the previous week, had to be cleared. He switched on his radio and dialed WGMS, thinking he'd try an injection of culture while he worked. He got four critics discussing the relative merits of several opera recordings, which to him had sounded identical. After twenty minutes of lisping sensitivity he was about to change the station, when Childress entered.

"What you listening to, Verg?"

"WGMS."

"What're they talking about?"

"Dunno. I think they're having a contest to see who's the biggest faggot. Wacha want?"

Childress had come to ask if he was still interested in the Wheelabrator machine in Petersburg.

"Yeah, sure, Jack. Why? What did you find out?"

"Well, I talked with a man named Lassiter, who owns the plant that owns the machine, and he says there is no way anybody could have used his machine for anything but polishing metal."

"How's that?"

"Because it's never empty, at least not at night. Some kind of health regulation says the plant can't run the machine while the men are working in the plant. Apparently it makes a hell of a mess—dust and metal filings flying all over the place. So Lassiter loads it during the day, then runs it all night while the plant is empty. He has a guy come in at six, turn it off and sweep up before the first shift comes on."

"Maybe Berg was getting there in the middle of the night. From two o'clock to four o'clock, something like that."

"I asked if that was possible, and Lassiter said no."

"Why?"

"Well, for one thing, Berg would have had to take the castings out of the machine before he put the money in. Otherwise, the castings would tear up the money. Then, when he was through with the money, he'd have to load all the castings back in. That's a hell of a job; it would take a bunch of people to do it quickly. The other thing is, Lassiter says he would have noticed if Berg had been doing that because the castings wouldn't have got fully polished."

"A couple of hours would make that much difference?"

"He says 'yes,' and I believe him. I went through the plant yesterday and saw what the castings look like when they come out of the annealing ovens. They are real rough, burrs all over them, big seams where the molds didn't fit right. If those things got only seventy or eighty percent polished, you'd notice it."

"Well, maybe you been looking at the wrong Wheelabrator. Maybe there's another one around here. You know, Carrington never said anything about Petersburg; Petersburg was our guess."

"I've checked that out, Vergil. You want to guess where the next closest one to Richmond is?"

"Not particularly."

"I'll tell you. It's in Wheeling, West Virginia."

"Did you check that one, too?"

"Vergil, you got any idea how far it is from Richmond to Wheeling, West Virginia? It's something like three hundred miles."

"So?"

"So how the hell does Berg drive back and forth from Richmond to Wheeling every day to get his money dirty?"

"Maybe he goes once a week, every two weeks. How the hell should I know? What are you getting at, Jack? You don't believe what Carrington said?"

"Vergil, you told me to check out the Wheelabrator; I checked out the Wheelabrator. I'm just telling you what I found."

"Okay, so now I know about the Wheelabrator. What else you got?"

"Nothing, except that I gather both the CIA and the FBI have been asked to look for Berg. I guess there's a good chance somebody'll nab him soon."

"You been to too many movies, Jack."

"How do you mean?"

"You ever try to look for somebody when you didn't have any idea where they were?"

"No."

"I didn't think so—'cause it ain't nothing like it is in the movies and on TV. All the stuff about the CIA being able to find anybody anywhere is a lot of crap. You hear about the ones they catch; but for every one they catch, there's twenty-five or thirty they're still looking for. Berg could be sitting on a bench in Lafayette Park feeding the pigeons and the CIA would never find him. You know what the people at the CIA are doing now? I'll tell you. You ever have to write papers when you were at the Citadel?"

"Sometimes."

"Ever have to write about something you didn't know shit about?"

"Yes."

"So what was the first thing you did when you sat down to do it?"

"I don't know. Make an outline?"

"Bullshit. You straightened up your desk. You got the pencils all sharpened up, you emptied the ashtray, you cleaned off all the junk and scraps of paper you didn't need. Maybe you even got something wet and wiped all the dirt and grit off the desk top. In other words, you fucked around getting ready just as long as you could 'cause you didn't have any idea what to say in the paper you were supposed to be writing. Right?"

"Right."

"Well, that's what's going on at the CIA right now. Only they're not cleaning up their desks. They're making little telephone calls to all the other spooks around town to tell them that they're looking for Mr. Berg. Then the spooks they call will make more telephone calls to other spooks to tell them that they're now looking for Mr. Berg, too. And pretty soon you got everybody callin' everybody else on the telephone and there ain't nobody lookin' at all. So don't you figure on that guy getting found, 'cause it ain't gonna happen."

Koenig had nearly managed to put Carrington, counterfeiting, and Berg out of his mind when at six o'clock the phone rang.

"Kurz here," said the voice on the other end.

"Who?" Koenig asked, momentarily unable to place the name.

"Ted Kurz, Mr. Koenig. You called several days ago asking about a company called Kieler Aktiengesellschaft."

"Oh, yeah, sure."

"Well, I had a heck of a time finding out about it."

"You did?"

"I sure did. You know why, Mr. Koenig?"

"Could you just tell me, please," Koenig said, trying to control his temper. Why did people always want to play Quiz Kids with him?

"Because there isn't any such company, Mr. Koenig. It's the name of a nominee of the West German Bundesbank. Do you know what a nominee is?"

"No."

Kurz explained that the West German Bundesbank, like the central bank of every country, routinely bought and sold foreign currency. In fact, under the Bretton Woods agreement of 1944, such banks were obligated to make whatever transactions were necessary to prevent their own currencies' values relative to the dollar from fluctuating more than one percentage point up or down. Normally, such transactions were open and undisguised. But there were occasions when a central bank wished to conceal the fact that it was in the market. To do this, it acted through a nominee, like the Kieler Aktiengesellschaft, which was nothing more than a name and a trading account number. Nominee accounts offered central banks the same anonymity and advantages that numbered Swiss bank accounts offered individuals.

"You understand what I'm talking about?" Kurz asked. Koenig said that he did and thanked Kurz. His initial impulse was to do nothing. What difference did it make who or what the Kieler Aktiengesellschaft was? It was obvious he was the only one who cared about Fang or about what already had happened. Why stick his neck out? Why let the bastards treat him like a dumb cop again?

It was against his better judgment that, before he left his office, he had picked up the phone and relayed the information to Walker.

Ruthie had codfish cakes waiting. With coleslaw and creamed corn, codfish cakes were one of Koenig's favorites, and he wasted no time getting into them.

"Vergil, Mimi's cat is up the tree in her backyard." Mimi was a friend Ruthie had met in exercise class several years before.

"Yeah?" Koenig's mouth was full, but he nodded as if to say, "So what."

"She called today; she wanted to know if she should call the fire department."

"Naw."

"Mimi says the cat can't get down. It's scared."

"It'll get down."

"Mimi says it's only a little cat, and it's going to starve."

"Mimi says, Mimi says, Mimi says! C'mon, Ruthie, you ever seen a cat skeleton in a tree?" Koenig mumbled through a mouthful of corn.

By the time he'd polished off the dessert of caramel tapioca and Reddi-Whip, he was stuffed.

"What's on the boober tonight, Ruthie?" he asked, wiping at a spot on his pants leg.

"There's a ball game, Vergil."

"Yeah, what else?"

"There's a pretty good movie."

"What movie?"

Ruthie couldn't remember and went off to check *TV Guide*.

"Never mind, Ruthie," Koenig called after her. "Let's watch the movie. Doesn't matter what it is."

Two hours later, the movie over, Vergil and Ruthie sat slumped in opposite corners of the couch watching the beginning of the eleven o'clock news.

During the first commercial, Ruthie had gone to the kitchen and got each of them one of her "magic" brownies. Now both of them were drifting under its effects, barely aware that a new program had come on.

"You've been working real hard, Verg."

"Yeah, I guess so."

"Is it something important?"

"There's a big international deal, Ruthie. The French government is going to try to do some things that will make dollars worth less and gold worth more. It has to do with exchange rates and reserves and all like that."

"Golly, Verg, you understand all that stuff?"

"Yeah, sure. Me and the Under Secretary of the Treasury and a big deal from the White House been working on it."

"No kidding? My little Vergil?"

"Yeah, ain't that somethin'?"

Ruthie shifted her position on the couch so that she was looking directly at him. "What's going to happen, Verg?" she asked.

"About what?"

"Well, about the dollars and all."

"I think it's going to work, Ruthie. The Under Secretary went to Paris yesterday, but he couldn't find out anything. So I guess they'll pull it off."

"That's terrible, Verg."

"Naw. If you want my personal opinion, Ruthie, it'll be a good thing. Course, that ain't the prevailing view; it's just the way I feel."

"Really?"

Koenig rummaged his memory for why Erlich had said it would not be a bad thing, but he could come up with nothing. So he just said "Yeah," gave Ruthie a knowing nod and let it go.

"I bet you could have done it, Verg."

"Done what, Ruthie?"

"I betcha if they had sent you to Paris, you could have found out what they want to know."

"Ruthie, I don't even speak French. How the hell would I be able to find out anything?"

"I betcha you could have done it, Verg."

"Ruthie."

"You're good at that kind of thing, Verg. What does some Under Secretary know about making people tell him what he wants to know? That takes an expert. Come on, Verg, let's go to bed."

"You go on up, Ruthie. I'll be right along."

He sat quietly on the couch and watched as his wife climbed the stairs. He heard her moving above him as she undressed. He heard the water and the sound that told him she was filling a glass in the bathroom at the top of the stairs. Then he heard her familiar gasp as the water ran between her legs into the toilet, where he knew she would be sitting. She always did that when she was in a hurry. She could never wait for the water to get warm.

Maybe Ruthie was right. Maybe he could find out. For that matter, maybe he could find Berg. Hawkins would be annoyed at being wakened at four-thirty in the morning. Still, it was worth a chance. Rising from the couch, Koenig went into the kitchen and called Paris.

CHAPTER 21

"I'm sorry, sir, we have no record of anyone named Joseph Berg. But we have only a sampling of government rosters. You might try the embassies."

St. Giles stood at the desk of the library in the main UNESCO building in Paris. The message was the same as he had heard in a dozen other places in the preceding two days. No one had heard of Berg. No one had a record of Berg. Without access to Interpol or to other official security records, he had just about exhausted his resources.

The preceding day, he had taken the agreed-upon advertisement in the *Herald Tribune.* It would run the rest of the week. According to plan, Majendie was to be at the Jackie Bar the following Sunday.

Would Majendie show? By now Carrington almost certainly had sung. The U.S. authorities would be beating the bushes for Berg. Majendie might have felt the reverberations and suspect something had gone wrong. Would he have smelled out the double cross? For days St. Giles had racked his brain for ways to make sure. Finding Berg had been his last hope. Majendie and Bosanquet were most likely just leg men. They would not appear on an official government roster. But Berg—if Berg was the mastermind—might rank high enough to show up.

From the UNESCO building he walked to the river and followed it along the elevated embankment. It was pleasantly cool under the shade trees along the quay, and as he strolled he browsed the bookstalls hoping to find something that might take his mind off the uncertain confrontation less than a week away. Poking through a pile of assorted magazine back issues, an illustrated sports journal caught his eye. He bought it and settled on a bench.

The magazine was not very entertaining, and his mind soon wandered back to Majendie. What if Majendie did not realize he had been double-crossed? What if Majendie really expected the plan to succeed and showed up at the Jackie Bar expecting to be handed directions to a warehouse full of counterfeit currency? Suddenly St. Giles was full of doubts. For months he had been trying to manipulate marionettes he couldn't see. For all he knew, the strings had become hopelessly tangled. He had no assurance any of his signals was having its intended effect. He wasn't certain even that he had an audience. . . .

Too late to look back now. Too late for second thoughts. Majendie would be insane to expect the money. No one could have counterfeited all that currency. Finding a warehouse would alone have been too great a problem. And what if something had happened to him in the middle of the project? St. Giles realized he was muttering to himself; it wasn't going to help to get excited. Majendie couldn't have expected him to succeed. What, then, would he expect come Sunday?

St. Giles's speculations were brought to an abrupt halt. The magazine lay open in his lap to a story about rugby. It featured a team called the Springboks, and a controversy of some sort. But what had caught his eye was the dateline, specifically, the name of the city. For nearly a minute he had been staring, without realizing what he was seeing, at the key to the Joe Berg mystery. It was right there, spelled out practically letter by letter.

Twenty minutes later, he was back in the UNESCO library. This time it took only a few minutes to get what he wanted. He then placed a telephone call from the pay phone in the hall. Within an hour he had learned all he needed to know. He could forget about Berg; he wasn't going to find Berg, and neither were the Americans. That didn't matter. What mattered was that he had Majendie on the defensive. The red-faced giant might not appear himself on Sunday, but unless St. Giles was very wrong, Majendie's remote-control hit man would be there with bells on.

What St. Giles had to worry about now was that Majendie's assassin have a target to shoot at.

To make certain of that, St. Giles, that afternoon, did something he had never before done in a dozen sojourns in Paris: he filled out a request for a *carte de séjour,* the document required of foreigners living in Paris. He then fetched half his luggage from the Gerson and took a room in the Hotel Lotti, on the Right Bank. In his room at the Lotti, he scribbled a note reminding himself of his Sunday-afternoon engagement at the Jackie Bar, crumpled it and stuffed it in the drawer of the bedside table, where even a cursory search would turn it up. Then, after rummaging through his suitcase, he reached under the table and pushed a straight pin gently into the bottom of the drawer.

For both the *carte de séjour* and the Lotti hotel registration, he had used the same name: Joe Berg.

The discovery that the payer of the check found on Fang was the West German Bundesbank threw the tiny circle of men around the President into turmoil. And it sent Walker, less than twenty-four hours home, winging back to Europe—this time to Bonn.

Were the Germans behind the scheme? Was the French coloration only camouflage? That possibility now seemed very real. Walker had only one man's word, thirdhand, that the French were involved. The check from Kieler Aktiengesellschaft argued at least as persuasively for Germany.

To Walker, airborne again, heading east, this thought was profoundly disturbing. Germany had far greater resources than France. With twelve billion counterfeit dollars plus fourteen billion of genuine dollar reserves, Germany could buy every ounce of U.S. gold and have dollars left over.

It was dawn on August 12 when Walker began his descent to Frankfurt. As the plane circled, he could see the city, side-lit and glowing in morning sun. One of those buildings below was the Bundesbank. Within an hour its employees would be at their desks. If his current suspicions were correct, some of those employees would spend this day, like military strategists, planning the timing and distribution of the sell orders that, like artillery fire, would precede the dump.

But he wasn't going to get anywhere talking to people at the Bundesbank. Twenty minutes after landing, Walker was in the air again, this time in a Lufthansa jet bound for Bonn. Central bankers might make important decisions, but they didn't declare economic war. That was a political decision.

From the airport in Bonn, Walker went directly to the U.S. Embassy in Bad Godesberg, a huge green-and-yellow complex that looked to have been built sometime in the early 1950s.

The ambassador, the only nonpolitical appointment running a major U.S. embassy in Europe, was waiting, and within five minutes they were in one of the embassy's green Fords headed back toward the city and the German Finance Ministry.

The Finance Ministry in Bonn was nothing like its Paris counterpart; no priceless antiques, no Oriental rugs, no high ceilings. It was as stark and utilitarian as a hospital.

But the meeting with the minister, a short, handsome chain smoker in his early fifties, was a replay of the Paris meeting—with one difference: this time there was no friendly chatter. By lunchtime, Walker and the ambassador were back in the embassy Ford headed again to the airport. As they sped across the flat, sodden countryside, Walker wondered what the old pro sitting next to him had thought of his conversation with the minister. His questions must have appeared naïve to the ambassador. He should have known better. He was dealing now with men to whom mendacity was an art form. One did not walk in on them and simply ask if they were planning to dump dollars next week. Candor elicited nothing from the sorts of men who reached the top in the Byzantine world of European politics; it offended their sensibilities, demeaned the sophistication and ear for nuance they had spent careers developing.

Walker had wasted time. In three days he had flown to Europe twice. All he had accomplished was to alert both of the dumping scheme's possible authors that the United States was moving to protect itself. If there had been doubt, there could no longer be any.

The dump would come now at the earliest possible date—Monday, August 16. He would have to tell the President.

CHAPTER 22

While Walker was wasting August 12 in Bonn, Hawkins was wasting it in Paris.

Koenig's call had been a stumper. Hawkins was tough, resourceful and street-wise. He knew how to find people, how to make them tell him what they would rather not and how to rattle the cages of the bureaucrats down at the local prefecture. The Hawk played rough. Once, six years earlier, he had suspected that someone was tampering with his mail. Though he never used the mail for official business, the thought that anyone would pry into his private life had angered him. After making conspicuous plans to go skiing, he had taken a train to Rome and mailed a letter bomb to his Paris address. It had cost his landlady a hand and a substantial portion of her chin, but Hawkins had found out what he wanted to know.

Still, his experience had been with criminals, society's flotsam and jetsam, people with whom one could take liberties. One couldn't do that with a finance minister.

Following Koenig's early-morning call, he had puzzled over how to extract what Walker had failed to get. This indecision had cost him a day.

At ten o'clock in the morning of Thursday, August 12, Hawkins left his apartment on Rue de Sully and set out on foot for the Finance Ministry a mile away.

After inquiring at the reception desk, he was directed to a second-floor room in the wing of the building farthest from the river.

The minister's *chef de cabinet*, Georges Bouladoux, saw him almost immediately.

In the French bureaucracy, a *chef de cabinet* is an executive assistant, the man who handles the schedule and keeps the paper flowing. The work is arduous, but the job is a plum, identifying its holder as a young man of promise, a comer in the new generation of civil servants. Hawkins had expected a young man. But the person who rose to meet him from behind his desk was scarcely more than a boy, twenty-six or twenty-seven years old.

"Good morning, Mr. Hawkins," Bouladoux greeted him.

"Morning," Hawkins responded, his eyes roaming for details. The office was of moderate size, but ornately furnished. The wall behind Bouladoux's desk was hung with a half-dozen framed diplomas, certificates and citations. On a side table, fronting a bookcase filled with financial journals and government reports, were two framed photographs, one of an older woman whom Hawkins took to be the boy's mother, the other of a house cat.

Bouladoux was a familiar type. Tall, preternaturally thin, narrow Gallic lips, high forehead, dark hair brushed straight back. In his dark blue tailor-made suit and elegant silk tie, he looked like a parlor fop. In ten years in Paris, Hawkins had seen hundreds of boys just like Bouladoux squiring their equally elegant young ladies around the fancier parts of the city. Though he admired the easy manner of these boys in the company of their women, he chose to attribute it less to savoir-faire than to serious hormonal problems.

Hawkins's conversation with Bouladoux was brief and to the point.

And it left the Frenchman puzzled. For the second time in three days, he had heard an American official ask the same questions.

But for Hawkins, who did not know Bouladoux had been privy to Walker's earlier conversation with the minister, the meeting achieved its purpose. The *chef de cabinet* now knew who he was and what he wanted. Bouladoux would have the whole day to think about it. On the street again, Hawkins glanced at the card Bouladoux had handed him. It was an official business card; the home address would be easy enough to find.

At four-thirty, having spent the afternoon napping in his apartment, Hawkins rose and began to make preparations. He spread a map of Paris on the bed and studied it. From the telephone directory he had ascertained that Bouladoux lived on Rue Théodule-Ribot, between Avenue de Wagram and the Boulevard de Courcelles, a few blocks north of Place des Ternes. It was not Hawkins's stomping grounds, but he knew what the area would look like—mostly large, late-nineteenth-century apartment buildings, two or three units to a floor, twelve to eighteen apartments per building. There would be at least two locks to deal with, no rear or side doors.

He put the map aside and dressed quickly.

Equipment was the next item of business. From the back of the bedroom door he took an old maroon bathrobe and stuffed it into the briefcase on the bedroom table. Then he went to the bathroom and from the medicine cabinet removed a dark green bottle and a small rubber syringe of the type used for administering enemas to infants. He squeezed the rubber bulb, drew off some fluid and replaced the bottle in the cabinet. Holding the syringe in one hand, he fitted its plastic stem with a rubber suction cup he had taken off a child's bow and arrow set at Au Printemps many years before. He studied the instrument in his hand. The center of the suction cup had been drilled out. With the syringe pointed at him, he could see, surrounded by rubber, the open hole in its stem. He sealed the hole with adhesive tape, returned to the bedroom and dropped the apparatus into the briefcase on top of the robe.

It was five-thirty when he emerged from the Courcelles Métro stop and began the short walk to Rue Théodule-Ribot. The area was typical of the wealthy parts of the city. It had none of the noisy street life of his own neighborhood, no stores or cafés, just an occasional dry cleaner or florist shop, provisioners to the peculiar needs of the rich.

Three-quarters of a block ahead of him on Rue Théodule-Ribot an old lady hobbled along the sidewalk. He slowed his pace, hoping she would turn the corner. Twice she stopped, put down her bag and picked it up with the other hand. He was ten yards from number fifteen now. The old lady had stopped again, and was standing still, resting, her back to him. There were no shop windows in which to feign interest. He hesitated. Then, taking the syringe from his briefcase, he peeled away the adhesive tape and stepped up to the door.

He had guessed correctly. Like most of the apartment buildings in Paris, this building had an electric lock. These locks worked on a simple principle. The key fit into an elliptical cam inside the lock. The cam, when turned, completed an electrical circuit, which popped the latch bolt and triggered a buzzer. Hawkins pressed the rubber suction cup to the keyhole and gave the bulb a gentle squeeze. Instantly the buzzer sounded. With his free hand he grabbed the door and held it ajar until the bulb had expanded again, recapturing its contents. He retaped the suction cup and replaced the syringe in his brief-case. By the time he turned back to the door, a globule of silver-white metal the size of a small pearl had gathered at the bottom of the keyhole. He brushed it to the floor and watched it scatter into hundreds of smaller balls. There was more than one way to complete a circuit.

The ground-floor layout was familiar. A concierge's apart-ment on one side; stairs on the other; in the center, behind elaborately filigreed gates, an elevator.

Bouladoux's telephone listing had included no apartment number. As Hawkins mounted the stairs, he saw the reason. The apartments, two to a floor, were not numbered. Brass nameplates on the left side of double doors identified the owners.

He found Bouladoux's apartment on the third floor. He assumed the young man lived alone. But for nearly five minutes he stood outside the door listening for sounds that might indi-cate an occupant.

Satisfied at last that the apartment was empty, he turned his attention to the lock. A two-inch shadow in the slit between the two doors told him what he needed to know. The door was secured by a key-activated steel bar bolted to the inside face of the door. Such bars could be cut with thin-gauge saber saws or abrasive wire. But both tools were messy and took time. Be-sides, he had neither.

At quarter of six, the concierge of the apartment building was surprised by loud knocking at his door. In twelve years in the building he had learned that during the afternoon his tenants were either at their offices or amusing themselves else-where in the city. These were hours he could safely appropriate to his own use and still appear to be guarding the property with vigilance. He had been asleep.

He splashed his face with cold water, pulled on his shoes and, still groggy, shuffled to the door.

The sight that greeted him did little to clear his fuddled mind. Before him stood a large man he had never seen. The man's presence was doubly confusing because he wore an old maroon bathrobe.

"Oui, monsieur?" the concierge ventured, staring at the unfamiliar face, then at the bare feet, then back at the face.

"I've locked myself out," the man in the bathrobe said.

"Pardon?" Embarrassed at being caught at his nap, the concierge's tone was more apologetic than challenging.

"I've locked myself out of Mr. Bouladoux's apartment," the man in the bathrobe said, making little key-turning motions with one hand, clutching at the bathrobe with the other. "I'm staying with Mr. Bouladoux. Third floor. Troisième étage," he added, pointing toward the ceiling with his free hand.

"Ahh, Monsieur Bouladoux, un ami de Monsieur Bouladoux?"

"Yeah, yeah, ami de Monsieur Bouladoux." Hawkins answered. "But no key, understand? I left the key in the apartment." Stick with the English and the sign language, he thought. Speak French, you'll get questions.

"Ehh, vous avez laissé la clé dans l'appartement?"

"Yeah, yeah, you got it; the key's in the apartment."

"Eh bon. Moment," the concierge said, at last abreast of what had happened.

With his back to the door and busy rummaging through his desk for a key that would fit Bouladoux's apartment, the concierge did not notice that the man in the bathrobe had stepped into the room and was busy scribbling something on a piece of paper.

After being let into the apartment upstairs, Hawkins waited until he was certain the concierge had reached the ground floor again before retrieving his clothes and briefcase from the fourth-floor corridor. He locked the door to Bouladoux's apartment behind him. It was nearly six now. He would have an hour, maybe more, before Bouladoux returned.

At the far end of the living room he spotted a large desk. He circled it, careful to stay away from the window, started to drop into a chair, then jumped up, startled by a piercing screech as a flash of grey shot between his legs.

"Goddamn cat."

A search of the desk produced nothing. He looked for files, found none, and began to explore the rest of the apartment. It was elaborate for a bachelor: two bedrooms, living room, dining room, kitchen, two baths, even a maid's room at the rear.

Hawkins returned to the master bedroom. If he had to get rough with Bouladoux, the bedroom was the place; its only window was on the rear of the building, rather than the street or the air shaft, an advantage if Bouladoux got noisy.

His foot caught something on the floor beside the bed. He leaned over. It was a wicker basket lined with quilted blue satin.

"Son of a bitch," he muttered, "the kid sleeps with his fuckin' cat."

This reminded him that he had not seen the cat since he nearly sat on it.

"Here kitty, come here, kitty, kitty." Hawkins located the cat where he had started looking, in the master bedroom under the bed. As he picked it up by the scruff of the neck he wondered if cats ever tried to attack people who beat up their masters.

He wandered about the apartment a second time. There were pictures of cats all over the place, on the bureau, on the bookcases, on the mantel. The kid must have a lot of cats, he thought at first. But no, the cats in the pictures all had the same fluffy grey fur, the same ribbons.

Having satisfied himself that he would not find what he was looking for, Hawkins helped himself to a lukewarm beer from the kitchen counter and settled into an easy chair from which he could watch the street. On the table next to him, by the telephone, he placed the scrap of paper he had brought back in his bathrobe pocket from the concierge's apartment. From his position in the shadows behind the sheer curtains, he would be able to see anyone approaching from thirty yards in either direction.

It was quarter after seven when he saw Bouladoux. He picked up the receiver and quickly dialed six digits, waited until Bouladoux was five yards from the door, then dialed the seventh digit. Laying the phone quietly on the table he headed for the kitchen, turned the oven on to one hundred and seventy-five degrees centigrade and returned to the living room.

If the concierge had intended to speak to Monsieur Bouladoux about his house guest's problems, he missed his chance. While Bouladoux was crossing the lobby and entering the elevator, the concierge was cursing a telephone prankster who had called and now refused to speak.

Hawkins heard Bouladoux's voice several seconds before he emerged from the entry hall.

"Sabine. Saabee . . . een, viens, mon petit minou."

Bouladoux was through the hall now and, though he was not ten feet from where Hawkins stood in the living room, he had not yet noticed he had company.

"Evening, Mr. Bouladoux."

Bouladoux whirled, then made a motion to retreat. But Hawkins had stepped between him and the door.

"What do you want? What are you doing here?" Bouladoux demanded, his voice shrill with fear.

"I want the same thing I wanted this morning. I want to know about Berg."

"I don't know Berg. Now get out." From the Frenchman's voice it was plain that his nerves were unraveling quickly.

"Sit down, Mr. Bouladoux; think about it," Hawkins said, shoving the young man backward into a chair. "You will be a lot happier if you remember who Berg is and where I can find him."

"Where is Sabine?"

"Never mind where Sabine is. Where is Berg?"

"I tell you I swear I don't know. I don't know who he is. I never heard of him until two days ago, when your Mr. Walker came to see the minister."

"I will give you two minutes to remember."

"I can't remember. There is nothing to be remembered. What is that smell?"

"Smell?"

"I smell something."

"That must be Sabine."

"Sabine does not smell."

"Mr. Bouladoux, at a hundred and seventy-five degrees, we all smell."

It took maybe five seconds for Hawkins's words to penetrate. Then, with a scream of horror, the Frenchman lunged.

Hawkins's forearm caught him flush across his skinny chest, dumping him back into the chair.

"Sa . . . abine, Sa . . . abine!" Bouladoux was sobbing now, his slender body heaving with each breath.

"One more minute, Mr. Bouladoux."

"I don't have one minute. I tell you I don't know. I don't know. Oh, my God, Sabine."

Hawkins looked at the blubbering form in the chair before him. Then, without speaking, he turned and headed for the door. Koenig had asked him to find the truth. He was satisfied he had it. Besides, the smell was getting disgusting.

Hawkins did not sleep well that night. But it was not Bouladoux's cat that kept him awake. It was thoughts of his friend in Washington.

Koenig had seemed certain that the ministry would know about Berg and the counterfeiting scheme. It wasn't like Koenig to be certain when he was wrong.

Something else Koenig had told him didn't seem right. It was one thing to print twelve billion dollars on a French press. It was something else altogether to move twelve billion dollars out of a printing plant and get it to a warehouse. That took men, lots of men; and, in Paris, "lots of men" meant "Frenchmen." In ten years in Paris, Hawkins hadn't met two Frenchmen he would have trusted with twelve thousand dollars, let alone twelve billion dollars. Some of the money would never have got where it was supposed to go; and in nearly a month some of it would have turned up.

Hawkins, claiming to represent an American reinsurance firm checking on the fire damage, was at the printing plant in Asnières the next morning when it opened.

"This thing count the paper?"

He had been poking around for twenty minutes. Most of the fire damage had been to the structure, the flames having scarcely touched the press except around its base. In the intervening weeks, repairs had nearly been completed. He stood now at the middle of the press, the plant manager at his shoulder, and pointed toward the device that recorded the paper sheets as they passed through the press. It was on the strength of this mechanism's accounting that the manager had noted the ten million missing sheets after the fire.

"Yes, yes."

"You ever take this thing apart?"

"Pardon?"

"You ever take the top off. Like this . . ." Hawkins said, tugging at the mechanism's protective cowling.

"No, never. Why?"

"Let's take it off, huh? Come on, get me a screwdriver."

The counting device was approximately six inches square, broken at the top by a four-inch plastic window through which a nine-digit number could be read. In design and appearance, it resembled a large odometer, the device that records the miles an automobile travels.

In a few minutes, Hawkins was peering into its works. Where nine digits had been exposed through the plastic slit, he now could see nine separate wheels, side by side, each with the numbers zero through nine etched about its circumference. All of the wheels were turned by the axial rod that ran through their centers, each at one-tenth the rate of that on its immediate right.

With his finger he tried the wheel farthest to the right. It would not budge. The only way to turn any of the wheels was by turning the rod. To advance the count in a hurry would require something mechanical, something capable of spinning rapidly. A blender? A router? A drill? With appropriate adaptation, any of a dozen electrical appliances could have done the job. That was theory, not proof.

Hawkins was about to replace the cowling when something caught his eye. In removing the cowling, he had exposed a dark, rectangular outline on the steel surface of the press. He touched it lightly with his finger. A ridge of grease, accumulated over the years. The outline perfectly described the shape of the cowling he had just removed, except in one respect; one side of the rectangle, the side closest to where he stood, had been smeared flat.

"You never take this thing off, huh?"

"Non, monsieur."

Hawkins stared at the plant manager, as though he might be able to read a lie with his eyes. Somebody was trying to fool somebody. . . . Somebody *had* fooled somebody.

He checked his watch. Eight-forty-five. In Washington it would be the middle of the night.

CHAPTER 23

It was not yet seven in the morning, and the grass on the helipad beneath the big Sikorsky VH-3A was still bathed in morning wetness. In a few minutes, the downdraft from the chopper's rotor would mash the lank blades flat. The sun would resurrect them, but by then it would be midmorning, by then the President and his party would be ensconced at Camp David. It was Saturday, August 14.

Late the previous afternoon, the White House press office had issued a release saying that the President and some of his advisers would spend the weekend at Camp David going over the next year's defense budget. A few reporters had picked up this lie and repeated it in the morning papers. No reporter had thought to check whether the men at the Office of Management and Budget who worked on defense matters were in town that weekend. Nor did any reporter note it when two senior White House speechwriters left town at noon the next day.

Since Wednesday, when Walker had left Washington for

Bonn, the dollar's strength had deteriorated badly. On August 12, it had come under heavy selling pressure in all European markets. By the end of the day its value had fallen to its lowest permissible level against every major nonfloating currency in Europe except the British pound.

On August 13, the Banque Nationale Suisse, alarmed at the volume of dollar demand for Swiss francs, had imposed one-hundred-percent reserve requirements on new foreign deposits at Swiss banks. It had also prohibited payment of interest on such deposits. Rumors that the dollar was in trouble were everywhere.

In the thirty-six hours since Walker had returned from Bonn, something else had occurred. The circle of insiders privy to the Berg Problem—as it was being called—had widened considerably. The reason was political. With each hour it became more likely that the President would have to take preemptive action. Whatever he did was sure to be controversial. It was important that he have the full and immediate support of his own Administration. The news media would pounce on any controversy. A Monday-morning dissent by some official piqued at being kept in the dark was a risk the President couldn't afford.

Two members of the Council of Economic Advisers were the first to arrive. They entered the grounds through the southwest gate and followed the asphalt driveway that cut across the south lawn. Halfway across, they left the drive and turned up the grass toward the White House and the waiting helicopter.

From their titles, anyone not privy to the meetings of the preceding twenty-four hours might have expected that the President would depend this day on the counsel of these two official economic advisers, this sparrowlike academic with the thinning red hair and his heavyset, sad-faced colleague. Both men knew better. Responsibility might be diagramed on organization charts; power could not be. Their invitations, received late the previous afternoon, had been *pro forma.* Neither had yet admitted as much to the other, but now, walking shoulder to shoulder and conversing in morning whispers, both knew it, and both took comfort from the fraternity of their extraneousness. Their views would be asked—simple courtesy demanded that—but their suggestions would not be heeded. Matters were too far advanced for the President to be interested in what economic theorists might tell him. It was "crunch time." Politics would govern.

Shortly after seven, these two were joined in the helicopter by the chairman of the Federal Reserve Board, a tintype figure with rimless glasses and thick grey hair parted down the middle. Even at this early hour the chairman would normally have been puffing on his favorite curved-stem Dunhill. This morning, out of deference to the President's known distaste for smoke, the pipe rode cold in his pocket.

There had been a period earlier in the Administration when pundits had described the chairman as the second-most-powerful man in the country. Then, his title had been counselor to the President; then, he had sat at the right hand. But the year before, he had been promoted up and out. Precisely how far out, few were certain, the reach of the chairman's residual influence being one of the few pieces of the White House power puzzle for which Washington's press corps had yet to refine a durable cliché.

At ten minutes after seven, the door to the diplomatic entrance to the White House opened, and five men emerged, obviously coming from a meeting to which the others had not been asked.

The secretary of the Treasury, back the previous evening from Latin America, led the way. Tall, smiling, already in midday form and showing no sign of morning puffiness, he clambered aboard, followed by Walker and Ferguson.

Though the secretary had been in Washington less than twelve hours, he had already captured the President's ear, easing Walker and Ferguson out of the picture. In a three-hour meeting the previous evening, at which Walker's and Ferguson's views had hardly been asked, the secretary had torn up the options paper drafted earlier in the week. What he proposed was more dramatic, more comprehensive.

"Stop thinking defensively," he had advised the President. "Look upon this as an opportunity," he had urged. It wasn't important what the President did; the important thing was what the President *called* what he did. That had been the gist of the secretary's advice.

The President had been enthralled, as he seemed always to be in the presence of this big, confident, politician-salesman he had chosen as his secretary of the Treasury.

"What you want to do, Mr. President, is to get on the TV" —the secretary always accented the first letter—"and tell those folks out there that you have a present for them," he had said. "Tell them it's going to be good for them, and good for the country.

"Start with jobs. Everybody wants jobs. 'Jobs' is a good word. There isn't anybody out there who is going to speak up for unemployment. So you just tell everybody you're going to cut their taxes so there will be more jobs. Cut the automobile excise tax; increase the personal exemption. Hell, this would be a good time to get back the investment credit. Only don't call it that; call it the job-creation credit. If you tell them it's turkey and cover it with gravy, folks will eat buzzard and beg for seconds.

"Then on this foreign problem, there's no reason in the world you need to say there is anything wrong with the dollar or with the economy. Don't mention going off the dollar standard, or devaluation. No need. Talk about the international speculators who have been disrupting the market. Ugly word, 'speculators.' Say 'speculators' and you've got people on your side. Then you hit them with how you're going to fix things: you're not going to sell the sumbitches any more gold. Not only that—until those foreign speculators shape up and things calm down over there, you're going to slap a tax on the stuff they sell us. Ten percent! You have to make this out to be some kind of financial police action. If you do that, people're going to line up behind you. You know people like to fight. They say they don't like it, but they do."

Walker had seen the secretary worked up before, but he had never seen him as persuasive, nor had he seen the President so excited. The President had agreed with everything.

"The beautiful thing about this," the secretary had said, "is that, with the import tax, we get our devaluation without calling it 'devaluation.'"

The President tried to interrupt, but the secretary waved him off.

"One more point, sir. The foreign stuff is going to wash okay if it's played right, but it isn't going to leave them bouncing in their chairs, because after they turn off the TV, most people aren't going to remember why the hell they were for it.

"You've got to leave them with a zinger. You've got to say there's one more thing you're going to do for them. You're going to freeze prices. Not forever; just for a little while. No more prices going up at the supermarket every day. You want to throw in a line about the average American family, about how hard they work, how they believe in the system; but the message you want to leave with them is that you're going to give everybody a better job and lower prices, and you're going to fix those foreign speculators at the same time."

224

Now, as he climbed into the helicopter behind the secretary, Walker reflected that the previous evening might have been the low point of his government career. He glanced toward the rear of the craft at the men already seated. He wondered if they suspected that they were participants in a charade—that the decisions they had been invited to help make had already been made, that the White House press office had already been alerted that there would be a press conference the following evening, that the Camp David meeting would be nothing more than a gathering of copy editors.

The remainder of the group now boarding consisted of the President, clad in slacks and the lightweight blue flight jacket he habitually wore on hops to and from his Maryland mountain retreat, and a jowly, dour-faced aide weighted down by two blocky, flap-over briefcases.

Quickly the men settled in, the President in his accustomed seat forward in the cabin, the others ranged behind him roughly in order of influence.

The engine was fired up and noise from the rotor overhead put an end to conversation. The men turned to their newspapers and the coffee a steward produced from the canteen.

Seated on a side-facing bench opposite the hatch, Walker brooded. Newspaperless, his great height hunched forward, he surveyed the group in the rear of the helicopter. None of them was going to be overwhelmed with regret. The chairman, the men from the CEA—they were academics. They had enjoyed having the world look to the dollar as its standard. But they had no commitment to principle. By their lights, policy and principle had parted ways with the demise of the gold standard; everything after that had been expediency. They could not be expected to argue.

For Walker, it was not so easy. He had spent twenty years on Wall Street, where a stable dollar was not merely a political convenience but an article of faith. On the Street, one believed in a nuclear financial universe, and the dollar was its center. Remove the dollar, and the other of the world's currencies would fly off at right angles to the radius. It was the first physical law of finance—one he and his kind would defend with Ptolemaic obstinacy.

The helicopter was lifting off, beginning its run down toward the Ellipse, where it would circle back for the thirty-five-minute flight north. The deed was as good as done. At their Washington offices, the Do Not Disturb signs were already out. Walker had left word with his secretary: the only calls he would accept were calls from the FBI or the CIA. The countdown was beginning. He checked the heavy stainless-steel Rolex he had set and reset four times in the previous four days. It showed seven-fifteen. Barring a miracle, the dollar standard had less than thirty-six hours to live.

CHAPTER 24

"You sure of that, Hawk?"

Koenig pulled the telephone onto the bed and propped his shoulders against the headboard. The clock on the table said five o'clock. It was the morning of August 14th, two days before the one on which Walker had advised the President the dump would begin.

"And the guy from the Finance Ministry didn't know anything?"

Koenig listened again as the man on the other end of the line repeated what he had already told him.

"Okay, Hawk, you did good. Thanks."

Ruthie was stirring now.

"Who was that, Vergil?" she asked, yawning.

"A guy who was checking something in Paris for me," Koenig said, slipping back down in the bed. "He couldn't find anything."

"Sorry, Verg."

"Doesn't matter, Ruthie. Probably there wasn't anything to find." For a while before he went back to sleep, Koenig thought about what Hawkins had just told him. It wasn't like Hawkins not to get what he wanted, not once he'd got his man. Maybe there wasn't any French plot. Then there was Hawkins's story about someone having fooled with the counter on the printing press. How did that fit in? Who was trying to fool whom?

"One egg or two, Verg?"

"Two."

It was after eight, and Koenig sat in the dining alcove watching his wife fix breakfast on the other side of the counter.

"Was that call this morning about the case you told me about the other night, Verg?"

"Yep."

"That didn't sound to me like a counterfeiting case, Verg. How come you're working on something that isn't counterfeiting?"

"It was counterfeiting, Ruthie. But the counterfeit money is all gone now. Except for a couple of hundred bills the police have, and these." He removed his two remaining Seydoux bills from his wallet and passed them over the counter to his wife.

"They look okay to me, Verg."

"Yeah, well, they look okay to most people, Ruthie, including your husband, but they ain't okay; they're phony. Somebody made about twelve billion worth of them and brought them into the country."

"Wow, that's a lot, isn't it, Verg?"

"Sure is. Probably enough to fill up this whole goddamn house. What are we going to do today, Ruthie?"

Ruthie didn't answer. The toaster had popped, and she was busy at the other side of the kitchen. In a minute she returned to the counter with his plate.

"That must have been a big plane, Verg," she said coming around the counter and settling down next to him to watch him eat, as she always did.

"What plane?"

"The plane that brought all that money. I mean it would take a real big plane to carry enough money to fill up this house. Wouldn't it, Verg?"

"The stuff's been coming in for a long time, Ruthie. It didn't all come at once." Koenig realized as he spoke that he was not telling Ruthie the whole story. The bills the police had found on Seydoux were probably the ones made by the new counterfeiter Berg had mentioned to Carrington. That had to be Fang. Koenig had no way of knowing how good the bills burned earlier by Swartzman had been. But Ruthie wouldn't care about details. "Where did you put those bills, Ruthie?"

"They're over there," she said, pointing across the counter.

"Better get them. I don't want to lose 'em. Kind of collector's items now."

"They're not going anywhere, Verg."

"Would you get 'em, Ruthie, huh."

While Ruthie went to get the bills, Koenig picked up the paper, slipped the sports section out of the middle and started looking for how the Red Sox had done the night before.

"Vergil."

He looked up. Ruthie was standing next to the counter. He could see something was wrong.

"I burned a hole in one of them, Vergil."

"You what?"

"I burned a hole in one of the bills. I left it on the toaster while I was fixing your plate. It must have still been hot. I'm real sorry, Vergil. I really am sorry."

"Lemme see."

She handed him the bills. Sure enough, in the upper left-hand corner of one of the bills was a tiny circular hole, in circumference no larger than a ballpoint pen would make. Except for a brown ring around it, it was neat enough to have been punched. He looked at the other bill. It was undamaged.

"Were these things one on top of the other?"

"When?"

"On the fuckin' toaster, Ruthie. Was one on top of the other on the toaster?"

"I don't remember, Verg."

"Try."

"I don't think so."

Koenig looked at his wife in exasperation. He examined the damaged bill again. Then he took the undamaged bill, walked to the window and pressed it against the glass, blocking out the light around it with his hands. For ten seconds he studied the bill, backlit by the summer sun. There was no doubt about it. The tiny area that had burned on the first bill appeared noticeably lighter on the second—as though the paper had been weakened, by abrasion or by chemicals.

"What are you doing, Vergil?"

Koenig had left the window and was heading for the toaster. "I'm going to burn this one, too."

It took thirty seconds for the toaster to reheat. Once the bill was placed over the slot, the effect was almost immediate: faint discoloration, a pinprick of light, then, almost too sudden to see, the appearance of a hole, as neat as the first and in exactly the same spot. The tiny circle of missing paper had evaporated, taking with it the bill's quadrant number.

"What is it, Vergil?"

"I don't know, Ruthie, but something's funny." Koenig had already picked up the telephone and was dialing.

"Who are you calling?"

"Shh . . . guy at Treasury."

Walker's line was busy. Koenig put down the phone and thought for a minute.

"Ruthie, go get my shoes and jacket would you? I gotta go down to the office for a while," he said.

Before leaving, Koenig went back to the kitchen and tried Walker's number one more time. It was still busy. He did not know that in the two and a half days since he had called Walker to tell him about the check found among Fang's effects suspicion had shifted from the French to the Germans. Nor did he know that a press conference had been set for the following evening, or that, even then, men were meeting at Camp David to formalize the President's decision. As he nursed the Mercedes through Rock Creek Park, he tried to make sense of what little he did know, but the facts didn't fit together.

To begin with, there was the Wheelabrator business. Childress was right; Wheeling, West Virginia, was a long way from Richmond. But Carrington had seen the money and had said it looked old. That much had to be true. The men at the Fed who cut the money up and burned it would have known something was wrong had the bills not looked old. They must have been aged somehow. If not the Wheelabrator, how?

There was also the press in Asnières. It was Hawkins's opinion that someone had monkeyed with the counter to make it look like a lot of printing had been done. What was that all about?

Something else had been nagging at Koenig. How had Swartzman gone for twelve years without being caught? Koenig had known a lot of crooks. He had known some nerveless, stare-you-in-the-eye crooks. But never had he known a crook who had been able to do his thing for more than a year or two. Something always went wrong: they got sick, they took the wrong person into their confidence, their Aunt Tilly pulled up

231

the floorboards looking for her hat pin. Nobody, in Koenig's experience, got away with anything for twelve years.

Now there were holes in the money.

Koenig didn't like it. A few days earlier, Carrington's story had seemed unshakeable. Koenig had run down every detail himself. He had believed it. Walker and Ferguson had believed it. And why not? People didn't admit to crimes they hadn't committed. Childress had had doubts, but what did Childress know? Everyone else believed . . . except maybe Erlich? What had Erlich said that evening in his office to give him the impression that the Treasury consultant also had doubts? Koenig couldn't remember.

He went back over what he had done since he'd learned of the Seydoux bills. He tried to recall the progress of his investigation day by day. What had he learned when? Which parts of the story had been confirmed, which not? Where had he relied on the word of others, where on his own knowledge or instinct? There was a chance he might turn out to be smarter than the men at Treasury after all. Carrington's story was cracking. One more little wedge in the right place and it might fall apart.

In the quiet of his empty office Koenig continued to reflect. He had been deep in thought for a good while when he rose to dig out and consult a folder from a file cabinet behind the door. Returning to his desk, he jotted a single name on his note pad and picked up the phone.

"Etta Swartzman." Koenig retraced the letters on the note pad as the phone rang. Nobody had really checked out Swartzman. The man was dead; with everything else that was going on he hadn't seemed a high priority. But it occurred to Koenig that he had only Berg's word, via Carrington, to implicate Swartzman. What if . . .

There was no answer at the New York apartment. It took

two more calls—one to the apartment-house superintendent, the other to Swartzman's cousin in Brooklyn—to find out that Mrs. Swartzman was visiting relatives in Florida.

Koenig took down the address, a place called Longboat Key, thanked the man, and hung up.

After a moment's deliberation he rejected the idea of a phone call. If Mrs. Swartzman had something to hide, she wasn't going to volunteer it over the telephone.

The map showed Longboat Key to be just northwest of Sarasota. Koenig checked his watch, then made two quick calls —a futile effort to reach Walker and the other to Ruthie. Ten minutes later he was in the Mercedes headed out New York Avenue in the direction of Friendship Airport.

CHAPTER 25

While Koenig was driving to Friendship Airport, Peregrin St. Giles was on his way back to the Hotel Lotti in Paris—for the first time since he'd checked in four days before.

The *Herald Tribune* had run his advertisement every day that week. But to be certain he had Majendie's attention, St. Giles had twice that week used the Telex number given him in Hong Kong—once to commission the murder of the South African prime minister, once to order the murder of the pope. Majendie could no longer doubt that his cat had turned on him, and that his piano was threatening to roll back down the stairs. He would know now that his scheme had been abandoned and would be afraid his government was about to be betrayed, with God knew what awful consequences. Majendie would see only one chance of averting disaster. He, or whoever did his dirty work, would have to intercept St. Giles by keeping the appointment at the Jackie Bar.

The Lotti was a quantum leap in class from the run-down

walk-up on Rue de la Sorbonne. But the elegance of the Right Bank establishment made no impression on St. Giles, who had other things on his mind as he made his way across the lobby to the elevator.

Months earlier, he had conceived a chain of events that would give him the name of his son's killer and free him from Majendie's grasp.

He had used Fang, with his comprehensive knowledge of a twenty-dollar bill's design, to create the illusion of counterfeit money good enough to escape detection, and done it by having Fang simply alter the quadrant numbers on genuine bills.

He had used the cables and Seydoux to alert the U.S. authorities to Fang's "counterfeits," and to plant the suggestion that they might be part of a politically inspired plot based in France.

With a few brief visits to Richmond and one call to Majendie's Telex killer, he had contrived to have an officer of a Federal Reserve Bank offer convincing confirmation of such a plot on a staggeringly large scale.

With these simple but carefully thought-out actions, he had brought the government of the most powerful nation in the world to the brink of decisions that would alter the course of history and along the way yield him the name of his son's killer.

There was just one more link in his plan. So as not to have to face other Majendies in the future, he had to arrange for the disappearance of what officially was left of Peregrin St. Giles.

He took the elevator to the fourth floor of the Lotti, then walked down the fire stairs at the rear of the building to the second. The precaution proved unnecessary. The second-floor corridor was empty. Moments later he was safely in his room.

There was no visible evidence of a search. His suitcase lay open on its stand just as he had arranged it. The bed had been turned down, doubtless the maid's work. His eye went to the telephone on the table by the bed. The receiver lay in its cradle with the cord to the right, as though replaced by a person seated on the bed. No professional would sit on the bed; the cracker under the mattress was one of the oldest tricks in the book. He approached the bedside table, reached under it and ran his fingers along the bottom of the drawer. He felt nothing. A few minutes of poking around in the carpet under the table produced the pin he had pushed into the drawer's soft wooden bottom four days earlier. Had it fallen out? He removed the drawer, retrieved the crumpled bit of paper on which he had penned the reminder of his meeting at the Jackie Bar and turned the drawer upside down on the bed. Using the bedside lamp, he examined the hole where the pin had been. On the side of the hole closest to the rear of the drawer the wood had been mashed where the pin had been forced against it. Someone had taken the bait. Unless he had miscalculated, the same person would be at the Jackie Bar the following afternoon. Until then he had only to stay out of sight.

St. Giles left the Lotti and walked the two blocks to Rue de Rivoli. He crossed into the Tuileries Garden and made his way up the gravel path, through the strollers, around the Jeu de Paume and across the Place de la Concorde. He had thought about the meeting many times in the preceding months, but always as a distant prospect. Now it was a bare twenty-four hours off. Would Majendie himself appear? Probably not. Whom would he send? And what about the American, or Americans? Only the Americans would have traced Berg to the Lotti, because only they believed Berg existed. They had read the note in his bedside table. They would be at the Jackie Bar, too.

After months of planning, the final act would still be an improvisation.

Hello, what's this? he thought.

Tired, he had turned toward a bench at the edge of the walk, thinking to sit and rest his knees for a few minutes, when he caught sight of a heavyset man in a trench coat starting to make a similar move behind him. Caught at a point where there was no bench, the man, after one hesitant step, resumed his course and continued on past. St. Giles watched, wondering if the man had been following him. A hundred yards farther on, the man turned from the gravel path into the trees and disappeared from his vision.

For a while he remained on the bench, reflecting. He had expected the Lotti room to be searched. He had expected it would be the Americans who searched it. But he had expected them to try to catch him at the Jackie Bar. He had not counted on being followed. What if the man in the park had been following him, and what if he was in too big a hurry to wait for the meeting at the Jackie Bar? His carefully planned timing was in jeopardy. He rose from the bench. He had to find some way to buy twenty-four more hours.

After Hawkins had finished his investigations at the printing plant in Asnières and telephoned Koenig in Washington, he had returned to his apartment. Crack-of-dawn trips to the Paris suburbs were not daily duty for the late-rising Secret Service agent, and it was with the pleasant anticipation of a few more hours of sleep that he had climbed the stairs.

Sleep had not been in the cards. He had not been in his apartment ten minutes when the Paris police called, responding to a request Hawkins had made through the embassy. The police had been checking hotel registrations. This morning, they had discovered that, four days earlier, a man named Berg had checked into the Lotti.

Hawkins had gone to the hotel directly. A telephone call from the lobby told him Berg's room was unoccupied. It took him less than half an hour to find the balled-up scrap of paper in the bedside table. That gave him a lead, but it did not give him Berg.

From the tidy look of the room, Hawkins reasoned that the maid had already made her rounds. Figuring the door would not be opened again until Berg returned, he set to work. Unwinding black thread from a small spool, he tied it to a coat hanger taken from the closet and lowered the hanger a few yards out the window. The hanger would be visible from other windows that gave onto the small air shaft. But there was no reason for anyone to take note. Closing the window all but a fraction of an inch, Hawkins backed across the room, paying out the thread. When he reached the door, he opened it, lowered the thread to a few inches above the carpet, backed out of the room and closed the thread in the door. Then, using a penknife, he trimmed the thread off flush with the face of the door. Minutes after he left the room, he was in a narrow passageway off the base of the air shaft. A little rummaging in the trash produced several tin cans, which he arranged on the ground underneath the dangling coat hanger. With his alarm clock in working order, he seated himself on the floor of the passageway, out of sight of the hotel windows but within easy earshot of the tin cans, leaned against the wall and closed his eyes.

It was midafternoon when the clank of the hanger hitting the cans wakened him. Quickly he moved to the mouth of the passageway. He could see the sheer white curtains in the window of Berg's room above him. After fifteen minutes, the curtains billowed, indicating that the door to the room had been opened and shut again. Thirty seconds later, Hawkins was in the lobby of the Lotti, in time to spot a tall man somewhere in his mid-fifties head from the elevator to the door. The man wore a rumpled suit, light in color and fabric, an outfit altogether more appropriate to the tropics than to Paris. Hawkins hesitated. The man was larger, older than he had expected Berg to be. Yet he looked . . . almost familiar.

He had seen Berg before! More than six months ago. Not in Paris, though. He'd seen him in . . .

An eerie thought gripped Hawkins. Was Berg Peregrin St. Giles? But that was impossible! He'd put six shots through the crook's blankets himself. . . . The only way St. Giles could have escaped his hotel room in Finale Ligure was as smoke through the window.

Quickly collecting his wits, Hawkins pushed his way through the hotel doors and stepped into Rue de Castiglione.

So this old man was the long-sought Berg. What to do next? With this question occupying him, Hawkins had been unprepared for the man's sudden decision to sit down on a park bench. Only by rapid footwork and doubling back through the trees had he managed to maintain contact.

From behind the trees, he watched Berg rise and resume his walk. Fifty yards apart they passed the Rond Point and headed up the Champs-Elysées. Though the sidewalk was crowded, Hawkins was careful this time to keep his distance. He deduced from the note he had found in the Berg's bedside table that Berg was not working alone. In twenty-four hours there was no telling whom Berg might lead him to. With luck, by the next afternoon he might be able to give Koenig a full cast of characters.

Several blocks up the Champs-Elysées, Hawkins watched Berg turn into the glass-faced Air France ticket office. From the sidewalk, he could see him speaking with an agent behind the counter. When Berg emerged, Hawkins was already in a taxi, idling at the curb.

The taxi that Berg took upon leaving the airline office did not head for the airport. Instead, it crossed the river, wound through the Latin Quarter and stopped in front of a small hotel, which green vertical lettering announced as the Gerson. Berg got out; the taxi waited. Was Berg picking up someone? No. A few minutes later he emerged with a suitcase and a briefcase, and the taxi was off again.

It was apparent that this time the destination was Orly. As they made their way through the afternoon traffic on the expressway, Hawkins wondered where Berg might be planning to go. He was excited. The origin of the Joe Berg problem had been its singular mystery. Koenig had said France. But after his episode with Bouladoux, Hawkins doubted that was true. No one in Washington had been able to find the answer. Berg might be about to yield it.

Hawkins waited until Berg had paid his driver and carried his bags inside the airport before following. At the check-in counter he watched as the older man pushed his suitcase onto the scale. He moved closer to catch the gate designation, then watched Berg, carrying his briefcase, move off in the direction indicated by the attendant. He glanced at the television screen on which departures were listed.

Cairo!

Hawkins blinked, thinking perhaps he was not seeing clearly, or that he had read the wrong line. But no, the attendant had said "Trente-trois." According to the television screen, the plane loading at gate thirty-three was going to Cairo.

By the time he had bought a ticket and reached gate thirty-three, Berg had boarded. Midway down the aisle, Hawkins spotted him still standing, folding the jacket of his suit. He pushed past and moved to the seat he'd requested in the rear of the plane, where he could command a view of the entire coach section. He watched the older man stow his jacket in the compartment above his head. He watched him remove his tie and roll his sleeves. He was surprised at the size and muscularity of Berg's forearms. Berg was powerfully built through the shoulders, too. Hawkins did not doubt that he could handle him, but ten years earlier it might have been different.

Berg sat down. For a moment his head disappeared from view. In a few seconds the reason became evident as he stood and in his stocking feet padded forward toward the magazine rack. Hawkins buckled himself in. He watched Berg, with two magazines under one arm, push through the curtain to the forward section to forage in the first-class rack. Berg might be working for the Egyptians, but he had good French if he planned to get through all those magazines, Hawkins reflected. He wondered what would happen when they got to Cairo. He wondered, too, what might have prompted the Egyptians to get involved in counterfeiting dollars. Was Egypt looking to finance another war? He was no expert on the Middle East, but if Egypt was contemplating another war, he was certain it was not in its interest to risk the enmity of the United States.

Perhaps Cairo was only a way station; perhaps Berg would be moving on from there. How, then, did he plan to get back in time for his meeting the next afternoon at the Jackie Bar? A whistling whine told him that the jet's engines had started. Maybe Berg had decided not to go to the meeting. Maybe it was a meeting between other people, one Berg had never intended to attend. Then why the note?

The plane was rolling now. Berg ought to have returned to his seat. Nobody could read that many magazines. Had Berg got into a conversation with someone in first class and sat down up there? When there were plenty of empty seats, the stewardesses sometimes allowed that. Hawkins leaned back and tried to suppress the half-formed thought that was working its way toward the surface of his consciousness. Berg had checked his big suitcase on this flight; his jacket was in the storage compartment, where Hawkins had seen him put it, and his shoes must be by his seat. There was no cause for concern. A man couldn't leave the plane without his jacket and shoes. If Berg had wanted to get off, he would have had to come back for . . . Unless . . . the briefcase! Where was Berg's briefcase? A carry-on luggage compartment was at the front of the plane. Had Berg left his briefcase with a second pair of shoes and a jacket up front? Had he got off the plane before they started? Ignoring the protests of the stewardesses and the stares of other passengers, Hawkins burst into the first-class section. There were a dozen seats, half of them full. None of them contained Berg. Hawkins slumped into an empty seat on the aisle. A few minutes earlier he had been on the brink of the greatest success of his career. Now he was on his way to Cairo. Alone.

CHAPTER 26

From Friendship, Koenig tried once more without success to reach Walker. He hung up, called Childress and instructed him to call Walker until he got him and to tell the Under Secretary that Koenig suspected that Carrington had not been telling the truth, that there was the possibility of a hoax.

Getting to Longboat Key was complicated. The flight from Friendship left Koenig in Tampa. There, he got a flight to Sarasota, rented a car and drove over the long bridge to St. Armand's Key, through the shopping center at St. Armand's Circle, then up the key and across the much shorter bridge to Longboat Key.

Swartzman's relatives' apartment turned out to be on the cheap side of the key—a condominium called "Key Coaster." If Swartzman had kept any of the money he had swapped all those years, he hadn't spread it around the family.

Several knocks on the door of the first-floor apartment brought no response. The lobby of the building opened onto

243

a central courtyard. Ignoring the dozen elderly residents sitting around the pool, Koenig circled the courtyard counting windows. Halfway around he stopped, raised one hand to his head and made little combing motions, as though using the window as a mirror. After a few seconds, he resumed his strolling, completed his circuit of the pool, and left the courtyard by the door he had entered. With his head and arms blocking the reflection, he had been able to see into the apartment. There had been dirty dishes on the table and a cat on the couch. Mrs. Swartzman and her relatives couldn't be far off.

The dishes reminded him that he'd had nothing to eat since breakfast, and he resolved to take care of that problem while he waited.

It was after eight o'clock when Koenig returned to the Key Coaster.

Mrs. Swartzman herself opened the door. She seemed confused. But after Koenig had explained who he was, she showed no reluctance to answer his questions. She had been in Florida since the day after the funeral. She had spent the entire time at the Key Coaster. No, she had never been to Florida before; Leonard hadn't liked Florida or the things old people did in Florida. They were New Yorkers; reading, watching and listening were their pleasures. With Leonard's back problems, they had no use for shuffleboard, golf, and outdoor things. . . . Leonard's back problems? Koenig didn't know? Leonard had had degenerating disc disease, had had it for years. She had had to lay out his clothes for him each evening, because he couldn't lift his suits off the rack in the closet. He hadn't been able to pick up anything heavier than the *New York Times*.

Koenig got back to the Sarasota airport too late to catch the last plane for Tampa. The man at the ticket counter explained that his best bet was the one o'clock flight out of Sarasota the following afternoon. He could then catch the four-thirty flight from Tampa to Washington.

Now, as the plane climbed north out of Tampa, Koenig struggled to make sense of things. He had the feeling of working on a jigsaw puzzle into which someone had thrown a handful of extra pieces. Too many bits of information didn't fit. Swartzman's widow had just described her husband as a man who could scarcely dress himself. How could a man like that carry a briefcase full of money?

At Tampa, the only available aisle seat had been next to a small boy flying with his mother. The boy, who looked to be about three, was studying the airline magazine, open upside down in his lap. Koenig fished for his own magazine in the pocket on the back of the seat in front. Gone. He looked back at the child, then at the child's mother. She was reading another copy of the magazine. Probably she has stuffed the third magazine in her pocketbook for some other kid who would be meeting them at the airport. Koenig tried reading over the boy's shoulder. He had just got oriented when the boy turned the page. He waited for the little thief to get bored. The boy turned the last page. But instead of putting the magazine down, he started back, turning the pages in the other direction. Jesus, Koenig thought in silent exasperation, it's not enough the little pecker reads upside down; he's gotta read backward, too. The kid was staring now at two girls in bathing suits hanging by the soles of their feet from a beach in . . . Koenig cocked his head as far as he could, but he couldn't make out where the beach was.

He lowered his seat and closed his eyes. Maybe it didn't make any difference to the kid if things were upside down, he reflected. The kid probably had spent half his life on his back, seeing things upside down. How could he know girls didn't look like that? Mommy looked like that when she leaned into the crib. Grownups had to have things right side up to recognize them. But a kid? A kid just saw what was there.

Koenig had forgotten the magazine now. With his eyes shut, he was going over what he had learned during the previous week. Maybe there was something upside down that he couldn't see. Maybe he had been asking himself the wrong questions.

How could Fang have done such fantastic work? Even with genuine paper, it was next to impossible. Something else didn't make sense, something that had been bothering him for months. Why would someone who could make counterfeit bills as good as the Seydoux bills bother to get involved with Carrington or a swap operation, with all the risk it entailed? If they could print Seydoux-quality bills in anything close to the volume that had been run off on the French press, they had no need to get involved with the Federal Reserve Banks. Not five people in the world would be able to tell their product from the genuine article. Somebody had gone to an awful lot of unnecessary work. And for what? All they had accomplished was . . .

Koenig was sitting upright now, his eyes wide open. Suddenly, a lot of things were coming into focus. Things had been upside down, or at least backward. . . .

Swartzman hadn't *had* to carry any counterfeit money. There never had *been* any counterfeit money. No wonder Fang's work had been so nearly perfect. Except for the part that the toaster had burned out, it *was* perfect. And no wonder Fang had been killed. Alive, Fang could have ruined everything. If Berg had been smarter, he would have killed the manager of the printing plant in Asnières, too. The only person Berg needed alive was Carrington. Carrington had been the key to the whole thing. Koenig checked his watch. It was a little before six o'clock.

246

The stewardess in the first-class section didn't know anything about radio calls. But Koenig's Secret Service identification quickly got him the attention of the pilot. Five minutes later, he was in the cockpit of the plane talking to the Friendship Airport control tower. His message would be relayed to Richmond.

When the plane touched down under heavy black rain clouds, Koenig was the first man off. He made straight for the bank of telephones in the airport's main lobby. Briscoe had had almost an hour to find the answer to the question Koenig had relayed.

"You got my message?" Briscoe had picked up on the first ring.

"Yes, sir."

"Did you talk to the store?"

"Yes, sir. I got the owner down there twenty minutes after I got your message."

"Did they have a record of selling Berg the case?"

"Yeah, and what's more, the man remembered the sale."

"And?"

"Berg bought just one case."

Koenig thanked Briscoe and hung up.

Just one case! Berg had been clever. But even the clever ones made mistakes.

Still standing at the bank of phones, Koenig placed a call to Walker.

Walker was not in. His secretary was terribly sorry, but Mr. Walker had left word the previous morning that he was at Camp David and not to be disturbed by anyone. Yes, she understood it was important; perhaps he would like to call back later.

Koenig hung up and called Childress at his home number. Something Walker's secretary had said alarmed him. Her mention of Camp David meant something big was up. And if Walker wasn't taking calls, Childress probably hadn't got through to him the previous day. Walker might not know even as much as Koenig had known the previous morning.

There was no answer at Childress's house, or at the office.

He tried the White House switchboard, this time asking for Walker, Ferguson or Erlich. All were tied up. Strict orders had been given not to disturb them until after the President's press conference.

Press conference! Koenig was close to panic now. He tried to recall what Walker, Ferguson and Erlich had discussed at the end of the meeting at the Treasury Department the previous Wednesday. Several actions had been outlined. Was the President about to announce one of them?

From the lobby of the airport it was a long way to the parking lot where he had left the Mercedes. It had started to rain. By the time he reached the car he was exhausted and soaking wet.

He checked his watch: twenty-five minutes to eight. The girl on the White House switchboard had not told him when the press conference was to be held. Probably the President had asked the networks for nine o'clock. He would get his largest audience then.

Koenig pulled out of the parking lot and feather-footed the Mercedes up to speed. He'd kill the kid in Takoma Park if the clutch chose this time to give out! The rain was falling heavily now, and the left front wheel threw a steady sheet of water up through the hole in the floor beneath his legs.

From the intersection of the airport road and the Baltimore-Washington Parkway, it was approximately twenty miles to the White House. In the rain, the drive would take twenty minutes flat out.

"Goddamn it!" Koenig exclaimed. The windshield wipers had gone out of sync and were banging into each other. Frantically he began to roll down the window next to him. The wipers had gone haywire before; he knew what to expect. Within seconds they would collide, and one of the little clips that held the wiper blades to their arms would snap.

"Fuck!"

The road in front of him dissolved into a blur. Where there had been cars in front of him there were just watery outlines. Gauging distance was impossible. He stuck his head out the window and tried using his left hand as a visor. No good. The water whipped around his hand. He leaned to his right and craned his neck. But the clear portion of the windshield in front on the other side was too far away. He eased up on the accelerator. The solid sheet of water on the windshield started to break into individual drops. But immediately, cars began to pass, throwing up road water, which made visibility worse than ever.

In a fury, he pulled the Mercedes onto the shoulder and slammed on the brakes. In a little more than half an hour, the President of the United States would go on television to announce his response to a threat that didn't exist. He was the only man who could warn him, and he sat soaking wet in a nine-year-old piece of German junk on the edge of the Baltimore-Washington Parkway.

Koenig leaped from the car, raced around to the trunk and took out the tire iron. Back at the front of the car, he began to flail at the windshield on the driver's side. He was right-handed, so he had to swing backhanded. It was an awkward business. He switched the iron to his left hand, but that lacked force. After eight or ten seconds of whacking away, all he had to show for his efforts were a dozen star-burst fractures that would have made driving difficult on a clear day.

To the trunk again, this time for something heavier. The spare tire? The jack? The jack! It was heavy, compact. Back at the front of the car, he raised the jack over his head and smashed it as hard as he could against the glass. There was no tinkling, none of the noise he associated with breaking glass; just a dull poof, followed by a crack as the jack hit the back of the steering wheel.

He scrambled back into the driver's seat, ignoring the thousands of glass fragments scattered about. He had cut himself; the inside of his right hand was covered with blood. As soon as he got into fourth gear, he pressed his wrist to his stomach to stop the flow. Rain pelted him on the chest, but by leaning back he could see the road ahead clearly. With his teeth, he pulled his left sleeve back. It was seven-forty-five.

By the time Koenig cleared Mount Vernon Square, the rain had stopped. The inside of his jacket sleeve was blood-soaked halfway to the elbow, but he felt no pain, only weakness and a disinclination to use the arm.

He was on Pennsylvania Avenue now, the White House ahead on the left. He turned down East Executive Avenue, circled the South Lawn, pulled up between the White House West Wing and the Old Executive Office Building and presented his credentials to the astonished guard.

Where would Walker be? Where were press conferences held? Away to the right he could see people disappearing into the White House's front entrance. He hurried after them. He was faint and exhausted from trying to remember all the things he had to tell Walker.

"Hey, are you press?" An arm seized him.

"Secret Service." Koenig flashed the plastic card he still clutched in his left hand.

"Are you all right?" The guard had turned to follow.

Koenig didn't hear the question. Down a corridor to his left, he could see a door and through the door bright lights and people milling around. By the door, talking to a little man with red hair, he spied a familiar face. It was Erlich.

"There's no money." He gasped.

"Mr. Koenig, what's happened to you?" Erlich turned his back on the red-haired man and took hold of Koenig by the shoulders, half supporting him.

"There's no money. There never was any money. It's all a trick." Koenig looked up at Erlich's concerned but uncomprehending face. "Berg fooled Carrington, like he fooled us. Carrington burned real money."

"Mr. Koenig, you'd better sit down. I think you are hurt."

"You've got to tell the President. You've got to tell him there's no money."

"Yes, yes, of course, but let's get you sitting down. You need medical attention." Erlich said something to the guard, then led Koenig from the corridor into a side room. "Now then," he said when they were seated, "exactly what do you mean when you say there's no money?"

Eyes shut with the effort, Koenig tried to explain to Erlich what he had figured out. There never had been any counterfeit money; only the illusion of it. The proof had come from Briscoe. If Berg had been swapping money, as he had convinced Carrington he was doing, he would have needed two cases. But he had bought only one. The case Carrington left in the locker at the bus station each evening was the same case he picked up the following morning. Moreover, it contained the same money. Berg must have had one case of old twenty-dollar bills to begin with. And Carrington had been carrying that one case back and forth between the Trailways station and his office for a month, exchanging money with himself. Except for those few occasions when he met with Carrington, it hadn't been necessary for Berg to be anywhere near Richmond. All Carrington had accomplished with his imagined swaps was to delay by a day the consignment of old twenty-dollar bills to the burn pile.

"Then how do you explain the counterfeit money you showed us, the money the police found on the Frenchman?" Erlich asked. The consultant had listened with surprising calm to Koenig's theory as it spilled out. The guard had returned now and with him a bespectacled man in a light business suit and carrying a medical bag.

"That wasn't counterfeit. That stuff was real, just like Verity thought it was. Berg got Fang to change the quadrant numbers on real money so we would think it was counterfeit. He must have planted those bills on Seydoux. He probably killed him, too. But not until he set us up with the cables. He had us looking for counterfeit money when Seydoux turned up dead, and he had us ready to believe almost anything by the time Carrington turned himself in with that crazy story."

"Why would he use real money, Mr. Koenig?"

"It was cheaper, easier. He only needed a little bit. My wife figured it out for me. Ruthie put it on the toaster. Hey, we gotta tell the President. What time is it?"

"The toaster, Mr. Koenig?"

"The toaster burned the quadrant numbers out. That was the only part of the bills that had been worked on. Listen"—Koenig's arm was throbbing painfully now—"you gotta tell the President. I busted my ass to get here in time!"

"Now calm down, Mr. Koenig. There are still a lot of loose ends that need explaining before we can interrupt the President."

"Like what? Why do we have to figure out everything?"

"Like what happened at the other Federal Reserve Bank, Mr. Koenig. Like Swartzman. Like the printing press that the French police found. I don't think we can lay this matter to rest just because in your own mind you are satisfied that it is a hoax."

"But it'll be too late," Koenig stammered. "Somebody dummied the press in France. Swartzman didn't have anything to do with it. . . ." Suddenly he was very, very tired, conscious for the first time that he was soaking wet and covered with grime, aware that the man in the light suit had peeled back the sleeve of his injured arm and was injecting something above the wound.

"What time is it?"

"It's about twenty after eight, Mr. Koenig."

Koenig looked at Erlich. The consultant's face was beginning to get blurry. He could feel faintness coming on like sleep. "You gotta tell . . ." He couldn't make himself finish the sentence. Why couldn't Erlich understand what he was trying to tell him? Why couldn't he see what had happened? Wasn't he listening? Had it all been for nothing? Was Erlich just another arrogant bastard like the others? Did no one ever care what he thought? Koenig felt the tears filling his eyes and a warm fuzzy feeling coming over him. Erlich seemed to be getting farther away. He had the feeling Ruthie was nearby.

"Yes, yes, I know, Mr. Koenig, but it's too late to tell the President now. Under the circumstances, it wouldn't be wise. The President's resigned to what is happening—convinced it's good for everyone, in the long run. The changes we'll see tonight should have come a long time ago. It took Berg to give us a push. You say the push is imaginary. But I doubt that we could ever prove that. Anyway, sometimes it's best we don't know the truth. You remember Begelman? My advice is to forget about it. We really should get you to the hospital. That wrist looks very nasty."

Koenig wasn't hearing Erlich any longer. He had slumped down on the couch with his eyes shut, a look of disengagement on his face. It was twenty years earlier, and he was back in the locker room at Colgate. The football team had just lost badly to Army, and the old white-haired trainer was cutting away the sweaty tape that bound Koenig's ugly blue-black arm to his side. "You did a helluva job, Vergil," the trainer was saying with avuncular warmth, "a helluva job. That kid Slater is all-East, and you stuck him cold; now you get some rest." Koenig could feel his pain giving way to contentment. Outside the locker room, Ruthie would be waiting for him. As soon as he could take a shower, he would hurry to see her. She would be proud of the way he had played. She would take him home and rub analgesic balm on his arm and tell him that he was brave and that she loved him. And while the unmarried students were out getting drunk, she would fix him a special dinner, like she always did on nights after games. Maybe Ruthie would fix him Salisbury steak.

CHAPTER 27

Hawkins glared out the window of the taxi at the grey apartment blocks flitting past alongside the elevated highway. It was three-thirty in the afternoon; he had not slept in almost thirty-six hours.

The Cairo airport had been a nightmare—dusty, overrun with beggars and pickpockets, and, even after dark, incredibly hot. Moreover, without his papers in order, he had been an easy mark for the Egyptian immigration officials; that had cost him an hour of acrimony and the Egyptian equivalent of about fifty U.S. dollars in "facilitation" fees. The worst of it was that there had been no direct flight from Cairo back to Paris; the earliest possible return flight had been via Beirut and Rome. Planes and trains made him feel dirty, even on short trips; after nearly a full day in transit, Hawkins was in a foul mood.

He had copied Majendie's name and the address of the Jackie Bar from the scrap of paper in the drawer of the bedside table at the Lotti. He was glad now he had it, because from the top of Rue Jules-Chaplain where the taxi dropped him he could see no evidence of a bar.

Ahead toward the end of the block on the right was a small cinema. It was either closed or in the middle of a showing, because the sidewalk was empty. Past the theater was the end of the street; it was only a block long. Hawkins stopped. Without the street number, he might have walked right past it. He was standing in front of a large set of wooden doors. A smaller door, cut into them, permitted him to see into what appeared to be a short alley or a narrow covered courtyard. Except at his feet, where the light from the street fell on the tiles, and at the far end, where a red neon sign glowed dimly, the courtyard was almost completely dark. There were no blinking lights, no awning, no advertisements, no *tabac* sign—just the dim red neon words "Jackie Bar."

Hawkins paused. The courtyard was perhaps ten feet wide and thirty feet long. The wall on his left was recessed at its far end to accommodate several trash cans. In the wall on his right was a door on which, as his eyes adjusted to the darkness, he could make out "WC."

He checked his watch; he still had twenty minutes before Berg's note said he was to meet the man named Majendie. He wondered if either was already in the bar. He wondered, too, if he should have notified someone about where he was and what he was doing.

Whom? He couldn't have told the embassy. What he was doing was totally out of order. The agreement under which the Secret Service kept him in Paris was explicit; playing free-lance cop was definitely against the rules.

Besides, the only security force the embassy had was the marine honor guard, barracked on top of a warehouse on the other side of the city. Even if the ambassador was willing to order the honor guard to the Jackie Bar, they could not be there in time.

Worrying made Hawkins nervous, which reminded him of the WC.

Locked! This wasn't his day for public facilities. Resolutely, he opened the door of the bar itself and stepped inside.

Hawkins was not prepared for what greeted him. The name, the neighborhood, the bar's location at the back of the alley and its tiny, secretive little sign had signaled a certain type of establishment. He had expected darkness, the wails of some Gallic torch singer, banquettes, booths and a bevy of used-up ladies in fishnet stockings and tear-away dresses wandering around looking bored. Whores in Paris rarely bothered to affect enjoyment, even in prime time. Sunday afternoon in August was not prime time.

The scene that met Hawkins's eyes filled none of his expectations. The bar, though dim, was not dark; there was no whorehouse music, nor were there banquettes, booths or women. None of this, however, surprised him as much as did the bar's size. The Jackie Bar was at most fifteen feet long and, including the space behind the counter, ten feet wide.

Except for a tall, thin bartender whose back was turned when Hawkins entered, the room was empty. As the door closed, the bartender turned from the shelf where he had been polishing glasses. For a moment he seemed to examine Hawkins, as though trying to decide whether he had seen him before. Then without speaking he nodded and turned back to his glasses.

Hawkins had counted on a dark corner from which to observe the rendezvous. He was uncertain now what to do. There were only six stools by the bar. On any of them his back would be to the door. Berg had seen him the preceding day; would he recognize him from the rear?

The bartender had finished polishing glasses and was waiting for Hawkins's order.

"Un demi," Hawkins said.

He watched the bartender draw the glass of beer. The man was tall for a Frenchman, he reflected; his long, slicked-back blond hair didn't look French either. Stereotypes were one of Hawkins's indulgences. After ten years in Paris, he still liked to think that all Frenchmen were short, with greasy black hair and little pencil mustaches. Devotion to this belief did little for his social life, but helped to sustain his self-esteem. Among the greatest compliments he was accustomed to bestowing was "You don't look French."

Nervous, he drank his beer quickly and ordered another. According to his watch, it was now five minutes after Berg and the other man were to have been there. Had they changed the time? Had Berg got hold of the other man and told him he was being followed?

The bartender had turned up the radio, and it was blaring loudly on the wall. Hawkins polished off the second of the beers and found his thoughts turning back to the WC. Either somebody would arrive soon or he was going to have to ask the bartender to unlock the door to the toilet.

Perhaps the bartender knew Berg. Maybe Berg was a regular. If so, the bartender might know if Berg had met someone there the previous afternoon, while he had been on his way to Cairo. He considered asking, but thought better of it. If the bartender knew Berg, he might tell Berg someone had inquired about him. Berg was already suspicious. Better to ask about the other man.

Hawkins fished from his pocket the scrap of paper on which he had copied down Majendie's name. Holding it below the bar, where the bartender could not see, he tried to decide how the name would be pronounced.

"Est-ce que vous connaissez un homme qui s'appelle Majendie?" he asked, putting the emphasis on the middle syllable. As soon as he had said the name he was sure his pronunciation was wrong. He did not have time to brood.

To Hawkins's surprise the bartender replied in English. "Are you looking for Majendie?" he asked, his emphasis confidently placed on the first syllable. His accent was distinct, but not French.

"You know him?" Hawkins responded.

The bartender did not reply. He had dumped another load of glasses into the sink under the bar and was leaning over with his arms in the water, his head separated from Hawkins's by no more than three feet.

"I asked you a question, pal," Hawkins said with irritation. There was an insolence in the bartender's silence that angered him. "I asked you if you knew somebody named Majendie," he repeated.

The bartender, still hunched over, stared fixedly at Hawkins now. Something about him had changed, something so slight Hawkins almost missed it. The rhythmical bobbing of his head and shoulders had ceased. The man's arms were hidden from view, but it was clear he was no longer washing dishes.

Hawkins didn't like it. Something was wrong. Suddenly he sensed that a lot was wrong. He wore his shoulder holster low, under his left arm; with his elbows on the bar and his arms dangling inward toward his crotch, his hand was only six inches from his gun. An upward flick of the thumb to throw the holster snap, a downward swipe of the thumb to kick off the safety, and he would be in business—no more than one second total elapsed time. He got as far as the snap.

The shot that stopped him had to have come from a powerful weapon. The bullet that ripped through the face of the bar in front of him split away a strip of wood the size of a yardstick.

Hawkins felt no pain, only a huge force crashing into his groin, knocking him off the stool. He tried to break his fall with his right arm, but the arm, which had been stretched across his stomach, did not respond. He hit the floor with his knees, then with his face.

There was no discomfort—a dream fall, concussion without pain. Footsteps told him the bartender was walking to the end of the bar. Was he limping? Dreamily, Hawkins wondered if the bartender had always limped. Had he limped since childhood? And where, he wondered, was he limping now? To finish him off? Would there be another shot? He hoped it would not hurt. Beyond that he did not care. He was comfortable, the center of him suffused with a familiar, soothing warmth. The last thing to cross Burton Hawkins's consciousness before he died was the realization that he was wetting his pants.

EPILOGUE

Late on the afternoon of August 15, the Paris police received an anonymous telephone tip. It led them to a tiny bar on Rue Jules-Chaplain, in the Sixth Arrondissement, and to the body of a man bearing papers that identified him as Burton Hawkins, a U.S. government employee. It led them to another body as well, this one alive and belonging to the bar's proprietor. The police located him, trussed and gagged, in a storage cellar beneath the floor of the bar.

According to the bartender, he had opened his bar at four o'clock, the normal Sunday opening hour. At four-twenty, his first customer, a blond man with a limp, entered. The man had not ordered a drink. Instead, he had drawn a gun and forced the bartender into the basement and bound and gagged him. As to what had happened after that, the bartender could only guess from what he had heard, but he was almost certain that only one other person had entered the bar before the shots. These facts the police duly recorded.

This reconstruction of events was muddied by the account

of a second witness. An elderly woman who lived in the apartment building across the street from the bar, and whose habit it had been for years to sit in her window and watch the comings and goings of the bar's clientele, also had noted the arrival of the blond man with the limp and of the American, Hawkins. But by her account, they were not the first two customers of the day; they were the second and third. The first customer, the old lady insisted, had been an older man with a bad stomach, tall and wearing what looked like the mismatched trousers and jacket of two light-colored tropical suits. What was more, the tall middle-aged man wearing this strange outfit had not left until after she had seen the blond man emerge and limp hurriedly up the street.

"With a bad stomach?" the investigators had asked. How could she know that the older man had a bad stomach? Because, she explained, he had never actually got beyond the courtyard outside the bar. As she had plainly seen from her window, he had spent the entire time, nearly an hour and a half, in the WC.

A full investigation would never occur. By evening, police contacts with the U.S. Embassy had uncovered the special nature of Hawkins's work. Since neither country's authorities wished it known that an agreement permitted the U.S. Secret Service to operate on French soil, inquiries were brought quickly to a halt. Within twenty-four hours, the body of Burton Hawkins was on a military aircraft headed for Fayetteville, North Carolina.

On August 15, at nine o'clock in the evening, Washington time, while the cable traffic regarding Hawkins was still en route, the President of the United States went on television to announce he was suspending the convertibility of the dollar into gold. This announcement, buried by design in a four-point program of dramatic scope, went over the heads of nine-tenths of the prime-time audience that had tuned in expecting to watch Jason Robards and George Segal in "The Saint Valentine's Day Massacre" or "Bonanza." Of those who kept their television sets on, the majority was most interested in the President's promises to create jobs and freeze prices. But to the money men who happened to tune in, the message was clear. The United States was giving up its defense of the dollar; a monetary system that had endured for more than a quarter century was dead.

The following day, August 16, every major money-trading center in Europe was closed. When they opened again on Tuesday, the price of gold jumped dramatically, the first in a series of increases that would in due time take the private-market price to nearly eight hundred dollars an ounce. In the economic history of the Western world, August 15, 1971, would be remembered as a watershed.

In Richmond, Virginia, Armistead Carrington was one of those who watched the President. For three weeks he had been under constant surveillance on Koenig's orders. To Carrington, the President's performance seemed a pageant to his personal treason. The President seemed to look directly at him, talk directly to him. His shame was too great to bear, and, long before the President had finished and the commentators had come on to expand and explain, he had turned off the set. He could not, at that moment when his life seemed bleakest, know that the steps he had just heard announced would keep him out of jail. He could not foresee—because he did not yet understand what he had done—that no President could let him go to trial if it meant admitting that the White House had been tricked into devaluing the dollar.

Vergil Koenig was not so fortunate. Of everyone involved in the Berg affair, Koenig had most nearly seen things as they were. He got little for his pains. Following his collapse at the

White House on the evening of August 15, he spent two days at George Washington Hospital, where the records show he was treated for a gash on his wrist and for nervous exhaustion. On August 17, he was transferred, on orders of the White House physician, to St. Elizabeths, a hospital specializing in care of the emotionally disturbed.

It took the threat of legal action to get Koenig out of St. Elizabeths. When at last he was discharged, it was not to return to his job in the Counterfeit Division, but to indefinite administrative leave. Appeals proved of no avail. Several times Koenig prepared papers. Each time the papers were stalled for lack of support from his superiors at Treasury. Somebody did not want Koenig back in the service. In March 1972, Vergil Koenig was given early retirement with full disability.

Peregrin St. Giles was the last of the survivors. Still wearing his rumpled tan suit pants with the mismatched jacket, he left Paris the night of August 15 and flew straight to Hong Kong. He had to wait nearly two weeks. But on August 27, an envelope appeared in the post office box to which Majendie had given him the key. As Majendie had predicted, the fall in the value of the dollar following the President's announcements had forced the bank from which he had borrowed Swiss francs to demand additional collateral. And, as Majendie had promised, the notice containing this demand gave St. Giles the name he sought. He read it with satisfaction. It was the name of a U.S. Secret Service agent, a good Anglo-Saxon name, but not a common name, like John Smith or Robert Thompson, that might be shared by dozens. It was Hawkins. There might be a number of agents named Hawkins. But there was probably only one named Burton Hawkins.

Standing in the post office in Hong Kong, St. Giles reflected that he had come full circle. Before Majendie and Bosanquet had found him in Hong Kong, he had felt secure, believing others thought him dead. He had been wrong. But now he was back where he thought he had been. The Americans might be looking for someone named Joe Berg, but to them St. Giles had been dead for better than half a year. And to Majendie? His blond hit man with the limp, whom St. Giles, through the hole in the door of the WC, had watched enter and leave the Jackie Bar, would have reported to Majendie that St. Giles was dead. Nothing Majendie would ever see would contradict that report.

St. Giles glanced at the notice in his hand and smiled. Majendie's name had been typed at the bottom of the page as the individual who had opened the account. But he was smiling at Majendie's address: Box 610, Jo'burg, South Africa. He wondered how long, without his chance perusal of the magazine article about the Springboks, it would have taken him to figure out who Majendie's and Bosanquet's employer had been, to figure out that the mysterious Joe Berg was not a person, but a place, that Majendie's real goal had not been to destroy the value of the American dollar but to increase the value of South African gold. Perhaps he never would have.

St. Giles's trail ended in the Hong Kong post office. It would not have taken a man of his resources long to discover that revenge on Hawkins had already been accomplished. But of this there is no record.

All that exists to suggest St. Giles's whereabouts after August 1971 is an entry in the visitor's log of a cemetery in Marin County, California, and a prepaid standing order to maintain flowers on the memorial stone of a twenty-one-year-old boy. The handwriting of the log entry is not good, and several of the letters have been smudged together; but the signature, dated January 14, 1972, a year to the day after the murder of St. Giles's son, appears to read "Joe Berg."

In the space provided for the visitor's address there is a single word, "Finale."